Black Redneck

Vs.

Space Zombies

Steven Roy

This book is dedicated to everyone who has
overcome where they are from.

ACKNOWLEDGMENTS

There's so many people to thank. I'm going to thank them personally so you ladies and gentlemen can get to the story without further interruption, but, hey, thank you for reading the book.

BIG BEAU'S LAST POOR DECISION

A single street light hung high over the Broke-Spoke saloon. Even though it was just starting to get warm, a cloud of bugs swarmed around the light and added their buzzing to the muted country music that escaped through the thin walls of the bar.

As late as it was, only a few pick-up trucks remained in the parking lot and, depending on which way the wind was blowing, you could catch the scent of honey-suckle or the foul scent of the dumpster on the side of the bar.

Big Beau Balladeer came stumbling out of the Broke-Spoke Saloon as if the bar had spit him out. He pushed open a tattered screen door hard enough to almost rip it off its hinges and picked up even more speed as he staggered down the rickety wooden steps.

As his boots crunched across the gravel parking lot, the screen door slammed behind him as loud as a gunshot.

He would have fallen face-first into the gravel, but he somehow caught himself on the door handle of his truck and pulled himself upright, though he still swayed from side to side as if he was trying to get a slow dance going with his '89 Ford.

Big Beau's name fit his stature. He made the large truck seem like a compact car. He was 6' 8" and wide all over, more like a bear than a bodybuilder. He wore a sleeveless shirt and the armholes were cut wider so he could fit his arms through. His weathered baseball cap looked like it was made for a child on his head.

He reached into his pocket and pulled out his keys. He started poking at the door with them, adding more scratches to the paint around the keyhole.

The key found the lock more by luck than guidance. The truck rocked from his weight as Big Beau pulled himself inside the cab.

He took a deep breath and leaned over the steering wheel as his chin drifted toward his chest. His head nodded up. He shook his head hard as if he could shake off the alcohol the way a dog shakes water out of its fur.

He started the truck. As the engine roared to life, his booted foot pushed the accelerator to the floor.

The spinning tires threw up a cloud of gravel and dust as the truck sped toward the narrow blacktop road. Big Beau's truck looked like it was headed toward the ditch on the other side of the road.

It didn't make it. A massive semi-truck smashed into the driver's side door. The steel caved in as easily as an aluminum can. The Ford flipped down the blacktop, throwing off small parts and glass.

Fifty yards away, what had seconds before been Beau and his truck was now a crumpled mess of metal and shattered bones.

Just like that, it was quiet again. The insects buzzed. The streetlight hummed. But there was a new noise - the drip, drip, drip of what was left of Big Beau leaking onto the shattered glass that lay around the truck.

JEFFERSON RETURNS HOME

Pearl leaned on the counter just to the side of the register and entertained herself by blowing her brown bangs out of her face as her hazel eyes stared off into space.

"What's with all the huffing?" someone with a voice as sweet as honeysuckle said from behind her.

Pearl turned and leaned her back against the counter and studied Anne.

Anne sat at small folding table behind the counter, leaning over a calculus book. Her hair, which was the color of a lioness and usually fell in long ringlets around her face, was tied back with a piece of thick string.

Pearl said, "Your eyes are as green as the grass. Mine are like the mud."

"Yep," said Anne as her hand quickly scratched out symbols with a pencil.

Pearl sighed loudly and turned back around and let her small body collapse across the counter.

"What, Pearl?" Anne said, without looking up.

"Well, I'm bored."

Anne met Pearl's eyes and asked, "Bored or boring?"

"I think both," she said, smiling.

Anne went back to her book. "You could study."

Pearl turned back and around. "I'm still too sad."

Her eyes grew misty.

Anne said, "We're all sad, but Big Beau wouldn't want you moping around the register."

She leaned back over her book.

Pearl said. "I know it ain't no use to try to bother you once you get into concentration mode."

She watched Anne, hoping to be acknowledged, but the blonde just kept writing. Pearl let her body collapse across the counter and laid there.

The bell on the door rang with a loud ding. Pearl gasped and sprang up.

She had never seen the tall, dark man who stood in the doorway, no one new ever came into Fast-Pick-Up convenience store. Even stranger, the man wore a tasteful, gray suit that fit his muscular form perfectly as it contrasted with his brown skin.

The man stared back at Pearl for a beat and said in a deep, smooth voice with no hint of an accent, "You are open?"

Pearl slowly nodded, her mouth slightly agape.

The man nodded back and picked up a hand basket. As he collected basic groceries, Pearl watched him intently. When he made it to the back of the store by the milk, she turned back to Anne.

Pearl whispered, "Hey, hey. Check out James Bond."

Anne raised her head and leaned out to see him.

"He's black," she said, and went back to her books.

Pearl said, "Hey, hey, check out *black* James Bond."

Anne raised her head again and nodded her approval as if to say, *"That suit does fit nicely."*

The man approached the counter, and Pearl unconsciously fixed her hair behind her ear. Even Anne turned in her chair.

The man said, "Good evening, I don't guess you'd have soy milk?"

Pearl's smile was on the verge of turning into a giggle as she looked back at her friend, then back to the man. Anne looked at her like she was crazy.

"You talk so funny," Pearl said in a thick, Mississippi accent.

Anne stepped to Pearl's side.

"You'll have to excuse her. We don't get your sort in here much."

The man scowled and raised an eyebrow.

Anne realized her mistake and chuckled.

"Sorry. I didn't mean... I mean you're in a suit, a tailored one at that, and you have all your teeth. Why, you're not even in desperate need of a shower."

The man relaxed.

"Thanks, I guess."

He turned to Pearl, "I had asked about soy milk."

"Is that a brand?" Pearl asked.

Anne chuckled. "No, genius. It's a bean."

"A bean? I'm guessing we'd have better luck milking a cow."

The man shook his head and set his basket of groceries on the counter. When the two girls continued to stare at him, he said, "Regular milk will have to do. You can check me out if you're ready."

"Sir, she's been checking you out since you walked in," Anne said.

As Pearl turned the color of a ripe strawberry, Anne handed her the groceries.

"Come on. This man probably has some place to be that ain't Picayune, Mississippi."

"You got that right," he said under his breath.

As Pearl started ringing up the groceries at a leisurely pace, the man loosened his tie.

Anne asked, "So, why are you so dressed up?"

"I was trying to make a funeral, but I missed it," he said.

Pearl stopped ringing up groceries.

"Big Beau's funeral?"

Her eyes started to tear up.

"Yes. Beau Balladeer's."

"How did you know Big Beau?" Pearl asked.

"Beau's my...was my brother."

Anne looked confused.

The man pointed at himself and said, "Adopted."

Pearl said, "Oh. My. God. You're Jefferson Balladeer."

Anne's look of confusion left her face and her eyes brightened as she realized who stood in front of her.

"You're the Black Redneck."

"No! Please don't call me that. My name is Jefferson."

"I heard you shot some Mexicans for a horse when you were just a little kid," Anne said.

"What? No. That's not true. It was a...look, can I just buy some groceries?"

"You know, Big Beau sure was proud of you," Pearl said. "He was always going on about how you were the best horse-rider and the best at shooting guns and how you were living in the big city now and writing stories about space-ships and such."

Jefferson said, "That's nice, but I really just..."

"Big Beau was like a big brother to me, too," she continued. "One time, those Spencer boys were giving me a hard time and Big Beau was like," Pearl made her voice low and gruff as she imitated Beau. "'You best leave Pearl alone or I'll stomp you 'til your guts squirt out your ass'. Let me tell you that was the last time those Spencer boys even looked at me funny."

"That sounds like Beau," Jefferson said.

"Is it true you put ten guys in the hospital by beating them up with a rodeo trophy?" Anne asked.

Pearl nodded. "Yeah, that's true."

"No. It's not."

Both girls went to say something else, but Jefferson held up his hand and the two young ladies both held their tongues.

"I'm glad to hear Big Beau made a positive impact on your life," Jefferson said. "But, I'm very tired and would just like to purchase some groceries and be on my way as quickly as possible."

"Oh, I'm sorry," Pearl said. "Listen to me just prattling on and on. My mom says I'm like a guinea hen. Just won't shut up."

Anne nodded enthusiastically. "I can attest to all she says."

Pearl pushed Anne playfully and giggled.

Jefferson didn't laugh or crack a smile. He just stared at Pearl.

She stopped giggling and moved quickly to get his groceries in a paper bag and told him the total.

He put down thirty dollars on the counter and grabbed the bag. He moved toward the door, trying to exit before either of the young ladies could say anything more.

He wasn't fast enough.

Pearl said, "I guess you'll be staying at the big farm now?"

"Only long enough to sell it," Jefferson said.

Jefferson got into his rental car and situated the groceries in the passenger's seat. He looked up to see Pearl still staring at him from the window. As soon as he made eye contact, Pearl smiled and waved enthusiastically.

He held up a hand and looked up at the sign for the Fast-Pick-Up convenience store. A Metallic pickup truck with flames shooting out of the back as if it were some sort of rocket ship loomed over the top of the store.

He shook his head and pulled the car onto the narrow blacktop road that led to the Balladeer farm.

It had been a long time since anyone had called him "Black Redneck". He had hoped after ten years the people of Picayune would have forgotten him as he had forgotten them, but in a place where hardly anything happens, everything is remembered.

Jefferson tried to concentrate on driving down the curvy country road, but he couldn't help but remember it was his fault that people ever called him "Black Redneck" to begin with.

FLASHBACK: 1989 PICAYUNE ELEMENTARY-BLACK HISTORY DAY

A very young Jefferson Balladeer sat at attention in his desk as his first grade Teacher, Ms. Swan, held up a large photo of an African American man in an orange space-suit with a NASA patch over his heart. Today just happened to be Black History Day in Mississippi.

Ms. Swan said, "This is Guion Bluford, Junior. He was the first black...er...African American Astronaut."

Jefferson was the only black kid in class, so everyone turned to look at him as if Colonel Bluford must be his uncle or something.

Glen, a chubby kid in camouflage, raised his hand.

Ms. Swan rolled her eyes and said, "Yes, Glen."

"It ain't the first black guy I've seen in an orange jumpsuit," Glen said.

"You be quiet Glen, or you can go to the principal's office, again," Ms. Swan said.

Jefferson raised his hand.

"Yes, Jefferson."

He said, "That guy's been to outer space, ma'am?"

"Yes," the teacher explained. "In fact, when they're in outer space he's in charge. He was the first African American to lead a shuttle mission."

Jefferson looked over at Glen and nodded proudly.

"Jefferson, is there anything you want to be the first African American to accomplish," Ms. Swan asked.

"Well, sure. I mean, yes ma'am."

"You care to share with the rest of us?"

Jefferson looked back at the rest of the class staring at him.

"I'm going to be the first black redneck," he said.

The whole class paused, then burst into laughter.

"Black people can't be rednecks," said Ambrose, a little, blonde kid and Jefferson's best friend since the first day of kindergarten.

"I'm going to be the first one," Jefferson explained.

Before Ambrose could protest further, Ms. Swan said, "Now, Ambrose, if that's what Jefferson wants, I'm sure he can do it, but, Jefferson, you're a very intelligent young man. There's nothing else you'd like to be?"

Jefferson didn't hesitate. He said, "No ma'am. I'm going to be just like Big Beau."

Later that day....

Big Beau and Old Ed worked with a young colt in the side field. Big Beau seemed as big as the horse. Old Ed seemed more like one of the tall, thin pines that stood beyond the fence line, and his skin was just as creviced.

"Look who's back," said Old Ed in a gravelly voice as he looked up from shoeing the horse.

Big Beau looked up from the horse to see young Jefferson walking down the dirt road that led to the farm with his head bowed. Big Beau's smile vanished when he saw the slump in the boy's shoulders.

Big Beau yelled, "Hey, what's the matter with you? Best friend get kilt?"

Jefferson raised his head and said, "No sir."

"Then, why you moping around?"

Jefferson shrugged.

"Get over here," Big Beau said.

Jefferson sat his books down by the fence and ran to where Big Beau and Old Ed stood.

"Well, spit it out," said Big Beau. "What's wrong?"

Jefferson hesitated.

"Come on, kid," said Old Ed. "We ain't got all day."

Jefferson spoke quickly. "Ambrose and the other kids said I couldn't be a redneck 'cause the fact that I was black."

"Did you punch them in the face?" Big Beau asked.

Jefferson shook his head.

"Well, that's what you should have done."

"Maybe I ain't a redneck," said Jefferson.

"Bullshit, you want to be a redneck?" Big Beau asked.

Jefferson nodded and said, "Yep."

"Then, I'm going to teach you to be the greatest redneck to ever walk this here earth."

"Now, wait a second," Old Ed said. "Maybe, the boy should aspire to more. He seems to like to read and..."

Big Beau cut Old Ed a glare that made old man fall silent.

"Old Ed will help too," said Big Beau.

Jefferson smiled up at the old man. "You will?"

"I reckon I just got recruited," said Old Ed. "but you have to keep up with your schoolwork."

Jefferson smiled. "This is so cool. What do I have to do?"

"Whatever me and Old Ed say. And no crying or belly aching, and we're starting right now."

Big Beau picked up Jefferson and put him on the colt's bare back. The young horse tried to move away, but Old Ed held his bridle in place.

Jefferson grabbed the reins as a look of determination came over his face.

Old Ed said, "I imagine when we let go of this horse its first action is going to be to relieve himself of your weight, but you hold on best you can, and, when he puts you in the dirt, you get back up on him. You have to make him quit 'fore you do."

Jefferson nodded.

Beau and Old Ed let the horse go. It bucked hard and threw Jefferson into the dirt face first. Jefferson got up slowly and spit out a chunk of grass.

Old Ed snickered and said, "How's being a redneck working out for ya?"

Jefferson didn't answer the old man. He ran after the colt and yelled, "Get back here, horse. We ain't finished."

END FLASHBACK

THE DEVOURER BREAKS FREE

About the same time Jefferson was getting his milk from Pearl, a large starship sped past Mars. Within the ship, in a containment cell as large as a basketball arena, two aliens sat across from each other. Though they were clearly different species, one tall and sleek with a face like a praying mantis and the other with a face as smooth as carved ivory with deep set, small, black eyes, they wore the same matte black armor. Their helmets were off and sitting on the table like a couple of decapitated heads. They weren't supposed to remove their helmets and they really weren't supposed to be drinking, but, on such a long journey, boredom often trumps discipline.

A large bottle sat between them. Inside the bottle a large, milky white, slug-like creature swam in a purplish liquid. Insect Face grabbed the bottle and shook it. The slug-like creature in the bottle thrashed around and slammed itself against the glass as it excreted a purplish, inky substance.

Ivory reached out a hand to still the bottle and said, "Do not agitate the slug so. The beverage will strengthen to unacceptable levels."

"Unacceptable for a species as weak as yours," said Insect Face.

Ivory let out a deep guttural growl and ripped the bottle from Insect Face's hands.

He shook the bottle. The liquid became darker and darker

until it passed beyond purple and became black. The slug could no longer be seen within the liquid.

Ivory opened the bottle and poured the thick, black liquid into two small glasses on the table.

"We will see which of our species is weak. Now, drink, bug-face."

A large proboscis shot from between Insect Face's mandibles, and he sucked up the purple liquid.

An orifice in the middle of Ivory's face opened in an almost perfect circular hole and he poured the drink back.

Ivory slammed the shot glass down hard on the table and glared at Insect Face. Insect Face turned his head sideways and studied Ivory. The orifice in Ivory's face opened and a stream of purple vomit shot out onto the table as he slumped over in his chair.

"The drink is too strong for you," Insect Face's mandibles fluttered with joy. "Your species is not as strong as mine."

Ivory slammed his armored fist on the table and staggered to his feet, overturning his chair.

"Do not dare to insult me, bug. My species was the first to move between the stars. We had colonies when your species crawled the fields of your world nibbling flora and thinking moons were gods."

Insect Face's mandibles grew still.

"Ours was not the first species to the stars, nor the second, nor the third, but the Bugs were the ones who spread the farthest and the fastest. We are the many. We are the brave, brave bugs."

Ivory said, "Brave? Brave? My species lifted yours from the grass fields to the stars. If it wasn't for my species, you would be in a grass and mud hut, not a starship."

"Ah, so it is your species that is intelligent and brave," Insect Face said.

"We are fearless," said Ivory.

"Prove it. Throw your glass at the Devourer."

Ivory looked to his left. There, behind a thick containment

glass sat a giant creature that was a mass of translucent tentacles pulsating with bioluminescence. Its great bulk took up almost the entire containment cell and seemed more like a mountain of tentacles and death than an actual creature. Within the mountain of clear flesh, the creature's *core*, what looked like a meter long walnut, floated in the ocean of flesh with bioluminescent filaments growing out of it.

"We are here to guard the Devourer, not disturb it," said Ivory. "This is a creature that has destroyed worlds and you want me to open the containment field to throw a glass at it?"

"You spoke of bravery, of fearlessness."

"There is a difference between bravery and idiocy. A devourer demands great respect. It is the ultimate predator. Its core is nearly indestructible. It took our scientists some years to develop a way to kill one without destroying the planets it infested."

"I know all about these creatures," said Insect Face. "I have killed more than I can count. I know how they spread themselves across a planet, using sentient species as host to make clones of itself. They consume all life and then go dormant. They wait epochs until that planet's sun explodes and the cores of the devourers are cast into the void like seeds on the wind. They drift for ages until they find a planet with life and the whole process begins anew."

"You know all this and want to open the containment cell," Ivory said.

Insect Face slid Ivory's shot glass to the edge of the table as if daring him to throw it at the creature.

Ivory stood and picked up the small glass. "Do you think such a thing rose from the chaos, or did something beyond our knowledge create it?"

"This is not known. That's why they mean to study this one. But, I do know this Devourer is sedated. If you are too frightened, I understand."

Ivory picked up his glass and walked to the containment field. He placed his armored hand against the transparent boundary. It came to life with a virtual control panel. He punched commands into the containment field and a portal two meters wide spiraled open.

Ivory drew back and threw the shot glass. It struck the clear, gelatinous flesh of the Devourer and bounced to the floor. The gargantuan creature did not stir and continued to pulsate a light-blue.

Ivory turned his back to the containment field. "That was anticlimactic."

Insect Face lurched to his feet so fast he overturned the table.

"Close it! Close it!"

Ivory turned back to face the opening. A tentacle rushed toward him and through the open portal. The tip of the tentacle opened like the mouth of a serpent and enveloped Ivory's head. It lifted him off the ground and toward the portal, but Ivory spread his limbs wide and pushed his hands and feet against the containment field in a desperate effort to not be pulled inside it.

Insect Face rushed to his side. A long vibrating blade slide out of the forearm of his black-armor. He swung the blade in a long arc. It severed the clear tentacle holding Ivory and one of Ivory's arms at the wrist.

As Ivory fell to the floor with the tentacle still encompassing his head and his wrist spurting blood, Insect Face sliced frantically at the other tentacles the Devourer shot through the small opening.

As the insectoid fought off the attacks with the vibrating blade, his other hand came up and punched commands into the containment field. The portal spun closed and severed a tentacle before it could reach Insect Face.

Insect Face leaned against the containment field in relief for just a moment, then looked back at Ivory, who convulsed violently on the floor as his wrist continued to spurt orange blood and the tip of the tentacle covered his head.

Insect Face ran to his side and grabbed the gelatinous tentacle that covered his face. He ripped it off his partners face.

A mask of clear, gelatinous flesh had replaced Ivory's face and burned away his eyes. Insect Face could see through the flesh to the skull beneath. As he stared, bioluminescent filaments slid into the empty eye sockets like pulsating worms.

Insect Face set his hand on Ivory's chest and bowed his head.

"Sorry, old friend."

Insect Face raised his arm and the vibrating blade emerged. He started to bring it down, but he was too slow. Ivory raised his good arm and pointed it at Insect Face. The vibrating blade shot out and penetrated the torso of Insect Face's armor and came out of the back, sending a splatter of brownish blood onto the clear containment field.

Ivory stood as the Devourer's cells continued to replace his own in a chemical process so violent and rapid that a mist rose from his face.

Blood still poured from the stump of his wrist. He touched the bloody stump to the gelatinous mask covering his face. The Devourer cells formed a seal over the wound and rapidly consumed the dripping blood to form a tentacle at the end of Ivory's wrist.

Ivory turned toward the Devourer in the containment cell. It pulsated with vibrate colors.

Nodules rose out of the clear flesh covering Ivory's skull. The jellyfish-like flesh began to pulsate with its own bioluminescence and in time with the Devourer's.

The vibrating blade emerged from Ivory's wrist, and he slammed it into the containment field, over and over. As cracks began to form in the clear field, the Devourer raised a mass of large tentacles and smashed them into the weakened containment field. The field shattered and sent Ivory flying backward. He slid across the floor and slammed into the wall.

Before Ivory could stand, a tentacle wrapped around his torso and pulled him from the debris of the containment field and set him upright.

The Devourer held the tip of a tentacle out to Ivory. He

raised the arm that now ended in a tentacle. The two tentacles intertwined and pulsated with green bioluminescence.

Ivory withdrew and sprinted out of the large containment area and disappeared out of an open entry way.

The Devourer raised her tentacles and pulsated with red before slamming her tentacles into the metallic walls that now contained her.

NOT ALL HEROES ARE TALL

Shorty, a short, barrel-chested alien stood in front of a complex control panel that was a series of nobs and levers mixed with touch panels that blinked with alien symbols. He wore the same matte black armor as Ivory and Insect Face, but Shorty's armor was marked with dents and deep scratches and his dome-like helmet was on.

Though the alien was short, no more than four and a half feet tall, he was almost as wide. Shorty's thick arms hung all the way to his ankles. He had no neck to speak of, making the top of his armor resemble the end of a giant, black bullet. If his hands hadn't been moving so quickly over the controls it would have been easy to think this alien was a high-tech, mini-fridge.

The ship shuddered. An alarm blared. Shorty stretched out a long arm and flicked a switch that abruptly ended the blaring noise.

Shorty turned and ran toward a closed bulkhead. As he stretched out his hand to pull the lever that would open the door, it slid open.

Ivory stood there (or at least what had been Ivory). Zombie Ivory swung his vibrating blade in a long arc down toward Shorty's head. The strange blade cut through the metal beam above the entry way and slowed the blade just enough for Shorty to get out his own blade and block Ivory's blade before it could cut into his helmet. As the two aliens stalemated each others blades, Ivory kicked Shorty in his wide chest and sent him flying back into the control panel. Ivory leapt across the cockpit and brought down his blade with great speed.

Shorty rolled out of the way. Ivory's blade sliced through the control panel sending up smoke and sparks.

Shorty continued his roll and used his momentum to swing his blade toward Ivory. Shorty's long arms meant his armor could house a longer blade, and the thickness of his arms meant that blade moved with speed and power. The blade hit Ivory in the chest just below his extended arms. The top part of Ivory's body collapsed straight to the floor as his legs and mid-torso fell backwards. Ivory's vibrating blade grew still and slide back into the armor, doing further damage as it withdrew from the control panel.

Shorty pulled Ivory's upper body free from the ruined machinery and studied the smoldering mess. His long fingers tapped at various dark touch panels but, when he got no response, he turned and ran out of the still open door.

A DEVOURER'S RAGE

The Devourer pressed her body flat and moved through the ship like a river of gelatinous flesh and tentacles. She came to a narrow corridor and grasped the opening with her tentacles, stretching it wide as the metal moaned in protest.

The Devourer pushed her way into a large room, large enough to let her mass reshape into a more natural form, a hill of writhing tentacles.

The tentacled horror moved forward slowly, studying the glow of the engine that shone like a small star suspended amongst all the machinery and sending out flares of orange behind a circular containment field.

The Devourer flickered orange as if in response to the engine and wrapped her larger tentacles around the tall columns that surrounded the engine's power source. She squeezed and the metal of the columns gave as easily as a man might crush an aluminum can.

Kaboom! The explosion that followed was violent. Even the massive Devourer flew back and was pushed flat against the wall of the engine room as the flames of the explosion charred her translucent skin to black.

The back of the starship tore away and the vacuum of space suffocated the flames. The ship began to spin out of control. The Devourer clung to the ship with her remaining tentacles but, when she sensed open space and saw glimpses of a purplish planet as the ship spun, she pushed off like a squid shooting across the ocean floor after a juicy crab. She drifted in open space as the ship spiraled out of control toward the purple planet.

The Devourer's tentacles wrapped together like a flower closing for the night as she slowly drifted toward Earth.

A STAR SHIP EXPLODES

As Shorty ran down the corridor, the ship shook hard enough to force him to reach out a long arm to steady himself.

When the shaking subsided, he dropped to all fours and moved quickly down the corridor with a motion that was one part charging gorilla, one part cheetah.

The ship shook hard again. The roar of an explosion and the scream of tearing metal echoed down the corridor. A violent wind blew Shorty down the passage like a piece of trash caught in a hurricane. He slammed into a wall and was held there by centripetal force as the ship spun out of control.

Shorty reached out a long arm and pulled himself down the wall of the corridor with great effort. He went hand over hand until he reached a small control panel in the wall. He placed his large hand flat against it, and the panel opened to reveal a cluster of black, metal cylinders a yard long, each with its own strap.

Shorty reached for one and pulled it out by the strap. The ship shook again as smaller explosions rippled down the side of the ship. The side of ship just across from him tore open. He grabbed the wall to prevent being sucked out into the void of space, but the black cylinders flew toward the tear in the side of the ship like thin capsules being thrown into a jagged metal maw.

He let of go of his hold on the wall and flew toward the opening with his long arm outstretched toward the last of the cylinders.

The cylinder bounced off his armored fingers and flipped out of the tear in the ship. Shorty followed the cylinder through the tear. At the last second, Shorty swung his long arm and caught onto the torn metal of the gap in the ship as he simultaneously swung his short legs and grabbed the strap of the cylinder with the long toes of his armored foot.

The torn metal onto which Shorty clung bent outward and threatened to tear off completely. He pitched the cylinder toward his head with his foot and caught it with his free hand. The squat alien pushed an arm through the strap so the cylinder was safe against his back, then swung his body so he could grab the tear in the ship with both feet and hands. A hard pull from his long arms and thick legs threw him back into the ship as it spiraled toward Earth.

He forced his way back along the corridor and back into the cockpit. The view screen flickered as he studied it. The purplish planet with the cluster of lights over its land masses grew ever larger, quickly. His armored hand wrapped around a lever and slammed it down. Another door slide open. He had to turn his wide shoulders sideways to fit into the small compartment but, once he got in, his fingers worked quickly at the touch panel. The door of the compartment slid shut.

Just as the ship crashed into the planet's atmosphere at the worst possible angle, Shorty pulled a lever down hard.

The side of the ship spun into Earth's atmosphere and broke apart as small explosions rippled down the side of the ship. The entire craft became a silent wall of flame. A small, pill-shaped escape pod emerged from the flames and rode the shockwave like a surfer. The pod stayed just in front of the flames that reached after it like angry orange fingers.

As the escape pod sped away from the planet, the flames from the explosion totally enveloped the pill-shaped craft. The craft shook so hard from the force of the explosion, shorty pushed his feet and hands against the wall of the craft to keep himself from being bounced around.

The escape pod emerged from the flames and the small ship sailed smoothly away from the planet. Shorty released his grip on the walls and floated in zero gravity as he entered commands into a control panel.

The ship came to a jarring halt, causing Shorty to be thrown around in the small capsule. As the escape pod spun wildly out of control, he spread three limbs to steady himself as he continued to enter commands into the control panel. The walls of the pod bent inwards slightly and the control panel flickered.

The walls of the escape pod continued to bend inward. Shorty pushed back against the walls of the small craft with his arms and legs.

As the Devourer floated in open space, she wrapped the escape pod in tentacles like a Kraken attacking a tiny boat. One tentacle was nearly overkill, but the Devourer had several wrapped around the pod. The alloy of the escape pod, built to withstand almost anything, bent inwards, but the engines of the pod grew brighter as if the tentacles were squeezing all the energy out of the craft.

The Devourer struggled with the craft and in the attempt to gain purchase without being burned by its engines spun the small ship spun back toward earth. The pod gave a hard thrust and slammed itself and the Devourer into the atmosphere of the planet.

The friction at such high speeds melted the Devourer's clear flesh as if it were butter held to the flame of a welding torch. As the tentacles that held the escape pod evaporated, the pod fell free and pushed itself through the atmosphere of the planet, glowing red from the heat.

The Devourer continued to burn after it. Before the core of

the Devourer hit the atmosphere, two long appendages pulled free of the clear flesh and pulled themselves inside the core, like two long serpents returning to the protection of their den.

The core pushed through the atmosphere just behind the escape pod. It could have easily been mistaken for a wrinkly meteor beneath the flames that surrounded it as it penetrated the magnetic field.

JEFFERSON SEES OLD ED

Jefferson pulled the rental car to a stop in a front yard that was as big as a football field. A large, red truck was already parked in front of the farmhouse.

He stepped out of the car and looked straight up into the sky.

Even with the moon almost full, he could see the band of the Milky Way and the twinkle of all the stars.

As he stared, a bright flare came from high in the atmosphere. It was the brightest falling star he had ever seen.

He chuckled to himself and made a silent wish. *I wish I were anywhere but here.*

The front porch squeaked with a booted step. Jefferson turned his eyes from the sky to the shadows of the unlighted porch.

A voice that was coarse as sand-paper came from the darkness.

"Look who's back."

Old Ed stepped out of shadows and walked down the concrete steps of the porch and limped until he was ten feet from Jefferson.

"Old Ed, been a long time," Jefferson said.

"Yep."

The two men stared at each other for a moment.

"You're looking..." Jefferson began.

"Like old leather."

"I was going to say well, but I do make up fantastic stories for a living."

The old man just stared at him.

"And I see your sense of humor is still intact," Jefferson said.

"You're going to sell the place?"

Old Ed said the words like he didn't want them to be true, but knew that they were.

"I had forgotten how fast news spreads in a small town."

The old man motioned toward the big red truck.

"Your developer is already inside putting price tags on everything. Tried to sell me a few acres, but I want you to sell me the whole thing."

"That would be a lot of money. You strike oil on your place?"

"Never been one for that kind of luck, and, no, I don't have the kind of money you'll be asking for this place, but I want you to give it to me anyway."

"Ed, I can't do that. You know..."

"Look, just listen. I'm an old man. I don't want to see this place broken up into a bunch of lots and turned into a subdivision. Makes me sick to think about it. Just let me look after the place. After I'm in the dirt, you can do whatever you like."

"I can do whatever I like now."

The two men stared at each other.

Old Ed grimaced. "Yeah, I reckon you can."

The old man limped past Jefferson and toward the gate in the fence that bordered the side field. He stopped and turned around.

"And, not that you care, but we're all real sorry that Big Beau is gone."

"I care," Jefferson said.

"You didn't even come to his funeral."

"My flight was delayed. They even lost my luggage."

"Lost your fancy luggage? That's what you're worried about? Your brother just died."

Jefferson said, "He got himself killed."

The old man just shook his head and said, "Well, he's on the back hill next to your parents if you want to say goodbye or sorry for never visiting, ever. Even though he was the one that raised you."

Old Ed walked off into the night toward his place.

FALLING TO EARTH

Inside the escape pod, Shorty pushed his hands and feet against the wall of the small craft. The walls shook hard. An alarm began to blare, and Shorty felt the heat of the friction against the outside of the craft even through the armor that surrounded his hands.

The roar of the flames suddenly ended and the shaking stopped. All that was left was the blare of the alarm and the whistling noise of the pod as it fell toward the planet.

Shorty entered commands into the touch panel, but it flickered and went black, giving off a little puff of smoke. The lights in the pod died, leaving Shorty in total darkness. A light on Shorty's armored shoulder glowed enough for him to see. He grabbed the speaker of the blaring alarm and crushed it in his hands and thought, *"Yes, imminent death. I know."*

He drew back both long arms as far as his confined area would allow and pounded on the door of the craft over and over. The door was already bent inward from the Devourer's grasp. Shorty continued his pounding until a crack showed in the door and air rushed inside. He put his back against the pod wall and pushed against the door on the opposite side with his feet. He strained with all his might. The door bent outward. He kicked again with both feet and it gave. Shorty flew out of the pod and struck the bent doorframe on the way out.

At first Shorty tumbled toward Earth, but he quickly gained control of his body as he fell toward the purplish planet. Even from this height he could see the shape of the continents and that they were speckled with bright, white artificial light.

Shorty scanned the area around him in free fall. The damaged pod was above him, streaking across the sky, trailing flame and thick black smoke but then he saw something else - the Core of the Devourer streaking toward the Earth like a meteor.

The armored alien pulled his arms tight against his body and leaned toward the Devourer. He shot across the night sky like a black missile headed toward the smoldering core.

He guided himself until he was in free-fall over the top of the devourer core. He spread his arms and legs to maintain his speed and position as he removed the cylinder from his back.

As his armored hand grasped the top of the cylinder to remove the weapon, a long, snake-like appendage whipped out of the core and slapped the cylinder out of Shorty's hands. As he reached for the falling cylinder, the appendage whipped back and struck him in the chest. The barbed end of the tentacle threw up sparks as it left another deep scratch in his battle-worn armor.

Shorty turned his attention back to the Core. The Devourer whipped the barb toward his head. Shorty caught the tentacle and planted his feet on the top of the core, pulling with all of his might to remove as much of the tentacle from it as possible. The tentacle undulated as it tried to pull free; Shorty raised his other arm and the vibrating blade emerged. He swung toward the base of the tentacle just as the escape pod blew up, sending out a shockwave and metal debris in all directions.

The shockwave blew Shorty's swing off course and his vibrating blade hit the hard, outer covering of the core. The blade threw up sparks but didn't so much as scratch the core.

Before Shorty could regain his bearings and swing again, a large, flaming piece of debris struck him in the head and knocked him away from the Devourer.

He fell toward Earth, flipping out of control as his long arms flopped about. His body was limp as he fell with the ground rushing up to meet him.

Shorty's head came up and he looked around frantically. He let himself flip over and regained control of his body. He spread his limbs trying to create as much drag as possible to slow his descent. Even with only the light of the single moon, he began to make out the detail of the large flora below. He opened his armor to allow more air and created more drag. Small panels opened all over his armor, but he still streaked toward the ground. He moved himself directly over the large trees and waited until the last second to seal his armor. Just as he touched the tips of the large flora, his armor sealed tight around him. He crashed down through the flora sheering off the branches as he went. The small branches slowed his descent, but he hit a branch large enough to bounce him in the other direction of a smaller tree. He smashed into the small tree and knocked it askew, then fell into a thick patch of briars and finally slid to a stop in an awkward position with the briars clustered all around his suit. He lay there as still as the dead.

A DEVOURER'S TALE

Not two miles from where Shorty lay twisted in the briars, the Devourer's core plummeted through the trees and slammed into the leaf-covered ground hard enough to the punch a decent crater into the earth. The force of the impact shot dirt and scorched leaves into the air. A flock of roosting birds in a nearly oak burst into the night air.

As the leaves drifted back to the earth through the fog of dirt, a tentacle shot out from the core and whipped back and forth, trying to gain purchase in the loose soil to little effect. Eventually the barbed end of the tentacle grabbed onto some exposed roots and winched the core out of the dirt that covered it. The tentacle on the opposite side of the core emerged and pushed as the other pulled and inch-wormed the core free so that it lay in the crater like a giant seed that wasn't yet buried.

The Devourer raised one of its tentacles high. The tip of the tentacle began to glow a bright white until the entire area was lit as bright as if someone had turned on a light bulb. The tip of the tentacle grew dimmer, then brighter. In just a few moments moths and other insects swarmed around the pulsating tentacle's bioluminescence. The other tentacle emerged from the core. The tip of the tentacle opened like a Venus flytrap and whipped back and forth amongst the swarming insects, catching them in its sticky maw.

As the Devourer continued to feast on insects, a rabbit moved through the briars not far from the crater. The rabbit emerged from the thorns and it rose on its hind legs. Its nose twitched. It hopped to within a long step of the crater and stood on its hind legs as if mesmerized by the glowing light.

The Devourer fell still, but the tip of its tentacle still pulsated.

The rabbit's large ears twitched. It leapt away from the crater, but too late. The barbed tentacle struck out like a cobra and blurred toward the fleeing rabbit.

The barb at the end of the tentacle slammed into the back of the rabbit's head. The rabbit twitched for a moment, then fell still. The tentacle rose back into the air. The dead rabbit hung limp from the barb. The second tentacle emerged from the crater. As it neared the dead rabbit, the mouth of the tentacle opened, latching on to the rabbit's stomach. A horrible sucking noise followed, like someone who just couldn't believe that they had finished their milkshake. The rabbit collapsed in on itself as its blood and internal organs were sucked out as if it was some sort of furry juice-box. The clear tentacle of the devourer turned dark red as it absorbed the cells of the rabbit. When the juicy parts of the rabbit were depleted, the tentacle slid around the carcass and squeezed hard, the bones snapped like twigs. The devourer sucked in the rest of the rabbit fur, bones, everything, except for one of the rabbit's back feet. It held the bloody rabbit's foot in the tip of her tentacle and lay the tentacle flat on the dirt. It undulated the tentacle back and forth gently until it was buried beneath the loose soil with just the rabbit's foot above the surface.

The devourer waited. She knew that, where there is life, there is hunger and something would come for the rabbit's foot.

DAN THE DEVELOPER

Jefferson walked to the farmhouse with just the carry-on in his hand. He paused at the door and almost knocked, but then remembered he owned all this now.

He pulled open the door and stepped inside. The walls in the front hallway were lined with all his old rodeo and marksmanship trophies. Pictures of Jefferson at various ages hung between the them. In all of the pictures, Jefferson wore a beige cowboy hat. It wasn't until the later pictures that Jefferson had finally grown into the hat. In most of the pictures Jefferson stood beside a large, gray stallion. The worn hat from the photos still hung on the wall just to the side of the trophies.

Jefferson stepped closer to the wall of trophies and photos and grabbed a framed photo that rested in the middle. A seventeen year old Jefferson smiled back at him while one arm was draped around Big Beau's shoulder and the other held up a rebel flag.

Jefferson shook his head and laid the photo face down on the cabinet.

He turned from the wall of memories to see a thin, middle aged man in a red polo shirt with Stockstill Realty inscribed like a badge on his chest.

"I didn't want to interrupt," the man said in a voice that was part Rhett Butler and part Foghorn Leghorn. "You seemed lost in your thoughts."

The man walked to Jefferson with his hand extended like he just couldn't wait to shake hands.

"I'm Dan Stockstill. It's my extreme pleasure to meet you, Mr. Balladeer."

"Jefferson is fine."

Dan picked up the photo and looked from it to Jefferson.

"You certainly seem like a different man now," he said.

"I should hope so," said Jefferson.

Dan put his hand on Jefferson's shoulder as if they were old friends and said, "Sometimes, the first thing a man has to overcome is where he's from." Dan sat the photo back face down and added, "You, sir, have overcome a lot. Picayune doesn't produce many novelists of note."

"I wouldn't say I was one of note," Jefferson said.

The developer smiled and walked back into the house. Jefferson followed.

"I hope you don't mind," Dan said. "I've been getting everything ready for the estate sale tomorrow. When we talked on the phone you seemed anxious to conclude your business here."

"You definitely got the right impression. The sooner I can go back to my real life, the better. Can you really do everything without me here?"

"Of course," Dan said. "I just need you to sign a few papers so I can get started."

"Where are these papers?" Jefferson asked.

The developer motioned toward the dining room. Jefferson took a step in that direction and turned back toward the trophy case.

"What is that?" Jefferson asked.

Dan walked back to Jefferson's side and stared with him at a giant revolver.

"Apparently, your brother had this weapon custom made for himself several years ago, along with the special ammunition. He called it Big-Bang."

Jefferson opened the case that held the large handgun and took it out. Even though he was a large person, the gun made his hand look small.

Jefferson chuckled. "It has a picture of Beau shooting the gun on the gun."

He held the gun out for Dan to see the image carved into the large grip of the monstrous pistol and shook his head.

Dan said, "It is a bit over the top, isn't it?"

"A bit?"

"I didn't price it for the estate sale tomorrow. I thought since it was your brother's special weapon it might have sentimental value for you."

"No," said Jefferson, "We'll sell it, assuming someone is gauche enough to buy such a thing."

"It is one big gun."

Jefferson sat the gun down on the counter with a heavy clunk.

"It's a useless piece of crap that demonstrates Beau's personality better than a ten volume biography ever could. You mentioned paperwork?"

Dan walked further into the house, and Jefferson followed.

POSSUM VS. DEVOURER

A gray and white possum scurried through the thick briars. It stopped, sniffed and changed direction, its long prehensile tail curling and uncurling behind it.

It stopped at the edge of the briars and sniffed again. It turned its head to see a rabbit's foot laying in some loose dirt. It charged out of the briars and into the opening as fast as it could go. The Devourer's tentacle rose out of the dirt and slammed its barbed end into the skull of the possum. The possum's limbs vibrated for a moment, then it went limp.

The Devourer lifted the Possum corpse into the air as the other tentacle rose out of the crater. The mouth on the tentacle opened wide, fastened onto the dead possum and began to absorb the animal. The blood and small organs flowed through the clear tentacle and toward the core of the creature. Soon, the possum was just a husk of fur and bone, but that was not to be wasted. The Devourer spun its tentacles around what remained and crushed the bones. The two tentacles worked as one to tear the possum to bits. The tentacle that ended in a mouth swallowed everything but the head and one of the back legs.

It dropped those two body parts onto the soil around the crater as the tentacle with the mouth stood straight up as if it was a stalk of corn growing out of the core. The mouth of the tentacle opened like a blooming flower and a thick, clear viscous fluid began to pour out of its mouth. As the fluid dripped out, it formed around the tentacle. New flesh. The fluid continued to drip out of the opening until the entire tentacle was covered in a thin layer of the jellyfish-like substance, and the base around the tentacle where it attached to the core was also covered in the same strange flesh.

SHORTY LIVES

The four long fingers of Shorty's hand twitched as if he was having a dream. He sat straight up, snapping some of the vines that twisted around his limbs. He remained in a seated position as his dome-shaped helmet turned like a turret on a tank. His armor had a few more dents and deep scratches, but it had kept him alive.

Inside the suit, the heads-up-display gave out all sorts of information on this environment and blinked a warning that he should stay immobile and seek medical attention.

Shorty grunted an emergency protocol and stood. He ran a hand over his armor and tested his range of motion. With a thought, the vibrating-blade slid out of his wrist and extended to its full length. He swung it, clearing away the vines that blocked his path and took a step as a piece of armor fell off his shoulder. He picked it up and with his long arm and beat it back into place. Shorty took off at a jog, only slightly limping.

A DEAL IS STRUCK

Jefferson followed Dan into the living room. On a long table, Dan had a large, colorful map of what the farm would look like once it had been turned into a subdivision.

The developer motioned for Jefferson to sit at the head of the table as he sat to his right.

Dan pointed at the map and said, "I've broken up the property to optimize profit. Here, around the catfish ponds, will be the more expensive properties. The catfish ponds and the surrounding area will be a centrally located park. There are some great oaks we can leave. It'll be beautiful."

The developer took a breath. "The properties closer to the roads and the edge of the property will be the cheaper ones," Dan chuckled. "But not too cheap."

He began to explain something else on the map, but Jefferson held up a hand, and Dan fell silent.

"I really appreciate the effort you've put into this," Jefferson said. "But I can't say I care about the specifics. I just want to be done with it so I can go back to my life. It'll be great to make some money, but the most important thing is to get this done."

Dan smiled. "Fine. I guess I'm just a touch excited about the property. You can depend on me to take care of everything. You can go back to your life. The only thing you'll need to do is cash the occasional large check."

"That's exactly what I had in mind," said Jefferson.

The developer opened a briefcase and pulled out a large stack of paperwork. He stood and placed the stack of documents in front of Jefferson as he stood over his shoulder.

The document was already highlighted where Jefferson needed to sign. Dan held out a pen to him. Jefferson took it and began to sign his name with certainty and a bit of joy.

"I like the idea of the park," he said. "But are you sure building those catfish ponds will be worth it?"

Dan paused. "We don't have to build them. Your brother already did. You didn't know?"

"I haven't been here in ten years," said Jefferson.

"Not sure why you're brother built them, but they are something else. The key point for us is that those ponds will greatly add to the value of the lots surrounding them."

Jefferson nodded.

"That reminds me," said Dan. "Tomorrow, we'll need to feed those catfish. Else they'll start eating each other."

"The ponds are that full?"

Dan smiled. "I've never seen so many fish in my life. It's a disturbing amount of catfish."

Some time later, they were finally making it to the back part of the thick document.

Jefferson rubbed his wrist and said, "I'm beginning to feel like I'm at a book signing, a really busy one."

"I'm sure you do quite well selling your books, but this is going to make you a pretty penny, several pretty pennies."

"And, I won't even have to be here," said Jefferson. "That's the best part."

"I'm going to handle everything," Dan said.

With a flourish, Jefferson signed his name in the last empty blank below Dan's finger. The developer quickly collected the papers, as if he was worried Jefferson would change his mind and put them into a leather briefcase.

"I'm looking forward to a prosperous partnership," he said. "I'll be back in the morning to help with the estate sale. I've marked almost everything, but, if there's something you want..."

"There isn't. I'm selling it all. Tomorrow."

"There were also some clothes in what I suspect might be your old room. If you don't want any of it, I can take it to the church for you."

"I would appreciate that," Jefferson said.

"I really didn't know what to do with the trophies and all those pictures."

"Don't worry," said Jefferson. "I know exactly what to do with them."

"I'll be back very early," Dan said. "Try to get some rest."

Jefferson stood and Dan shook his hand again.

"I really appreciate you doing all this."

"Say nothing of it. I'm going to make a lot of money too. A lot. I'll be the one handing out the gratitude." Dan chuckled. "Well, tomorrow."

Jefferson said, "Tomorrow."

The developer showed himself out, and the old farmhouse fell quiet. Jefferson could hear the crickets outside.

AN OLD PAIR OF BOOTS

Jefferson walked around, feeling a bit like a burglar as he explored the old farmhouse.

He pushed open the door of his old room. Besides a coat of dust, it was just as he left it. Even the old movie posters from the original Star Wars and Alien movies were still pinned to the wooden paneling. The framed picture of Colonel Guion Bluford, Junior hung crooked on the wall. Jefferson stepped into the room.

A wooden bed rested in the corner. A gun belt hung off the headboard holding a pair of revolvers. At the end of the bed sat an old pair of boots. Jefferson stood over them and looked down at them. One of the boots was stained with maroon splotches. A deep scratch marred the leather. Jefferson stared at the stains on the boot and knelt by them, touching the grooves.

FLASHBACK: 2001, PICAYUNE, MISSISSIPPI

Seventeen-year-old Jefferson wore all black cowboy gear and a worn, brown cowboy hat on top of his head. He led a big, gray horse to a trailer. Jefferson held the horse's reins loosely in one hand and a tall rodeo trophy in the other hand.

Jefferson wrapped the reins around the saddle horn and opened the door of the horse trailer.

He turned to his horse. "'Go on, Gray Man, get in.''

Jefferson patted the horse as it calmly entered the trailer.

"Good job, Gray Man. Couldn't win without you."

He closed the trailer door behind the horse and walked around to the old, green pickup that was in front of the trailer. As he was opening the door, he saw three figures wearing cowboy hats reflected in the window of the truck.

Jefferson looked over his shoulder at the three young men.

He turned around. "Glen and his two friends. Good evening to you gentlemen."

He tipped his own worn cowboy hat at them and opened his truck door.

"Look here fellas," said Glen. "It's the famous Black-Redneck."

"Just locally famous, for now," Jefferson answered.

"Me and the fellas were talkin'. We decided we like you playing basketball better. You need to stay out of rodeo."

Jefferson sat his trophy on the seat of his truck, turning to face them as he leaned on the truck and folded his arms across his chest.

"Is that so? Is that what you and the fellas decided?"

"Yep," said Glen.

Glen spit and the tobacco juice landed on one of Jefferson's boots. Jefferson looked down at his boot and scowled. He could feel the adrenaline course through his body and he had the sudden urge to rip Glen's head off, but by the time Jefferson raised his head his face was wearing a smirk.

"Even if I did quit, Glen, you still wouldn't win. Eleven other guys finished before you. That means you came in last. You going to go visit those guys next?"

"Those eleven other guys are white. I can take getting beat by them, but I can't take getting beat by no n..."

He never got the chance to finish the word. Jefferson covered the distance between them, and his fist connected with Glen's chin. A spray of tobacco and spit flew out of his mouth as Glen staggered back and fell on his backside in the gravel parking lot.

Jefferson glared at Glen's two friends. They kept waiting for the other to attack him first. Glen slowly got to his feet and screamed, "Let's kick his ass."

The young men charged at once, but Jefferson lurched to the left and pushed one of the guys hard into his truck. Glen threw a punch, but Jefferson ducked and kicked him in the thigh with the heel of his boot. Glen went down holding his thigh. The last of the young cowboys held up his hands apologetically and started to back away as Jefferson stalked him.

The boy that had been thrown into the truck picked up Jefferson's trophy and swung it like a bat into the back of Jefferson's head. His hat went flying as the trophy snapped over his skull. Jefferson sank to his knees. Glen's two friends grabbed Jefferson by the arms and threw him against his truck as Glen got to his feet and limped toward Jefferson.

"Now, you're going to learn a lesson, boy," he said.

He punched Jefferson in the stomach as hard as he could, but it didn't seem to have any effect against the muscle of Jefferson's stomach.

Jefferson smirked, "What's the lesson? You don't punch very hard."

Before Jefferson could raise his leg to kick Glen in his other thigh, a fourth young man in a white cowboy hat crashed into Glen and brought him to the gravel. The boy punched down and hit Glen in the eye.

The young man turned to where Jefferson was pinned on the truck and showed his face to be that of Ambrose Hill.

"Since when can three guys like this take you down?" he asked Jefferson.

"I had it under control."

He stomped the feet of the guys holding him with the heel of his boots. As they loosened their grip, he pulled his arms free. He threw one guy to the ground and kicked him in the ribs. The other guy tried to run, but Jefferson punched him between the shoulder blades and the boy went down, writhing in pain.

Jefferson said, "See."

"Now, that's the Black-Redneck I know and love," Ambrose

said.

Jefferson and Ambrose turned to see Glen trying to crawl away.

"Where you going, Glen?" Ambrose said. "We still want to have a word with you."

Glen turned over, continuing to scoot away on his butt as he said, "Now, fellas. You know I was just joking around."

"I don't find you funny," said Jefferson.

Glen started crying and held up his hands as Ambrose and Jefferson closed in on him.

BAM! A gun went off. Both Jefferson and Ambrose jumped back.

Old Ed walked out of the darkness with a rifle in his hands.

"That's enough, you two. I think ya won your little skirmish."

"They started it," said Ambrose. "We were just finishing up."

"I don't doubt it," said Old Ed. "But you'll be the two in jail when you hit one of them hard enough to shatter a jaw or kill one of 'em."

Jefferson walked back and picked up this broken trophy and snatched up his hat.

Old Ed walked around to the other side of the truck and got in the passenger's seat.

"See you tomorrow," said Ambrose. "We can ride the horses to the creek."

"Sure, and thanks," said Jefferson.

Ambrose waved and walked away as Jefferson stepped toward the truck.

Glen still sat on the ground holding his thigh.

"You know why the Balladeers adopted you?"

"Glen, I figured out long ago I was adopted."

"I ain't talking about that," said Glen. "I'm talking about why."

Old Ed yelled, "Just get in the truck. We don't have time for this idiot."

"He doesn't want you to hear, but I heard Mr. Balladeer talk about you 'fore he died. Said he was going to adopt some unwanted black baby so you could haul watermelons and cut wood for him." Glen laughed and said, "That's you Jefferson."

Jefferson took a step toward Glen.

Old Ed said, "Hey! Get in this truck."

Glen kept talking. "Big Beau may have raised you, but the man that adopted you just wanted a slave to pick watermelons."

Jefferson took two steps and kicked Glen in the mouth. A spray of blood splattered one of Glen's friends as Glen's eye-tooth dug into the leather of Jefferson's boot like a tiny plow marring the boot before the tooth pulled free and flipped into the air and came down in the gravel of the parking lot. Jefferson raised his boot to stomp Glen's throat..

Old Ed screamed, "No! No, Jefferson. Stop!"

Jefferson slammed his foot down, but into the gravel alongside Glen's head.

He leaned down. "You ever say a cross word about the Balladeers again and there won't be nothing that can save you."

Old Ed said, "You gone crazy? Get in the truck."

Jefferson stomped back into the truck, slammed the door, and sped away.

Old Ed sat quietly until they were on the dark country road that led to the farm.

"Can't say I remember being so proud of someone and so disappointed all in the same evening."

"What?" said Jefferson. "What was I supposed to do? Just let him badmouth the Balladeers. They kept me from starving, gave me a life. I won't listen to anyone lie about them."

"If you know it's just lies, why do you get so upset? Balladeer, the man you called Pa until he died, was a complicated man. Weren't perfect. Nope, not by a long shot."

They were silent until Jefferson pulled the truck to a stop in front of Old Ed's house.

"Is it true what Glen said?" Jefferson asked. "They raised me to pick watermelons?"

Old Ed got out, but then leaned into the open window.

"What starts as one thing often becomes a whole 'nother thing. You should ask your brother to tell you the whole story."

"I'm asking you. I know you ain't the one to sugar coat things."

"What makes you think the truth needs sugar-coating?" Old Ed said. "But your brother should tell you, and I should probably keep my old mouth shut."

He turned away and walked toward his house.

Jefferson yelled, "Hey, Old Ed."

Old Ed turned.

"Thanks for keeping me from killing Glen."

"Glen's life is going to be its own punishment," said Old Ed. "No need to cut it short."

Young Jefferson walked into the farmhouse. Big Beau sat at the dining table drinking a beer. His big hand made the beer can look tiny.

"There he is," said Big Beau. "There's the rodeo star. How'd you break your trophy already?"

Jefferson said, "Someone hit me in the head with it."

"What? I hope you stomped the shit out of 'em."

"I took care of it."

Big Beau reached into the cooler at his feet and popped the top on a beer and sat it at Jefferson's spot on the table.

"I know you ain't a drinker, but looks like you need one. Hell, did someone shoot Gray Man? What's this look on your face?"

"Why did your father adopt me?" Jefferson asked.

Big Beau stared at him for a long second and leaned forward. "You mean why did *our* father adopt you?"

Jefferson nodded.

Big Beau leaned back in his chair and said, "Guess you needed adopting, and Ma wanted to do it, so he didn't have much choice."

"Glen said it was to have someone to haul watermelons."

"Glen? Asshole-Glen? If something comes out an asshole it's liable to be shit. Why are you worried about what he says?"

"I'm not," said Jefferson. "I'm worried about what's the truth."

"Well, sit down," said Big Beau. "You're making me nervous. I'll tell you the honest truth, but you have to promise not to get upset. You can be a spot sensitive."

"I ain't sensitive."

"You are. Just someone usually gets punched in the face when you get upset instead of you crying. It's like other people's blood are your tears or something."

"Well, go on then," Jefferson said. "I ain't going to get upset."

"Pa was at one point what you might call a racist."

Jefferson lowered his head. He clinched his fist and banged it on the table.

"Well, there you go already getting upset and that was just the first sentence of the story," said Big Beau.

"A racist? He was a racist?"

"Wait, now. It's not like he was some Grand Wizard in the KKK or something. He just thought...well..whites were better, and the races shouldn't mingle."

Jefferson took off his hat and rubbed his temples.

"So, it's true. They got me to haul watermelons and cut wood."

"No," Big Beau said. "Well, yes, Pa told people that but..."

Jefferson stood up so fast his chair overturned.

"I think I would have rather starved."

"See, now you're upset. Just calm down. The story ain't done by a long shot..."

"I'm done," Jefferson said. "I've heard enough."

He stormed into his room, stripped off his rodeo gear and threw his boots in the corner of the room. He put on a plain pair of jeans and looked through his closet for a shirt that wasn't western cut. He found a Ghost-Busters T-shirt, slipped it on and put on his basketball shoes.

He pulled a wad of cash from a cigar box and stuck it in his pocket, then marched out into the long hallway toward the door.

Big Beau blocked the way.

"Now, you just relax. We got a lot more talking to do."

"We don't," said Jefferson.

"How you gonna get around me?" asked Big Beau.

Jefferson launched himself forward and grabbed Big Beau by the front of his sleeveless shirt, driving him against the wall. Even though Big Beau had a hundred pounds on him, he kicked Big Beau's feet out from underneath him and threw him out of the way.

Jefferson stood over him and said, "Everyone else in this town is afraid of you, but I ain't. You're just a big piece of shit. This whole family is shit."

"Stop it. We're brothers, you asshole. Now, help me up."

Big Beau extended his hand. Jefferson slapped it away.

"We're not brothers. I wasn't part of this family. I was free labor, and, you know what, I don't think I even like this cowboy shit, and I ain't doing it anymore."

Jefferson turned and walked out the door. Beau got to his feet quickly for such a big man and went to the open door.

Big Beau yelled as Jefferson made it to his truck, "You come back when you calm down. We got more talkin' to do."

END FLASHBACK

Jefferson sat the boots down and stood up. He stepped out of the dusty room and marched into the kitchen. He opened cabinets until he found a container of garbage bags beneath the sink and went back into his room. He began to stuff his old clothes into the bags like they had done something bad to him. In a way, they had. They made him remember.

Not long after, Jefferson dropped several bags of clothes by the door. He pulled out another empty garbage bag and started dropping picture frames and trophies into it.

He stopped as he picked up a picture of Ma and Pa Balladeer holding him as a toddler. Everyone was all smiles in the picture as both Balladeers looked at Jefferson like it was true love, the look only parents get.

Jefferson stared at the picture for a long moment then crumpled it up in his hand and dropped it into the garbage bag.

COYOTE VS. DEVOURER

The coyote eased into the area around the crater setting one paw softly on the ground, then pausing before moving the next paw forward.

Its nostrils flared and the fur around its neck and back bristled. Its lips curled to reveal yellowed fangs as it growled.

The animal took another step toward the chuck of meat at the edge of the crater.

A tentacle sprang out of the dirt just below the forepaws of the coyote and wrapped around its neck. The coyote dug its front paws into the loose soil and tried to pull backwards as it thrashed back and forth. The tentacle tightened and yanked forward. The vertebrae in the coyote's neck made a crunching noise and the animal fell limp. Its tongue lolled from its mouth as its back legs twitched.

The tentacle shortened and pulled the dead coyote into the crater.

The sound of snapping bones and a wet sucking noise rose from the crater. A moment later, a tentacle rose straight from the bottom of the crater like a transparent stalk of corn. The tip of the tentacle opened like a horrible flower and it exuded a clear goo that ran down the tentacle and thickened the layer of clear flesh that coated the core of the Devourer.

The creature shook. The translucent flesh vibrated like a jello mold in an earthquake. Small appendages emerged from its sides as the clear flesh lengthened behind it like a thick tail.

The two tentacles that protruded from the core rose out of the clear flesh like long antennae. When the transformation was complete, the Devourer looked like a giant, translucent trilobite.

As the appendages at her sides pushed against the soil in time like tiny oars, her tail swished back and forth like a serpent.

The Devourer pushed forward and emerged from the crater, moving toward the woods with a horrible smoothness. As she reached the trees, the Devourer stretched out her two tentacles and wrapped them around the low-hanging branches to pull herself forward even faster.

She was no longer content to wait for her food to come to her. She was on the hunt and that was bad news for anything that lived.

SKEETER AND TATER GET BLOWED UP

Skeeter stepped out of the makeshift, metal building that was mostly welded together sheets of tin. He wore a respirator and gray coveralls. The bottom of the coveralls barely reached to the top of his cowboy boots. The sleeves of the coveralls barely covered the prison tattoos on his forearms.

He collapsed in a folding chair twenty feet from the door of the building. His excessively long legs making the chair seem like it was something meant for kids.

He pushed the respirator back on his head to reveal a face that spoke of cheap drugs and hard living.

Just as he leaned back in the chair and closed his eyes, the sound of an approaching engine came from the woods.

A moment later, Tater let the four-wheeler coast to a stop alongside Skeeter's chair.

Tater hopped off the ATV and practically danced with excitement. Skeeter smiled, revealing that his teeth were rotted, black and brown nubs.

"You won't believe it," Tater said. "It's crazy, man. Crazy."

"I would ask what's got into you, but I imagine that it's some of our product which we both agreed to no longer sample."

Skeeter stood. The difference in their height and shape gave one the impression that these two were the Laurel and Hardy of homemade, illicit drugs.

"Were you followed?"

"No way, man. I left the truck just where you said. No way I could have been followed."

"You get the donuts?" Skeeter asked.

Tater held up a white bag. "Yeah, but you won't believe what happened. I was driving back and something fell out of the sky right into the middle of the road. It must have bounced fifty feet in the air, and then, where did it fall but right in the back of the truck."

Tater laughed as Skeeter grabbed the donuts and reached his skeletal hand inside the bag to pull out a chocolate donut. He shoved half of it in his mouth and said with a full mouth, "You're really high."

"No, well, yeah," Tater said. "But that don't mean it ain't true."

"Could mean it ain't true."

Tater reached into a canvas bag on the side of the four wheeler and pulled out the black cylinder.

"Then, explain what this is?" he said.

"What the hell?" Skeeter mumbled, almost dropping the other half of the donut.

Tater giggled in a high-pitched voice that would have better suited a middle-schooler. "I told you. I told you, man. It's crazy right."

Skeeter took the cylinder. "And, it just fell out of the sky?"

"Yeah, that's what I'm trying to tell you," said Tater. "Crazy right? Maybe it fell off a plane or a satellite?'

"It looks like one of those things you keep a painting in."

"Yeah, a little, but why would that be falling from the sky?"

"Well, how I am I supposed to know?" asked Skeeter. "Wouldn't be so mysterious if it made sense."

The two men just looked at each other for a moment.

"You try to open it?" asked Skeeter.

"'Course I did, but it's on tight as a mutha," said Tater.

Skeeter wrapped his long fingers around the top of the cylinder. He bent at the waist and strained until his face turned red and his knuckles turned white, then he gave up.

"Damn!"

Tatter cackled. "Told you, told you, it's on tight."

"You try both ends?" asked Skeeter.

"Yeah."

"I bet it's something valuable inside."

"Yeah," Tater said. "Like the Moaning-Lisa."

Skeeter gave him a look like he was stupid. "That's in a museum, you big dummy. It's probably just one of those blurry flower paintings, but some asshole will still give us a million dollars for it."

"Maybe just tap the edges. My granny use to open jars like that."

"I got a better idea," Skeeter said.

He inhaled another donut and pulled down his respirator while he was still chewing and walked into the building.

A second later he came out with a large monkey-wrench.

Tater held out the cylinder with both hands as Skeeter fastened the monkey wrench onto the end of the cylinder and tightened it.

"Hold it tight" Skeeter told him.

Tater squeezed the cylinder with both his fat, little hands. When Skeeter turned the wrench, the cylinder just spun.

Skeeter said, "Damn it, Tater. Hold it tighter.

"Think I ain't trying?"

Both men relaxed when they realized it wasn't going to work.

"Well, shit," said Skeeter. "That things on tight."

"What if it ain't a painting, but some government plans or something, you know, like top secret."

"Whatever it is someone went to the trouble of sealing it up tight," said Skeeter. "Must be valuable."

"Maybe we should call the FBI?

"And invite 'em out to our meth lab?" Skeeter said.

"No," said Tater, "we'd meet them in town."

"No, you big-dummy, we're getting the thing open. Then, we'll know what to sell it for and who to sell it to."

Tater snapped his fingers. "We have the welding torch."

"And, that would burn up anything inside," said Skeeter. "Jesus, you're stupid."

"Oh, right."

Skeeter poured some white powder on the back of his hand and snorted it.

"You said we shouldn't use our own product no more," said Tater.

"Well, it helps me think."

Tater thought. "Maybe Glen could get it open?"

"And, once he did he would keep whatever's inside," said Skeeter.

"Oh, yeah," said Tater. "He would do that."

Skeeter stared down at the cylinder in his hands. "Just be quiet and let me think."

Tater turned to go back to his four-wheeler. Shorty stood not ten feet away from them. The fat man just froze and stared at the short, wide, armored creature. His mind took a long time trying to figure out what he was looking at as his jaw hung loose. Tater started to back away.

Skeeter looked up and followed his partner's confused gaze. When he saw the armored alien, his whole body tensed, then he jumped back as if a copperhead was slithering across his boots.

Shorty extended his large hand, palm upward. His long arm covered half the distance between them.

Still holding the cylinder, Tater turned and ran into the building, unconcerned about the deadly fumes.

Skeeter held the monkey wrench up like a club and walked backwards into the meth lab pulling down his respirator as he went.

He disappeared into the building and slammed the door.

Shorty lowered his hand and walked toward the building. He pushed gently at the door but it wouldn't open.

Inside, Tater fell to his knees and started coughing

something fierce. Skeeter stood over him and slipped a respirator onto his head and over his face, then pulled him to his feet.

"You big-dummy, you trying to kill yourself?" said Skeeter. "This stuff's poison."

Tater adjusted his respirator. "What the hell is that thing?

"I don't know, but it wants that black thing. I knew it was valuable."

"Just throw it outside," said Tater. "Maybe, it'll go away."

"What? No way! We're going to capture it. We'll be famous, rich," Skeeter said.

The sound of someone walking on the roof echoed on the tin as it bent in with each step.

Tater looked up. "It's on the roof, man. How did it get up there?"

The sound of bending metal was followed by white smoke pouring into the building.

"Damn, he's blocking the exhaust, trying to smoke us out," said Skeeter.

The room started to fill with white smoke that would have been deadly to inhale.

"Shit," said Tater, "Will these masks work in this? I don't think so. Shit, Skeeter, it's getting foggy in here."

"Quiet, I'm trying to think, stupid."

The sound of bending tin came from the roof. Light streaked in from the new opening as smoked swirled out of the hole.

A large, black form dropped into the structure just behind the chemistry set and disappeared in the thick white smoke.

Tater's yell was muffled by his respirator, "Jesus, it's in here."

"Get away from it!" Skeeter ran to the other side of the room and pulled up a shotgun.

Tater wasn't exactly fast. Shorty easily grabbed him as he ran by and snatched the little, fat man up as if he weighed as much as a child and held him to his armored chest with one long arm.

Tater screamed, "Skeeter, Skeeter. It got me! Help!"

Skeeter raised the shotgun and walked toward them through

the smoke.

He yelled, "Best put Tater down. Right now."

Long, thin black wires emerged from Shorty's helmet. The black, sinewy wires waved around like Shorty was a metal medusa, then the wires jabbed into Tater's skull at various points. Tater's eyes rolled back in his head and his body went limp just before his limbs twitched like he was having a bad dream.

Skeeter yelled, "Tater! Tater! Let him go you...metal man."

Shorty didn't budge. As more of the white smoke ventilated out of the tear in the tin roof, Skeeter saw blood running down Tater's forehead bad as a pro-wrestler that got hit in the head with a steel chair.

Skeeter took another step closer.

He pointed the shotgun right at Shorty. He wasn't so much concerned about Tater as he was concerned that he was next, and, if there's a scared meth-head with a shotgun in a room full of explosive chemicals, something bad might happen.

Tater raised his head, though his eyes still just showed white. He extended a open hand toward Skeeter. His body stopped twitching and his jaw went slack.

Tater said softly, "No. He's here to..."

The wires withdrew from Tater's head and disappeared back into the helmet. Shorty let Tater sink to the floor.

Skeeter pulled the trigger. The shrapnel of the shotgun blast scratched up Shorty's armor as the force of the blast staggered him backwards. Tater screamed as a few of the pellets struck him in the leg.

"Skeeter, no. Don't!"

Shorty rolled out of the way as Skeeter fired again.

"No. Wait!" Tater yelled.

Skeeter aimed and fired. Shorty leapt out of the way and flipped toward the wall.

The brunt of the shotgun blast hit the chemicals.

Boom! Flames engulfed the entire space. The force of the blast slammed Shorty through the wall and high into the air.

Every piece of tin that had been welded to the metal structure flew off and twisted through the air like giant, metal leaves.

Shorty hit the ground thirty feet from the meth lab and slid to a stop at the tree-line. A piece of scorched tin landed on top of him.

A moment later, Tater staggered out of the wreckage, some of his clothes still smoldered. The skin that showed was charred black. He held a hand to the side of his neck as blood spurted between his fingers.

He swayed on his feet and muttered, "Skeeter, you're the stupid one."

He fell face first into the dirt surrounding the structure and the woods were as quiet as if they had never existed.

EVERYTHING MUST GO

The first light of day spread across the lawn in front of the farmhouse, revealing all of the household items – furniture, appliances, even a long table with more guns than it could hold – sitting in rows in the yard.

Dan pulled up in his big, red truck to find Jefferson leading a large, brown horse into the yard to tie it to a fence next to other horses and a few cows.

The developer got out of his truck in a hurry and jogged to Jefferson's side. "I thought I was going to get here early enough to help you set up, but you've done everything."

"It's not a problem. I really couldn't sleep."

Jefferson tied the horse next to the others. He turned to find Dan with his hand extended to force another hand shake.

"You're an industrious young man."

"I mean to sell everything today," Jefferson said. "And I do mean everything."

Dan walked past a large antique armoire and pulled up the white tag. The price he had written had been marked through and replaced with $100.

"Now, it's your stuff and far be from me to tell you your business..."

"I know," Jefferson said. "I'm giving it away, but my goal is not profit, but expedience."

"In that case, I'll be your first customer. I'll take that rather fine dining table and the chairs that go with it."

"It's on the house," said Jefferson. "I'll help you put them in your truck."

"I wouldn't hear of it," Dan said. "I'll pay what you marked and no less, but we'll put it back in the house, and I'll take it later."

"I know better than to argue the point, but, I need your help with one of the horses. I tried to move him earlier, but he...tried to kill me."

Dan laughed. "Horses, some of them are just seven hundred pounds of mean, but I'll go get him."

"Be careful," Jefferson warned.

"Don't worry. I know a thing or two about horses. You can take a break if you like."

"We should deal with the horse together. I mean, he is really something."

Dan smiled and walked toward the barn. "You take a break. I'll be right back. I have a way with animals."

Jefferson sat down on a recliner and waited for Dan to scream for help but, a moment later, the developer came leading a large, gray horse out by his bridal.

"This horse gave you trouble?" Dan yelled. "He seems pretty tame."

Jefferson hopped off the recliner. "Maybe you do have a way with animals."

Dan tied the large, gray horse to a post. "Now, help me move this table and chairs back in the house before someone tries to buy it."

Jefferson and Dan came outside from moving the table and chairs and found several ladies roaming through the aisles of unwanted furniture.

A short woman with gray hair who was probably not quite five feet tall looked up at him. "Are these prices a joke?"

"No ma'am," said Jefferson. "I'm quite serious about selling everything."

"I want this armoire," she said.

She rushed to Jefferson and handed him a hundred dollars. She pulled out her cellphone.

Jefferson said, "That's not going to work. You have to drive five miles up to get a somewhat shaky signal."

The woman looked at her phone and nodded. "Don't let that armoire go anywhere. It's mine, and I'll be right back."

"I'll guard it with my life," he said.

Word spread fast in the small town and soon the front yard of the farmhouse seemed more like a festival, minus the cotton candy and funnel cake. Even the giant front yard could barely contain all the trucks as a line of people formed to give Dan money as Jefferson watched satisfied.

At a folding table lay all manner of firearms, rifles and handguns. A man in overalls held up a nine-millimeter pistol and yelled, "It says one hundred dollars, but I only have seventy four."

Jefferson pointed and the man and yelled, "Sold to the man in the lovely overalls."

The man smiled, took his gun and got in line.

The little old lady who had purchased the armoire got out of a giant truck with three massive men.

Jefferson recognized them immediately. The Tillman Boys. It was odd that they were called boys since they had been the size of men since they were in junior high.

Mama Tillman directed the boys to the armoire.

"Get it in the truck boys, and you better not scratch it, or I'll do the same to your eyes."

The little woman bossing around the men made Jefferson think of a Chihuahua giving orders to three lions.

Samuel, the largest Tillman boy, stopped and looked across the yard at Jefferson.

Samuel yelled, "Must be rough on you to be back amongst the country folk. Better watch out. You might scruff your shiny shoes."

"It's no trouble," said Jefferson. "I'm not going to be here long."

Samuel went to say something else, but his mother slapped him on the shoulder and said, "We ain't here for you to puff up your chest. Just get the armoire."

Samuel pointed at Jefferson. "Make sure you don't stay long."

Jefferson smiled but not on the inside. He wanted to leave as fast as he could, but he wasn't keen on being told to leave. On the inside, he was a balled up fist and clenched teeth. A small part of him - the part that would always be part of Picayune - wanted to call Samuel over and kick in his teeth, but he wasn't that person anymore. He wasn't the Black-Redneck.

The Tillmans loaded up the armoire and all three brothers glared in Jefferson's direction. Jefferson made a point of not making eye contact, just like you don't want to make eye contact with an aggressive dog.

No sooner had they left and Jefferson was able to relax a bit, than Old Ed stepped onto the property and whistled loud enough to burst eardrums.

"So, that's it," Old Ed yelled. "You're going to help him, help him sell this place off and turn that beautiful wood into some shitty subdivision."

The man in the overalls turned around. "Old Ed, it's his. We can't stop him. We might as well get cheap guns."

"Yeah," a redneck lady said. "He's practically giving this stuff away."

"Beau's stuff!" Old Ed shouted.

"Sir, you can't stop progress," said Dan. "And, why would you want to. A lot of families are going to enjoy this place, and it's going to be great for the local economy."

"Your and Jefferson's economy."

"No," Dan argued. "Everyone is going to..."

"Shut your mouth, carpet bagger," Old Ed cried out.

"Sir, I am from the great state of Mississippi. I am no carpet bagger," said Dan.

Jefferson placed a hand on Dan's shoulder. "I've got this."

He walked up to Old Ed. "I know your natural state is pissed off, but I hope you know this is for the best. More little kids will be able to run in these woods, just like I did."

"They ain't going to leave any woods. Don't think they will and don't pretend you care."

"I'll make sure there is," Jefferson said. "Look, I really appreciate you taking care of this place after Beau...got himself killed."

Jefferson held out a wad of cash to Old Ed.

Old Ed slapped the money out of Jefferson's hand and it flew into the yard.

"I wasn't doing it for your money. I was doing it because Big Beau would have done the same for me, or any one of us. But, you all enjoy your new trinkets. Bunch of assholes."

"I can't stay here, Old Ed. This town...isn't for me."

Old Ed pointed at the large gray horse. "And, you're selling Gray Man? What kind of man sells his own horse?"

"It's not my horse. I haven't seen the animal in ten years, and he seems to want to kill me."

"Did you always hate it here?" Old Ed asked. "Did you always hate us? Me?"

Jefferson shook his head. "No, I don't hate you, never have. You taught me a lot, how to ride, how to shoot a gun, but I'm just not that person any longer."

The old man said, "You're certainly no one I know."

He limped away.

Jefferson sighed. His goal of getting away without an altercation was becoming a larger and larger failure.

He bent to pick up his money, but two little boys were already bent over and snatching it up like they were picking strawberries. As one little boy ran after some of the money that was blowing in the wind, the other turned and held out the money to Jefferson.

"Here you are, sir."

The other little boy ran back and held out the money he collected.

Jefferson took the money and said, "Thanks, thanks a lot."

The youngest boy asked, "How come nobody likes you?"

Jefferson ignored the question and held out two twenties. "Here's your finder's fee. Thanks for your help."

"Really?" one of the boys asked.

Jefferson nodded.

"Thanks, Mister."

EVERYTHING DOESN'T GO

Jefferson looked up from counting money from the cigar box. The yard that had not long ago been filled with all manner of items and people was mostly empty of shoppers. The only two items left were Big-Bang and Gray Man. As the few remaining shoppers eased toward their trucks, Jefferson stepped from behind the table.

"Everyone, wait." He said loudly.

Some people ignored him and others turned to look at him. He walked to the gun table and held up Big-Bang.

"Can't I interest any of you in this custom-made...handgun. It even has a picture on the grip of the gun of Big Beau shooting it and everyone loves Big Beau."

One of the farmers said, "Bad luck to own another man's gun."

"You bought two of his rifles," Jefferson said.

"Yeah, but those were guns he owned, not *his* gun. That one has his picture on it."

Jefferson sat the gun down and said, "Okay, I can understand why no one wants that eye-sore of a hand-cannon, but." He walked toward the large gray horse. Gray Man faced away from Jefferson as if he didn't want to look at him. "This is a Lipizzan stallion, known for their strength, their longevity, and their intelligence."

One of the farmers came over and looked at the horse. The beast did look like one of the horses that would carry a knight into battle.

"Fine horse," said the farmer. "But I happen to know it's almost thirty years old. Could die any moment."

"Ain't no small thing to bury a horse," said another.

"You're right," said Jefferson. "But if you could just breed him once, it would be worth it. Because you can take him for...free. That's right. Free."

The farmer looked back at the other man, and they both shrugged as if to say 'it's up to you'.

Jefferson could see the first farmer was considering it. "And this horse is smart. It's so smart it can train your other horses by himself."

Jefferson grabbed the horse's bridle "Gray Man, bow for the nice men."

Gray Man jerked away from Jefferson's touch so hard and fast that it almost pulled him off his feet. The horse spun quickly and kicked its back hooves toward Jefferson's head. Off balance, he had to fall backwards to avoid having his head smashed. The horse turned and tried to stomp him, but Jefferson scooted back and regained his feet. The horse tried to pursue him, but his reins were tied to a post.

The farmers laughed hard as Jefferson got to his feet and moved quickly away from Gray Man.

"Don't need no horse to train my others how to murder me," said the farmer.

The farmers got in their trucks and drove away.

As Jefferson tried to brush the grass stain off of his designer pants, Dan came over. "Well, overall a great success, and it didn't take long."

"Rednecks love cheap guns and livestock," said Jefferson. "I don't guess I can interest you in an aged, somewhat homicidal horse?"

Dan said, "I'll buy a horse when they make one that comes with air conditioning. 'Til then I'll be keeping my truck."

Jefferson looked at Gray Man. "I don't know what I'm supposed to do with him."

Dan went and grabbed Big-Bang and walked back to Jefferson.

"It's not my place to say, but maybe the one other thing that didn't sell could help."

Dan pulled the giant handgun from its holster. "You and the horse go for a walk in the woods; only you come back. You could just take the gun apart and throw it in the catfish ponds."

"Might lose my PETA card for that," he said.

"Well, for whatever the reason, the horse seems fine with killing you. At this point it could be considered self-defense."

As Jefferson seemed to consider the solution, Dan said, "I'm going to get the sign for the new subdivision put up. If I come back and there's no horse, it'll be our secret."

Jefferson nodded as Dan put the gun back in the holster and draped it over his shoulder. The developer walked to his truck.

"Cheer up," Dan said from inside his truck. "You're almost out of here and we're going to make a lot of money. Oh, and can you feed those catfish? Those ponds are going to be a big selling point."

"You got it. I could stand to go for a walk."

THE DEVOURER FEASTS ON BIRDS

The Devourer moved through the woods eating everything that wasn't fast or smart enough to get out of its path - squirrels, mice, insects. Some creatures were drawn to the pulsating bioluminescence of the creature. Their curiosity led to their deaths as their cells were added to the Devourer's mass. Like a snowball rolling down a hill, the Devourer grew rapidly.

As the sun began to rise, the Devourer froze at the sound of chirping birds. She turned toward the sound and moved silently toward it. The creature moved slowly and silently beneath them as the birds pecked happily away amongst the vines of a blackberry bush.

The Devourer slowly stretched up its tentacle and, grabbing a bird without the others noticing, swallowed it whole. She picked the birds out of the thorny vines as easily as a man might gather the berries. One of the birds fluttered and chirped as it was consumed. The others took off into the air. The Devourer fell still beneath the foliage, its clear flesh making it practically invisible and waited. The birds fluttered back to the bushes. The Devourer would feast off of them until one would finally notice and they would all take to the air. This process went on for some time until there were no birds in the area left and the ground around the berry vines was covered with so many feathers that it looked like a serious pillow fight had occurred.

The Devourer's core shook, rocking the rest of its body back and forth as it sprouted new tentacles from its clear flesh. She rose her bulk off the ground with the new appendages and moved quickly into the woods with the grace of an octopus moving along the ocean floor.

HORSE-ICIDE

Jefferson wore the holster that held Big Bang draped over one shoulder as he led Gray Man deeper into the woods.

It was no easy task for Jefferson to get Gray Man into the woods. The large horse fought him almost every step of the way but, while it had been a while since he had dealt with horses, he hadn't totally forgotten how to manage an unruly horse. Every time Gray Man would rear up, Jefferson would pull him back down by the reins.

He pulled the large horse into a copse off the trail. He held the reins with one hand and pulled Big-Bang with the other and placed the barrel of the giant handgun between the horse's eyes. Gray Man turned his head to the side. The horse's large, black eyes reflected Jefferson's image. He slowly lowered the gun and bowed his head.

FLASHBACK: 1992 PICAYUNE MISSISSIPPI-THE HORSE SHOW AND AUCTION

The black eyes of the Lippizan Colt reflected the image of a nine year old Jefferson. Young Jefferson smiled as he reached through a wooden fence to scratch the ears of the colt. The young horse put his head through the gap in the fence and nuzzled Jefferson affectionately. It was love at first sight.

Jefferson looked up from his new friend when he felt the pounding of horses' hooves hitting the ground in time.

Dark haired men rode massive, gray horses. They wore thick, gray tights with black leather boots to the knee and black waist coats with matching derby hats.

Jefferson burst into laughter and held his belly. One of the men with a curly mustache looked over his shoulder and glowered at the boy.

Young Jefferson climbed onto the fence and pushed back the cowboy hat that was way too big for him.

One of the riders yelled, "Levade! Levade!"

The rider's horse rose onto its hind legs and took short, choppy steps forward. The rider barked another order and the horse collapsed back to the ground and pranced raising it legs high.

Jefferson burst into laughter again so hard that he almost fell off the fence.

The rider turned his horse to look in the direction of the laughter. Jefferson tipped his hat to the man and gave him a big smile, almost bursting into laughter again at the sight of the man's curly mustache.

Fancy Mustache broke from the other riders and galloped to where Jefferson sat on the fence.

He pulled up in front of Jefferson and spoke in a thick Spanish accent, the kind of accent that could steal your girlfriend in about two seconds.

Fancy Mustache asked, "Do we amuse you?"

"No, sir. Just ain't...well, you guys are about the strangest cowboys I ever did see. How long did it take you to grow such a fancy mustache?"

"We are *not* cowboys. We are Lippizaners."

At the click of the rider's tongue and a slight flip of the reins, his horse went up on its hind legs and spun in a circle.

Young Jefferson laughed and clapped.

"That sure is something," he said. "How did you train your horse to do that?"

"It takes a thousand years to do such a thing."

Young Jefferson shook his head. "Mister, I might be just a kid, but ain't no horse live a thousand years. What are they? Dracula horses?"

"It does take a thousand years," the rider said. "You see, such a horse cannot be trained. They are bred, and it took a thousands years to do so. So, much like great men, great horses are bred. When I ride this horse, I sit upon the efforts of my ancestors."

"Wow," said young Jefferson, " I'm not really sure what you said, but I sure do want one of these horses." He pointed at the young colt, "That one. Him and me are already friends. My big brother, Big Beau, is going to buy me a horse today. How much is he?"

It was the rider's turn to laugh.

Jefferson said, "I guess that means it's expensive."

"We do not sell our horses. Especially not that one. That one will be a great horse, and only a great man will ride him, not you."

"I got some money," Jefferson said. "We had a bumper crop of watermelons this year. With all the rain and all, and I shot any coon that thought to pilfer a melon."

The rider laughed again. "Run along, boy. Go buy one of these nags. That will suit you better."

Even though Jefferson was just nine, he still felt his face burn with anger. Just because someone had a fine horse and a fancy mustache didn't mean they could say anything they wanted. If Big Beau would have heard him talk like that, he would have snatched him off his horse by his funny, little hat, but Jefferson's teachers had told him it wasn't right to settle everything with a fist fight.

Jefferson jumped off the fence. He turned his back and was going to walk away, but the young, gray colt neighed and pawed the wooden fence with his hooves. He turned around to see the horse put his head through the fence and stare after Jefferson like it didn't want him to go.

Young Jefferson ran back to the fence and climbed it so he could look the rider in the eye.

"Hey, Fancy Moustache man!"

The rider galloped back to the fence.

"What is it now, boy?"

"I'll shoot you for him," Jefferson said.

"Are you threatening me?"

"No. I mean like a contest."

The rider scoffed. "I do not think so. There is no honor in beating a mere boy. Go grow into your hat."

Fancy Moustache turned to ride back to the others, but Jefferson yelled, "Mister, I think you're scared."

The rider ignored him, but the other riders laughed at Jefferson.

"Go on and laugh," he said. "But, if he shoots against me, he'll be shy one fancy horse."

Big Beau walked up behind Jefferson, casting a wide shadow over him. Jefferson looked up at him.

Big Beau stared at the men. "What's going on here?"

"I'm going to shoot against him for a horse if he's got the courage," said Jefferson.

The rider galloped back to the fence.

"Boy, do not question my courage." The rider turned his eyes away from Jefferson to Big Beau and asked, "Large one, do you happen to know this boy's parents? They need to come collect him."

"He ain't go no parents, but I'm his brother," Big Beau said.

The rider looked confused.

"Well, obviously I'm adopted," said Jefferson.

Big Beau leaned against the fence and looked up at the rider. "I don't blame you, Fancy Mustache. I wouldn't shoot against him either. He's what you might call a *pro-di-gee*."

The rider spoke Spanish to his fellow riders and they all had a good laugh. He turned back to Jefferson.

"And, when you lose to me and you will, what do you have to give up?" asked the rider.

"I ain't got nuttin' but my hat and my guns," Jefferson said. "Both belonged to the man that adopted me and ain't nobody getting those from me, no way."

"Ah, so it is you, you who lack courage once you have something that is valuable to you at stake."

Jefferson looked up at his big brother. Big Beau shrugged. "You started with him. You decide how to finish it."

"We have a show to put on tonight," said Fancy Mustache. "Watch our show. At the end, if you still wish to challenge me, we will go mano a mano...if you have the courage."

Jefferson stood with his head bowed but, as the rider turned his horse, Jefferson raised his head and yelled, "I'll see you after the show Fancy Mustache."

The rider nodded and trotted off.

"I was watching these guys earlier," Big Beau said. "If he shoots like he rides, I reckon you're going to have some empty holsters and the sun in your eyes, but Pa left those things to you. They're yours to lose but, if you lose them, I'm going to be sore at you for a long time."

Jefferson looked down, deep in thought. "Well, I can't back down now, can I? You wouldn't."

"Hell, kid, if you go on whether I would do something or wouldn't, you're going to do all manner of stupid things."

Jefferson smiled. "It's only stupid, if I lose."

The Lippizaners put on a hell of a show, a fine demonstration of riding and shooting. Fancy Mustache was by far the best and the star of the show. He shot targets like it weren't nothing while his horse was doing horse-ballet beneath him.

One of the Spaniards had pulled Jefferson and Big Beau out of the stands and sat them next to an old Spaniard with white hair and large gold rings on his fingers. He didn't speak English, but would occasionally smile at Jefferson and say something in Spanish.

Jefferson took off his hat each time and said, "Yes sir." He didn't know what else to do.

On the field, one of the Lippizaners lit a cigarette and pretended he was taking a break. Fancy Mustache galloped by on his large white horse and shot the cigarette out of the man's mouth.

Fancy Mustache rode to the front of the stands and his horse rose on its hind legs. "Kids. Don't smoke. It is bad for your health."

Everyone laughed and clapped.

Beau put a large hand on young Jefferson's shoulder. "Reckon that guy's pretty good."

"Yeah, guess it won't be easy to beat him," said Jefferson.

"Nope," said Big Beau.

At the end of the show, everyone in the stands leapt to their feet and cheered. The people of Mississippi had never experienced anything like it. More than a few of the women in the stands fanned their faces even though it wasn't hot at all. People were about to leave, but Fancy Mustache rode to the microphone and grabbed it.

Fancy Mustache's voice echoed as he spoke into the microphone. "Ladies and Gentlemen! Tonight I have been challenged to a contest of marksmanship by one of your own."

The rider motioned for Jefferson to join him.

Jefferson stood up, strapped on his gun belt and walked over to stand at the rider's side.

The crowd fell still and quiet.

Fancy Mustache said, "A mere boy, a brave boy who calls himself..." The rider moved the microphone away from his mouth and said, "What do they call you, boy?"

Jefferson pushed back his hat. "Black-Redneck."

The rider just looked at him and then held the microphone to Jefferson's mouth. "I'm going to let you say that."

Jefferson said shyly, "Umm, I'm the Black-Redneck."
The crowd burst into laughter.

Jefferson and the rider walked side by side.
"We will begin with plates," the rider said.
Jefferson nodded but really had no idea what was coming.
One of the other riders with a stack of white plates stepped off fifteen paces from where Jefferson and Fancy Mustache stood.
Fancy Mustache pulled his sidearm and nodded. The other horsemen threw two plates straight into the air. Bang. Bang. The two plates rained down in shards.
He holstered his weapon and smirked at Jefferson.
"You may want to pull your weapon," suggested the rider.
"I'm good," said Jefferson.
The horsemen grabbed two more plates. He looked a bit nervous and said, "Un momento."
Fancy Mustache and the other horsemen spoke furiously in Spanish. Jefferson couldn't understand a word, but it seemed the guy wasn't too keen to stand in front of a nine year old while he shot off live rounds from his two Colts.
Jefferson said, "Dude, I won't shoot you. Promise. I'm good."
The man sighed and grabbed two plates. He threw them into the air.
Before the plates even had time to teach their apex, Jefferson pulled his two colts. Blam! Blam! The plates exploded into a hail of white shards.
The boy spun his colts and slide them back into the holsters. He didn't look up, but he could feel Fancy Mustache looking down at him.
"Maybe you will beat me," Young Jefferson said. "But it ain't gonna be easy."

What followed was a veritable plate holocaust. Horsemen threw plates into the air and Fancy Mustache and Jefferson shattered them with bullets. They had worked their way up to six plates and had no problem shattering all six. It was decided that round was a tie, and at some point the crowd turned on the rider and everyone started rooting for Jefferson. Every now and then someone would yell, "Go, Black-Redneck."

They set up plates on top of rods and stuck each of the rods in the soft dirt. Two aisles of plates extended down the arena at ten feet apart, the closest being ten yards away from where Jefferson and the rider stood. The plates extended away from them until the last couple seemed like white dots against the dirt of the arena.

Fancy Mustache explained, "This is simple. First one to miss loses. I shoot, then you shoot."

Jefferson nodded.

The rider shot first. A plate exploded.

Jefferson shot the first plate easily in return.

The rider shot the second plate with little effort.

Jefferson took a deep breath and pulled the trigger. The plate shattered and the crowd cheered.

The rider used both hands for the third plate. Boom. Crack. The plate shattered.

Jefferson smiled and nodded. He took aim, but didn't over think it. Bam. The plate shattered.

The rider sighed in frustration. The crowd grew deadly quiet as he took aim. Boom. The plate shattered. He sighed in relief.

It was Jefferson's turn to worry. From this distance the plates started looking like snow flakes. Jefferson aimed and fired. Blam. A small chip was taken out of the top of the plate, but it didn't shatter.

As the crowd gasped and murmured about whether that was a hit or not, Jefferson spun his colt in his left hand and returned it to his holster. He unbuckled his belt and wrapped it neatly around the holsters. He took off his hat, dropped the guns inside, and held it out to the rider.

"That was some fine shooting, Fancy Mustache," said

Jefferson. "Ain't no shame in losing to you."

Jefferson walked back toward Big Beau. The crowd cheered for him. Some people chanted, "Black-Redneck! Black-Redneck!" Jefferson waved to them.

Fancy Mustache walked back to the microphone and grabbed it.

He said, "Earlier tonight I said there was no honor in beating a nine-year-old boy. Now, I just feel lucky that he was not ten."

The rider walked away holding Jefferson's hat and guns.

Jefferson made it back to Beau's side. The old Spaniard seemed about to say something, but Big Beau said, "Thought you had him for a second there."

"Yeah, I guess you'll be sore at me now, but, before you start yelling, I plan on practicing a lot and tracking that guy down to get Pa's guns back."

"I ain't as mad as I thought I would be. Hell, that fancy lil' Mexican just got lucky."

Jefferson started to walk off with Big Beau, then he ran back and extended his hand to the Old Spaniard. The Old-Spaniard smiled and grabbed Jefferson's hand in his own. Jefferson could feel the cold rings on the man's hands.

"I imagine you understand me about as much as I understand you," he said. "But I reckon it was you that taught these guys how to ride and shoot, so I guess that makes you a bad ass. Just wanted you to know, I'll find you guys some day and I'll be getting my guns and hat back."

Jefferson ran back to Beau's side. "One day, one day I'll have a horse like that."

"There's plenty of horses for you to ride on the farm," Beau said.

"Yeah, but not like that."

Beau and Jefferson walked back to the truck. Beau loaded the horse he had bought in the trailer as Jefferson watched.

Fancy Mustache called out from the darkness, "Black Redneck."

Jefferson turned to see the Rider and the Old Spaniard leading the young colt and coming toward them.

Jefferson said, "Evening, Fancy Mustache and you sir."

The boy went to tip his hat, but then realized he had lost it and smiled at his own mistake.

The old Spaniard walked to Jefferson's side and placed his hand on Jefferson's shoulder.

He spoke and Fancy Mustache translated.

"He says in the old times men of bravery were given horses, not just for what they had done, but to give them the opportunity for more bravery. He says you are very brave and very talented. He says the horse can tell this about you, too, and longs to carry you. He thinks it is important you have the horse. He thinks the two of you will do something important one day. He feels it in his blood. I think he has gone mad in his old age."

"He's giving me the horse?" asked Jefferson.

"Yes. Against my vehement pleas to do otherwise."

The old Spaniard knelt in front of Jefferson and spoke Spanish smoothly.

"He says you must promise to properly train and care for the horse and that a man always keeps his word," Fancy Mustache said.

Jefferson smiled and nodded.

"I swear. I'll keep him safe and take good care of him. He'll have a great life with me."

The old Spaniard smiled and handed the reins to Jefferson before shuffling away.

The rider glared at Jefferson one last time and dropped Jefferson's cowboy hat on the ground. He followed the old man into the darkness. "I'm keeping the guns. Come for them when you are man enough to take them."

"I will," said Jefferson, "You better keep practicing, cause that's what I'll be doing."

End Flashback:

Jefferson holstered Big Bang and leaned against Gray Man, and the horse let him.

"I can't believe I was going to shoot you," he said. "Is that the person I've become?" He shook his head if that wasn't true. "I don't break my promises. I don't kill things out of convenience."

Jefferson sighed and led the animal back to the trail. He rubbed Gray Man's ears. The horse turned his head so he could scratch the other ear.

"Yeah, I remember how much you like that."

He stepped to the side of the horse. The horse shied away and neighed, but Jefferson rubbed the horse's neck softly and spoke even softer.

"Easy, big guy. Easy. If you're going to stick around, you'll have to earn your keep. You'll have to help an old friend carry some catfish food."

Jefferson put a dress shoe in the stirrup and swung onto Gray Man's back. He didn't get his other shoe into the other stirrup before the horse started bucking fiercely and threw him into some of the tall weeds along the trail. Jefferson hit the ground hard and wanted to lay there for a bit, but Gray Man turned and charged toward him.

He rolled to his feet and ran into the woods where the giant animal couldn't follow. Jefferson looked back from between two trees. Gray Man stood proudly and stomped his front hooves as he blew air harshly out of his snout. The horse reared up on his hind legs and then sprinted down the trail.

Jefferson watched until the horse was out of sight. He stepped from the woods and sighed and started walking back toward the farmhouse.

SCAVENGERS

Shorty laid in the tall grass just at the tree line with a sheet of scorched tin covering his wide frame. The twisted tin wasn't quite up to the task and his shoulders stuck out on either side.

Not ten yards from where Shorty lay, a long, clear tentacle emerged from in between two tall pine trees. The tentacle hooked the trunk of one of the trees and pulled the Devourer's bulk between the two trees.

The Devourer let her body rest between the two trees as she slowly moved the rest of her tentacles to grab the sides of the trees.

A few steps in front of the Devourer, buzzards clustered around Tatter's corpse like hogs at a trough. The birds jostled and squawked at each other as they tried to gain access to Tatter's round belly.

The tentacles grasping the trees tightened. The Devourer pulled with all her tentacles at once and threw her body toward the carrion and scavengers alike.

The Devourer collided with the corpse hard enough to send a wet thud echoing through the clearing. Most of the birds didn't even have a chance to raise their heads from where they were buried in Tatter's torso, but one of the birds launched itself skyward. The Devourer shot up a tentacle that wrapped around the large bird's body. The buzzard screeched and flapped its wings frantically. The tentacle tightened like a python and a crunching noise followed. The buzzard fell limp, but the Devourer held it high as it wrapped the other birds in tentacles and pulled them away from the corpse.

The Devourer kept the big, black birds held high as she wrapped another tentacle around the corpse's neck and dragged it toward the burnt out Meth-Lab.

As the creature entered the destroyed building, the crows that had been pecking at Skeeter's long corpse shot into the air. They came to a rest on the high beams and looked down as the Devourer continued to pull Tater's corpse across the dirt floor of the building.

The Devourer grabbed Skeeter's corpse as she went and pulled them both against the wall. She stacked the dead buzzards and corpses on top of each other and climbed on top of them. She reached out with her longer tentacles and grabbed sheets of tin. The monster covered herself and her meal with a lean-to of loose metal. Horrible sucking noises and the sound of bones snapping echoed from beneath the tin.

FEEDING CATFISH

Jefferson let the fifty pound bag of catfish food slide off his shoulder and fall to the trail with a loud crunch. His white dress shirt was soaked through with sweat and the bag had left a film of brown dust on his shirt and his sweaty face. He tried to brush off his shirt to no avail, then gave up. He used his clean, dry shirt tail to wipe the sweat out of his eyes.

Over the hill, a rudimentary fish sculpture on a tall pole rose high into the air.

He stretched his arms over head in a stretch and picked up the bag as if it weighed nothing. As he restarted his trek, he looked down at his shoes and saw the expensive leather covered in mud. He shook his head in disgust.

Next time the catfish can just starve.

His frustration increased his pace. He soon emerged at the top of a small hill. Before him lay the four catfish ponds. At first glance Jefferson knew they were man-made, as the ponds were perfectly rectangular. His second thought on seeing the ponds was that Big Beau had made them because the first pond was big, the second pond was bigger still, the third pond even bigger, and the last pond was ridiculously big. He smiled and shook his head at the excessiveness of the ponds as he walked toward them.

Jefferson walked to the pole on which the fish sculpture was mounted and set the bag of food down by it. He tore the bag open. At the sound, some catfish began to strike at the surface of the murky water. Many more shadowy shapes swam just below the surface.

Jefferson eased down the steep, muddy bank of the largest pond while trying to hold the cumbersome bag of catfish food against his chest. His dress shoes weren't up to the task. His foot slipped in the mud. He fell on his back and slid down the muddy bank toward the water. He dropped the bag of feed and put his hands in the mud, clawing at the ground for purchase. He stopped his momentum, but not before one foot went into the water up to his knee.

Jefferson yanked his foot out of the water and his foot came out of his shoe.

"Shit."

He spun around to the edge of the pond and reached after his shoe, but the bank wasn't cut at an angle. It went straight down like the edge of a swimming pool. Jefferson reached into the murk to try to find his shoe, but all he got for his trouble was his shirt sleeve covered in brown murk. Jefferson sat up on the muddy bank in his suit pants.

"Great, that's just great."

Jefferson pulled the bag of catfish food to the edge of the pond. He grabbed two handfuls of the catfish feed and cast it onto the water. The catfish food looked like dry dog-food floating on the surface of the water, but not for long. A thousand catfish rose to the surface of the pond and formed a writhing mass of slimy fish flesh as they all pushed at each other to get at the food. The catfish were stacked so tight that it seemed you could walk right across them.

He grabbed even more food and threw it. Again, the writhing mass of fish flesh rose and consumed the food and then vanished beneath the surface.

Jefferson looked at the bag of catfish food. "I need a bigger bag."

Sometime later, he stepped out of the woods and into the side field that sloped up to the farmhouse. He walked in mud-encrusted silk socks and held a single dress shoe in his hand.

He muttered to himself how much he hated Picayune and how he couldn't wait to leave. Every time he looked down at his muddy clothes, his scowl turned downward a little more and the lines on his brow grew deeper.

Gray Man appeared behind him at the trailhead. The horse took off at a sprint toward Jefferson. At the sound of the pounding hooves, Jefferson turned his head to see the large beast charging toward him.

Jefferson took off at a sprint and it was easy to tell he was a man that kept himself in fantastic shape, but he was no match for the horse. The big animal was right behind him in just a few long strides. Jefferson felt the heat of the air coming from the flaring nostrils of the horse. He turned hard to the right and his feet came out from under him and he fell on his side as the horse ran by him.

He rolled and leapt to his feet. The horse turned sharply and faced him but didn't charge. The large beast stomped his hooves into the field, pulling up big divots of grass.

Jefferson stood tall. "Get out of my way. Yah!"

The horse turned his head sideways at Jefferson.

"Seriously, I've had a bad day. I don't have time for some homicidal horse, so shoo."

Jefferson took a step toward the fence and the horse charged. Jefferson sprinted right back at the horse as if he was playing a game of chicken with two tons of herbivore. At the last second, he dove to the left, rolled and came up running. The horse turned in a tight circle and charged after him. Just as he was about to be overtaken, Jefferson leapt for the fence and sailed over it like Superman. He landed on his stomach and laid there for a moment, groaning, then slowly rolled over on his back.

The horse stopped at the fence, stomped his hooves, and then galloped back into the woods with his tail and head held high.

Jefferson sat up and pulled a thorn out of his foot, wincing. He got to his feet and brushed the grass from his already ruined clothes and saw Old Ed standing there.

Old Ed was never much on smiling, but something like a smirk had formed on his face.

"Beautiful day, isn't it?

"Yeah, just lovely," said Jefferson.

The old man began to say something else, but Jefferson said, "If you're going to ask about the farm again don't waste your time. The paperwork has already been signed. It's a done deal."

"Ain't here about that. I heard you were having trouble selling Gray Man."

"Sell him? I can't give him away. He's gone crazy. Keeps trying to kill me."

"Well," said Old Ed, "Is he crazy or just a good judge of character?"

"You want him? Take him. You and the horse can discuss how horrible I am."

"There's lots of folks to have that conversation with, but, yeah, I'll take the old fella."

"Good, he's all yours. You just have to catch him. Preferably, before he murders me."

Old Ed shrugged. "He'll come back to his stall. Always does. I'll collect him then."

The old man turned and limped away. He turned back toward Jefferson and said, "I hope your day stays pleasant."

Jefferson waited until Old Ed was gone and walked to the Old Farmhouse. He stripped off his clothes on the porch and carried them into the shower where he rinsed the mud off and hung them to dry. When he jumped in the shower and turned the water on hot, he hoped it would wash away the stress, but it only got rid of the mud.

BAD TO WORSE

Only part of the meth lab still smoldered with a bit of white smoke. The few sheets of tin the Devourer had stacked on top of itself and its meal rose and fell as if it concealed a giant beating heart.

Two crows perched at the top of the burnt out meth lab turned the black orbs of their eyes toward the shifting tin. The sheets of tin exploded outward to reveal a translucent, tentacled horror. The crows leapt for the sky, beating their wings frantically, but not fast enough.

The Devourer climbed the frame of the destroyed meth lab in a blur of clear flesh and pulsating bioluminescence. As some tentacles pulled her mass to the top of the roof, others whipped toward the fleeing crows. The tentacles struck the birds so hard that a cloud of black feathers burst into the air as the crows' broken bodies spiraled toward the ground.

The Devourer slid down the wall and scooped up the two birds with tentacles that ended in snake-like mouths.

The dead crows traveled down the tentacles and came to a rest in the clear flesh around her core. The large birds rapidly dissolved and bubbled as if they had been dropped in acid. The skull and femur bones of Skeeter and Tater dissolved at a slower rate nearby.

She stretched some of her tentacles forward as she pushed with the tentacles at the back of her body. The pulling and pushing of tentacles made the Devourer seem like a giant, clear Medusa's head floating across the ground as she crawled out of the ruins of the Meth-Lab.

Not only was she larger, her body was transformed. A mass of tentacles stood out from her back. Some ended in Venus flytrap-like mouths. Others ended in hooks and barbs. A long, thin tentacle that rose from her body just over her core ended in a cluster of spaghetti-like tendrils. She held this tentacle out before her like a dowsing rod. The tendrils waved back and forth like sea anemone.

The Devourer pulsated with vibrant colors and moved toward the edge of the woods where Shorty laid covered in a sheet of scorched tin.

As a tentacle reached out for the piece of tin, another thin tentacle lurched in the other direction. The Devourer spun her strange body.

A deer and her fawn moved toward the creek to drink. The Devourer sped toward them, sending up dust in her wake and leaving Shorty safely beneath the tin.

WELCOME TO SHADY PINES

Dan stepped back and wiped his brow, his red polo shirt stained with sweat under his arms and around his collar, but he was too pleased with himself to even notice. He continued to stare at the large sign advertising the new Shady Pines Subdivision with lots starting at $20,000 like he was in a museum staring at a Monet. When Dan thought about his share of the money, he smiled even wider.

The developer turned when he heard the crunch of tires on the gravel road that led to the farmhouse. The Sheriff's car pulled to a stop just off the black top, but this wasn't just any sheriff's vehicle. It was a modern day, black hot-rod with sheriff decals on the door and the windows tinted almost too dark to see through.

Dan smiled and waved. He tried to look through the dark tint of the windows, but could barely make out the two shapes sitting in the front seats.

"Sheriff Hill, is that you? It sure would be great to have a law enforcement officer living here. We should discuss..."

When Dan got a few steps from the sheriff's cruiser, the engine of the car roared and the tires spun, sending up a cloud of dust and gravel. Dan tried to back away, but still got coated in a fine coat of white dust that stuck to his sweaty skin.

He coughed as he back peddled out of the cloud of dust and used the bottom of his shirt to wipe the grit from his eyes. By the time he looked up, the sheriff's cruiser sped down the gravel road at high speed as it kept just ahead of a plume of dust.

"Asshole," Dan said, but only because he knew Sheriff Hill couldn't hear him.

OLD FRIENDS

Jefferson felt his dress shirt and pants. They were still very wet, but at least he had gotten most of the stains out.

He slipped into his athletic clothes and looked like he was about to star in a North Face commercial. It wasn't that feeding the catfish and getting chased by a homicidal horse hadn't been a decent work out, but his muscles still felt full of stress and, since he was dressed for it, he thought why not go for a run.

He stepped off the porch and saw what looked like a mix between a cop car and a drag racer sitting in the yard waiting on him. The windows were too dark to see through, but Jefferson tried to look past them.

The door of the car opened and a man in a brown and beige sheriff's uniform stepped out. It had been ten years since Jefferson had seen Ambrose Hill, but he would have recognized that jawline and curly blonde hair anywhere.

"Hey, Ambrose."

The passenger side door opened and a tall, thin woman with long, wavy blonde hair stepped out wearing a similar uniform. She held a bundle of thick books under her arm.

Ambrose looked over the roof of the car at the woman. "Ten years, ten long years, he doesn't call, he doesn't write, and he's like, 'Hey, Ambrose' like he saw me yesterday."

"I've been really busy," said Jefferson.

"Too busy to accept my Facebook request?"

Jefferson and Ambrose just stared at each other. Jefferson had imagined Ambrose would be wearing a beer belly by now, but his waist was still narrow and his shoulders were still wide.

"So, you're the sheriff. Can't say I'm surprised."

"Really?" said Ambrose. "Why's that?"

"You always did like to push people around."

Ambrose took a step toward Jefferson. "Is that right? That why you left? You get tired of me pushing you around?"

Jefferson scoffed. "You never pushed me around. Remember when you tried and I beat your ass?"

"That was the eighth grade, Jefferson," Ambrose said, raising his voice. "Maybe, it's time for a rematch."

Ambrose took off his badge and unbuckled his holster to lay his gun next to the badge on the hood of the hotrod.

Jefferson shook his head as he said, "This. This is exactly why I left. Bullshit like this."

"Ambrose, you put your gun back on," the woman said with a heavy Mississippi accent.

"You're right," Ambrose said. "I should just shoot him."

"Ambrose!" the woman yelled. "You promised to be nice."

The sheriff put his gun belt back on and picked up his badge. When the woman gave him an angry look, he gave her a fake smile and leaned against the car looking anywhere but at Jefferson.

The woman approached Jefferson with her books. On closer inspection Jefferson could see they were the books he had written.

The woman said, "Geez, I'm so sorry about that. His feelings are hurt is all, you leaving and never seeing him again. He was under the impression the two of you were best friends."

There was something familiar about the woman, but Jefferson couldn't place her. He certainly didn't remember such a woman when he lived here.

When Jefferson didn't say anything, the woman continued,

"You probably don't remember me on account of me having the body of a malnourished twelve year old boy when you saw me last, but I'm..."

"Daisy?" asked Jefferson.

She smiled. "That's right. Ambrose's kid sister, but I'm all grown up."

Jefferson's eyes passed over her and he thought how she had grown in some very convenient places.

"It's so cool you're back. Do you think you could sign these for me?" She held up the books, "I'm a huge fan."

Daisy had always been a fan of Jefferson's.

"Sure. It's always nice to meet a fan," he said.

"Or in this case be reunited with one," Daisy said, handing Jefferson a book and a sharpie. "I'm always prepared."

He signed the book and handed it back to her.

Daisy took the book and held it out to Ambrose to take. When Ambrose ignored her, she cleared her throat and shook the book at him.

"Ambrose Hill, you be nice."

The sheriff gave her another fake smile and snatched the book out of her hand.

Daisy turned back around to Jefferson and said softly, "Yep, feelings are really hurt."

"So, you're a cop too," said Jefferson.

Daisy leaned to show off her badge and to flash a bit of cleavage as she explained, "No, I'm just the Game Warden, only kind of a cop."

As Jefferson took the next book to sign, Ambrose turned the thick book he held over in his hands and said, "Ha, this book has your picture on it, but it says here your name is Emerson and that you're from Portland. Seems like I remember going to kindergarten with you and throwing the football right in this very yard..oh about a million times."

Jefferson and Daisy ignored him.

Daisy said, "I sure am curious about where you're going with the Laser-Sword Chronicles. Maybe we could get some coffee and you could give me a special preview."

Before Jefferson could answer Daisy, Ambrose blurted holding up the back of the book, "Hey, Jefferson. I don't think the back cover is supposed to be fiction too."

When Jefferson looked around Daisy at Ambrose, the sheriff asked, "You ashamed of where you're from, Jefferson?"

Jefferson leaned around Daisy. "Short answer, yes."

He handed Daisy the last of the books.

"So, how about that coffee?" she said.

Jefferson looked up at Ambrose who shook his head and put his hand on his gun.

"I won't be here that long," he answered.

He went to step around her to start his run, but she stepped into his path.

"Well, if you need anything while you're here, be sure to call."

"Thanks."

Jefferson stepped around her and started his jog.

She yelled after him, "Great seeing you. Hope to see you later."

Daisy turned to Ambrose and scowled at him.

"What?" he asked. "I didn't make him an asshole."

"You promised to be nice," she said.

He said, "Well, I couldn't take my sister throwing herself at some guy that abandoned us both."

"I wasn't throwing myself at him. I was expressing my interest. It's the twenty first century. I can do that if I want."

She walked to Jefferson's rental car and put her card underneath the windshield wiper, then walked to the screen door and inserted another card between the door and the frame.

"And, what are you doing now? Expressing your desperation," said Ambrose.

Daisy said, "No...let's just go."

"Wouldn't be surprised if you had his picture up with a lot of candles around it," he said.

"I don't."

Ambrose raised an eye brow at her.

"Well, there's no candles."

Ambrose shook his head and got into his cruiser.

A JOG IN THE WOODS

By the time Jefferson made it to the trail, he was already in a rhythm. He let his mind empty and focused on his breathing and staying relaxed. He repeated his running mantra over and over: The mind is empty, the breath is soft, the feet are swift.

Time seemed to vanish and before he knew it, he was deep in the woods. He stopped at a flat grassy spot in the trail and began doing yoga. The up and down motion of the yoga emptied his mind further and he felt the stress of all the imposed reunions leaving his body.

The woods were surprisingly quiet, not even a bird song, but he could hear the chirp and buzz of insects.

Jefferson moved to more complicated yoga positions. He went into crane with his hands supporting his full weight as his knees rested on his elbows. From here, he pushed into a handstand and held the position as if his body was just another tree and the fingers of his hands were roots. He closed his eyes.

In the thick of the bushes just off the trail, a tentacle that ended in the cluster of tendrils rose above the foliage like a periscope in a sea of green. The bushes swayed back and forth as the Devourer eased closer to Jefferson.

Jefferson's legs dropped to ninety degrees and he curled his body right into a cross-legged seated position and sat the back of his wrists on his knees as his eyes remained closed and he took slow deep breathes.

A tentacle that ended in a large, jagged barb rose above the foliage and positioned itself to strike.

BOOM! A shotgun blast sounded, and the tentacle withdrew into the bushes as the Devourer retreated. A dead squirrel tumbled out of the tree above Jefferson and landed on his shoulder before sliding into his lap.

Jefferson's eyes sprang open as he cried out in frustration, "Arggguhhh."

He sprang to his feet and pushed the squirrel away from him where it fell dead on the trail. Jefferson's pristine white workout shirt was spotted with squirrel blood.

He looked up to see an eleven year old boy holding a shotgun. A girl about half the boy's size stood in her bare-feet at his side holding five dead squirrels by their fluffy tails. Both had clothes that were tattered and too big. They looked like they had been cutting each others hair or maybe just escaped a Mark Twain novel.

Jefferson yelled, "What do you think you're doing?"

The two kids looked at each other like it was the dumbest question either had ever heard.

The girl said, "We huntin' squirrel." she held up the dead squirrels and added, "They ain't gonna kill themselves, are they?"

"No," said Jefferson, "I mean why are you doing it here?"

"Well, we're here on account of all the squirrels," the girl said.

"No, you can't be here. Not on my property."

"It aint your property," the girl said. "Big Beau said we can come back here whenever we like."

"Big Beau is dead," said Jefferson. "I own all this." He waived a hand at the woods. "And, I didn't say you could be here."

The girl said, "Oh yeah, well, we the ones got the gun, so you shut up."

Jefferson stomped across the distance separating them and ripped the gun out of the boy's hand. He unloaded the shotgun before shoving it back into his hands.

"Hey, you can't..."

Jefferson pulled the dead squirrels away from her and threw them back on the trail by the other dead squirrel.

"Hey! Those are ours."

"No," said Jefferson, "They aren't. All this is mine, including those squirrels. You're trespassing and if I see you again, I'm calling the sheriff."

The girl went to step around Jefferson to collect the squirrels, but Jefferson blocked her path. The boy put his hand on her shoulder. "Best go."

The girl drew her fist way back and threw a wild punch that landed right between Jefferson's legs.

As Jefferson exhaled a large amount of air and staggered backwards a few steps, the girl took off at a full sprint into the woods, laughing as she went. The boy gave Jefferson an apologetic shrug and ran after her.

Jefferson said, a few octaves higher than usual, "That's right, get out of here. Don't come back."

The girl turned around and yelled, "We don't like you, and I got you good."

Jefferson stood straight until the little kids were out of sight, then leaned against a tree and sighed heavily, waiting for the pain to subside. He stood and took a few deep breaths. He tried to restart his jog but took a few strides and bent at the waist. He stood straight again and started walking.

As Jefferson tried to walk it off, a few, long, clear tentacles stretched out of the foliage and pulled the dead squirrels into the brush.

PREPARING FOR A PARTY

After about ten minutes of walking, Jefferson restarted his jog. He ran even deeper into the woods and had almost burnt off the stress of running into the little kids, when he spotted a large fire pit just off the trail.

He slowed to a walk and moved toward the fire pit that was a least five feet across and held the charred remnants of a few large logs. Scattered beer cans lay strewn all about the area. Jefferson grimaced at the stale smell of beer and kicked one of the cans. It made a loud noise and he heard a gasp from behind one of the large pine trees.

Jefferson turned toward the trees. "Come out," he said.

There was no response.

"Don't make me come get you."

Anne, the beautiful girl from the Fast Pick Up convenient store, jumped from behind a tree. She motioned to someone behind a tree nearby, but, when they didn't step out, she reached out and pulled Pearl next to her. Pearl looked down at her shoes and fidgeted. She looked like she didn't know whether to run or throw up.

Anne gave Jefferson a big smile. "Hello, we're with...the woods clean up crew."

"The woods clean up crew?"

Anne nodded. "That's right. We're an organization that goes into the woods and...cleans up."

"Seems like a fine task to take on. Why were you hiding then?"

"We..Well, you could have been...a bear or one of those Satanists."

"Or, maybe you're just cleaning up for the next party."

"We're sorry," Pearl blurted out.

Anne cut her a look. "Right. We're sorry you would think that nice, young ladies like us would intoxicate ourselves in the middle of the woods, but we're just here to clean up. With your permission, of course."

"By all means," said Jefferson. "I'm sorry to interrupt your good deed, but don't let me catch you here again."

"Yes, sir," said Pearl. "You won't." She started picking up cans as quickly as she could.

Anne smiled and waved.

Jefferson turned his back and jogged away.

Anne looked up from picking up cans and ran to the trail to make sure Jefferson was gone. She giggled and said, "Oh my god. I thought we were going to pee yourself and pass out, again."

"It's not funny. He looked so mad. A vein in his forehead was throbbing, and he has so many muscles," Pearl said as she stared off into space.

Anne laughed. "Oh, you like his muscles." She started helping her friend pick up cans. "Maybe tonight we can drop you at the farmhouse and you can keep him distracted."

"I can't imagine anything that could get me to go to that farmhouse. Besides, that guy would just yell at me," Pearl said.

GLEN'S SHITTY HOUSE

The worn back door of the house eased open with a slow creak as light filtered in through the crack in the door, revealing a wooden floor that had seen better days.

Mary peeked through the gap in the doorway and eased silently down a hall that was slightly less dirty than her feet. She made it to the end of the hall and peered into the living room. She looked back over her shoulder and made hand motions like she was in the special forces, then mimicked someone sleeping.

Tom stepped into the hall with the shotgun and set it down carefully as his took off his boots. He picked the gun back up and snuck down the hall in his tattered socks.

He made it to the end of the hall and Mary eased behind him as he took in the scene.

Glen slept like a walrus that had been hit with a tranquilizer dart in a worn recliner as a poker-tournament played on a giant, flat screen TV.

Tom took a deep breath and carefully placed each foot on the worn wooden planks of the floor as he headed toward a gun rack on the wall.

He made it halfway to the wall and stepped on the floor wrong. It made a loud creak. Tom froze and looked over his shoulder. Glen didn't even stir. He laid motionless with his large belly slowly rising and falling with each snore.

Tom eased to the gun rack and placed the shotgun gently back into its spot. He sighed with relief and started to step backward carefully into the steps he had made on his way in.

As he moved alongside the recliner, Glen's hand came up and grabbed Tom's wrist hard enough to make the boy wince.

Glen said groggily, "Go get me a fresh beer, boy."

Mary disappeared into the darkness of the hallway like a frog slipping into the water when some boys come running around its pond. Tom ran to get the beer and held it out to the fat man. Glen sat up in the recliner and snatched the beer away. He snatched the boy's wrist again, squeezing it harder than he needed to.

"What were you doing in here, boy?"

"Nothin', sir."

Glen pick up a metal pipe that had several railroad spikes welded and twisted around the top of the pipe as if it was some sort of redneck mace.

He rested the weapon on Tom's shoulder, letting the tips of the spikes brush against the boy's hair. "Best not be thinking you can get one of my guns away while I'm sleeping. That's what you think?"

"No sir."

"If you did try to get one of my guns and cause me some trouble, I'd have to let Sweet-Darling here give you a kiss." Glen let the sharp points of the railroad spikes brush against Tom's cheek. "That what you want?"

"No, sir. I was just looking."

Glen pushed away Tom's arm. "Go look somewhere else. And, I don't want to hear that girl's smart mouth while I'm watching my shows so take her with you."

"Yes, sir."

Tom just stood there.

"Got something to say?" asked Glen.

"Mary, she's hungry."

"She ate yesterday," said Glen.

RETURNING FROM A RUN

Jefferson ran back toward the farmhouse by the Eastern trail and, though his muscles should have been tired and loose, his run in the woods had done little to relax him. His nuts were a little sore, too. He ran to where the trail head met the lower side field. He looked in both directions to make sure Gray Man wasn't waiting in the field like a little kid making sure the school bully wasn't lurking in the school yard to take his lunch money.

He didn't see the horse, so he took off toward the fence at a full sprint.

He got about half way when his foot came out from underneath him and he almost face planted in the field. He looked down to see what he had slipped on, but there was no need. He could already smell it.

The thick, brown paste of horse shit covered his high tech running shoe.

He jumped up and tried to wipe his foot on the grass, but that just made it worse, as he could feel the warmth of the fresh manure pushing in through the mesh of his shoe.

"Great, that's just great."

Jefferson stomped to the yard, pulled off his shoes and hung them on the fence. Gray Man had gotten him without even being there.

NO TRESPASSING

Dan drove his big, red truck into the front yard, pulling it next to where Jefferson had tied his shoes to the fence-line by the laces and was busy hosing them off.

The developer said with a big smile, "Looks like you stepped in one of those organic land-mines."

"Yeah, it's just been good fortune all around since last I saw you," Jefferson said.

Dan got out of the truck. "You should walk down to the end of the road. When you see the lovely sign advertising the new Shady Pines subdivision, it'll put a song in your heart."

"I feel better already, but we got a new set of problems."

A look of concern fell over Dan's face. "What is it?"

"Trespassers. I took a jog around the property, and I ran into two little kids hunting squirrels."

"That's really not surprising. Your brother was rather carefree about property lines."

"Yeah," said Jefferson, "but these were really little kids. One of them looked like she was in the first grade, and she was barefoot. Barefoot."

Dan shook his head. "Well, that just ain't right."

"It gets better. I also ran into some teenage girls getting ready to throw a party in the woods."

Dan's eyes widened. "Really? Where abouts?" then quickly added as he noticed Jefferson's serious look, "I'm just joking. We can't have that kind of liability."

"My thoughts exactly. If someone got hurt on the property..."

Dan said, "I'll go get some 'No Trespassing' signs and splatter 'em everywhere. You should call your buddy, the sheriff, and get him to run off anything that doesn't look like someone who is interested in buying a lot."

"I don't know if that'll work," said Jefferson. "When we were in high school we were tight, but...let's put it this way, I don't think I'll get any special treatment."

"Fine. We'll just have to ask him to do his job."

He got back into his truck. "I'll come check on you when I get those signs up."

CALLING THE COPS

Jefferson walked into the farmhouse and pulled out his cell phone. He knew there wasn't any signal, but it was force of habit. He put the phone back into his bag and walked around until he found the phone laying on the floor in the empty living room.

He looked at it for a moment, then went and took another shower. He got out of the shower and felt his dress pants and shirt. The clothes were only a touch damp, but he didn't put them on. He had a better idea. He walked to where he had bagged up his old clothes for the church donation and ripped the bag open.

He pulled out his old cowboy boots and a pair of well-worn jeans. He slipped into both of them and dug through the bag trying to find something that didn't look like he was going to perform at the Grand Ole Opry. He settled for a brown shirt with pearl snaps and blue stitching.

He told himself that he didn't care if he was dressed like a cowboy and besides, if these clothes got ruined that was fine because he could just throw them in the trash. He even planned to keep the boots because they were damned comfortable.

He walked back to the phone and saw emergency numbers on a sticker beside of the phone. He dialed the Sheriff's office.

Rotary phone, are you serious?

The phone rang twice before a pleasant, old lady's voice answered the phone. "Sheriff's office."

"Yes, hello. May I please speak to Ambrose..er..Sheriff Hill?"

"Who might I say is callin'?"

"Tell him it's his best friend."

The hold music was Hank Williams Sr., but Jefferson didn't have to listen to much of the song before he heard a familiar voice pick up. "This is Sheriff Hill."

"Hello, Ambrose. This is Jefferson. I need a favor."

In the Sherriff's office, Ambrose and his two deputies sat in front of a large television. On the screen, Hercule Poirot played in *Murder on the Orient Express*. Ambrose picked up the remote and paused the video as he said, "Jefferson. Jefferson Balladeer needs a favor. I can't wait to hear what it is."

Back at the farmhouse, Jefferson frowned as he held the phone to his ear and said, "Well, not so much a favor as to just ask you to do your job. I went for a jog and I ran into some little kids hunting. I mean, they were really little. Six and ten I would say."

"So what?" said Ambrose, "Me and you were hunting those woods at that age and poking at copperheads with sticks."

"Yes, we did, and that was messed up. Some adult should have intervened on our behalves, but that isn't all. I also found some teenage girls at a fire pit...on my property. Looked like they were getting ready for a party."

Ambrose's smile was almost as wide as his big screen TV. "Do you mean to tell me that some kids from Mississippi plan to drink some beer in the woods. This is just shocking. What other breaking news you got?"

"Ambrose, they're trespassing. Last time I checked that was against the law."

"Hell," said Ambrose, "It ain't nothing we ain't done a thousand times."

"I don't care if they do it," said Jefferson. "They just can't do it here. I don't need one of them wrapping one of their trucks around one of my trees. I'm not going to be liable for that."

As Jefferson when on about the legalities of things, Ambrose held the phone away from his ear so the deputies could hear and opened and closed his hand as if it was an overly talkative puppet. The deputies both smirked.

As Jefferson finally took a breathe, Ambrose said, "That does sound very serious, Mr. Balladeer, and I really would love to help, but," Ambrose waved a hand at the television and said, "I'm in the middle of a murder investigation."

As the deputies chuckled, Jefferson said, "Murder?"

"Murder most foul, my friend. This one looks like it's not going to be easy to solve. Hell, it could be anyone or maybe even everyone."

As the deputies started laughing, Ambrose joined in.

"I'm glad you're so amused by barefoot first graders and shotguns," said Jefferson.

"You're right. The hunting of squirrels out of season is a serious offense, but one that is unfortunately outside of my jurisdiction. You should call the game warden."

Ambrose hung up and looked to his deputies.

"Man, I love hanging up on that dude."

"Yeah," said Deputy Leon. "But did you just send your sister to the farmhouse alone? Doesn't she have a thing for that guy?"

"A thing? She's got some sort of obsession, but I know what you're thinking, Leon. But Jefferson won't enjoy her company. He's going to be annoyed and uncomfortable."

"I don't know," said Deputy Leon, "Daisy's one fine game warden."

Deputy Kirby added, "And two legged doe is always in season, but you know who is even hotter than Daisy."

Ambrose and Deputy Leon said in unison, "Anne Taylor."

Ambrose continued, "Oh, my god. You're worse than Daisy talking about Jefferson, except Jefferson ain't in high school."

"I have to agree," said Deputy Leon. "It's creepy, Kirby."

"Being a law enforcement agents, you both know the age of consent in Mississippi is sixteen," pointed out Deputy Kirby.

"Don't make it right," said Ambrose.

"She turns eighteen on November twelfth," said Deputy Kirby. "And, when she does, I'm going to get all up inside that. I assure you. She likes me a lot."

Deputy Leon shook his head. "She doesn't."

"Okay, please, shut up," said Ambrose. "Especially about my sister. Remember, I am armed. Now, pay attention boys." Ambrose picked up the remote. "This lil' French guy is pretty good."

I AIN'T THE SIGN WARDEN

A large, beige SUV with a game warden's star painted on the door pulled off the black top and onto the dirt road that led to the farmhouse. The door opened and Daisy jumped out.

She sauntered over to the sign that advertised the new subdivision and smirked. Someone had already defaced it to read "Shitty Pines-Outsiders go away!!!"

As Daisy was still chuckling about the sign, Dan screech to a stop in his big red truck. He stared at the defaced sign and looked like he was about to blow a fuse as his cheeks turned the color of his truck. For some reason this increased Daisy's mirth. She had to stifle a giggle. Dan cut her a mean glare.

"Don't look at me," she said. "I would have thought of something much wittier, maybe something like Shady Developer? Yeah, that's good. I'm a fan of ad hominem attacks."

He got out of his truck and stomped over to her.

Dan spoke too loudly to be standing right next to her. "I just put this up. I want you to find who did this and arrest them."

She pointed to the badge on her chest. "See, I'm the game warden, not the sign warden. You'll probably want to report this to Sheriff Hill. I hear he loves a good mystery."

"I hear he just watches them," said Dan.

Daisy shrugged. "He thinks of them as educational videos, but this will be a difficult mystery to solve since everyone in town hates you and your subdivision. Yep, lots of suspects for this one."

Dan stormed off and got in his truck, slamming the door.

He yelled from the truck, "You tell that brother of yours I want this dealt with."

She turned and squared her shoulders toward him. "Tell him yourself. His number is nine-one-one."

Dan peeled out and sped away.

Daisy smiled and waved as she walked back to her truck. She studied her image in the mirrored windows and ran her fingers through her thick, blonde hair. She undid one of the buttons of her uniform. She took a step toward the driver's side door, but then looked to the four wheeler strapped in the bed of the truck. It was clear from the smile on her face she had just got a good idea.

JEFFERSON AND DAISY INVESTIGATE

Jefferson sat on the steps of the porch, typing away on his fancy aluminum laptop. The roar of a loud engine came from the front yard. He turned his eyes from the words on the screen to the long front yard. Daisy rode toward the farmhouse on a large ATV. Her blonde hair fanned out around her head like a lion's mane as a cloud of dust rose up in the wake of the four-wheeler.

He closed his laptop and set it inside the screen door and walked into the yard as she turned off her engine.

Daisy spun on the seat and hopped off the ATV as she asked, "Did I catch you working on a novel?"

"It's what I do," Jefferson said.

"More of the Laser Sword Chronicles I hope. I can't wait to see what happens. That cliff hanger at the end was a dirty trick."

"It's not really a cliff hanger."

"For you maybe, you know what's going to happen," she said.

"I think you'll like the conclusion."

"I like everything you do." She smiled and held his gaze.

He looked away and his eyes fell on the four-wheeler.

"You drive this thing everywhere?" he asked.

Daisy laughed.

"Heaven's no. My truck is at the end of the dirt road. I just thought since we were going into the woods." She pointed a thumb at the four-wheeler and added, "It's more practical."

"The trails are plenty wide for a truck," said Jefferson. "Wait, you said, 'we'."

Daisy nodded. "That's an awful lot of woods out there. You'll have to show me the scene of the crime."

She got back on the four-wheeler. Her pants leg rode up to reveal the hilt of a large, Bowie-knife.

She followed his eyes to the hilt of the blade.

"Oh, that. I mostly use it for cutting rope, marking trees, and cutting off the occasional snake's head. I promise not to use it on you."

Jefferson hesitated.

"Hop on," she said.

Jefferson got on, doing his best not to touch the shapely game warden as he got situated on the seat behind her. She started the engine and took off quickly, causing him to wrap his arms around her to keep himself from going off the back.

Daisy felt his arms squeeze her tight. Jefferson could hear the smile in her voice as she yelled, "Hang on tight, could get bumpy."

Not too much later, Jefferson looked around on the trail like a man who had lost his wedding ring.

Daisy stood against a tree with her arms folded, leaning against one of the tall pines. He looked up to see her staring and smiling at him.

"I'm sure they were right here," he said. "There was a pile of dead squirrels right here. Look, you can still see a bit of blood. I bet those kids circled back around, or maybe some animal..."

Daisy interrupted him, "Well, no bodies, no crime or as we like to say in the game warden business Squirrelius Corpus."

He just stared at her until she smirked.

"You can't be serious," he said.

"We don't really say that. I made it up. I thought it was pretty witty."

"No. I mean aren't you going to do something about the armed first graders trespassing on my property. One was barefoot. Barefoot. You're not even taking this seriously."

Daisy sighed. "Fine. It was a girl and a boy?"

"Yeah."

"And the boy didn't say much, and the girl was the opposite," said Daisy.

"That's exactly right. Their clothes were too big too. They looked they had time traveled here from the depression. The little girl, she threatened to shoot me and...assaulted me."

The game warden turned her head sideways. "You were assaulted...by a little girl."

"She punched me while I wasn't looking. I certainly wasn't expecting it."

"Still, a punch from a little girl can't be that bad?"

"Depends on where that punch lands."

Daisy thought for a second then did her best not to laugh.

"It's not funny."

"No," said Daisy, trying desperately not to smile. "Not funny at all." She broke in a slight giggle and covered her mouth.

Jefferson just stared at her.

She composed herself. "The perpetrators you described definitely sound like Tom and Mary. I kind of had a feeling it was them."

"If you know who it is, just go talk to their parents."

Daisy sighed and explained, "Well, they have what you might call a unique family dynamic. They live with their Uncle Glen who is not what you'd call an ideal caretaker. Some might even say he's a piece of shit."

"Not Glen Spears?"

"That's right," said Daisy. "I think you kicked out his tooth. Some others have fell out on their own since then."

"What kind of place would let that guy raise children?"

"Don't look at me. I'm the game warden, not the kid warden."

"Fine. I'll go talk to Glen. Does he still live..."

Daisy laughed. Jefferson fell silent.

"So, you're going to walk onto Glen's property. How do you think that's going to go? I imagine you'd beat him up and then he'd shoot you."

"I'm not the same person who left here. I don't solve problems with violence."

"I get that. You're all self-actualized, enlightened. But Glen is still the same asshole, even worse. I'll run over there and talk to him, make sure those kids don't bother you."

"They don't bother me," he said. "I just don't want a kid getting shot on my property."

"Because that sure would slow down you selling this place off as fast as you can," said Daisy.

"Yes. That's true, but I'm also generally against dead children."

"Fair enough," said Daisy. "But Tom's a good shot, not as good as you..."

Jefferson didn't seem impressed.

"I'll go talk to Glen," Daisy said.

"That would be good. Come on. I'll show you where those teenagers were setting up for the party."

"Nah, that's okay. If they come back, just call Ambrose."

"Call Ambrose? That's not going to be very effective," said Jefferson.

"Well," said Daisy. "If he doesn't come, call me. Or, you could call me even if they don't."

She took a step toward him and pushed her hair out of her face.

"Look, I appreciate your interest," said Jefferson. "I do, but I'm not going to be here long. It wouldn't be fair to you. You've grown into something special, but I could never stay here. Never."

Daisy frowned and took a step back. "I get it, you know. Bailing on this place and putting it in your rearview like it never happened."

"You do, huh?"

"Yeah, thought about doing it myself. Think it's hard to be a black guy here? Well, you're right it is, but it ain't easy being a chick with a brain in her head, not a lot of intelligent conversation here."

"You can leave," said Jefferson. "You're not a serf. Just leave."

"You see," she said. "The thing is, if all the good people leave, run away. Well, this place won't get any better." She motioned toward the woods. "Look how beautiful this place is. It shouldn't be populated by mostly assholes. People here need a touch of enlightenment. That reminds me, they're looking for an English teacher at the high school. Maybe..."

Jefferson interrupted with a loud scoff. "The last thing I want to do with my life is teach rednecks how to read. File that under lost causes."

Daisy's face grew serious. "You used to be a redneck. Remember, Black Redneck?"

"I'd prefer if you didn't call me that."

Daisy said, "I preferred you when you were a redneck. Now, you're just a jerk."

She jumped on her four-wheeler and started it. She peeled out and started to speed away, but she stopped and looked back at Jefferson.

"And, my long term crush on you is officially over."

She peeled out again and made it about twenty feet. She slid to a halt and looked back.

"You know, it's actually a very long walk. You want a ride?"

"I'll take the short cut through the woods," said Jefferson.

"You'll get lost."

"I won't. I still remember the way."

Daisy yelled, "Fine! Suit yourself," and sped away on her four-wheeler.

STRANGE TRACKS

J efferson pushed through a thick part of the woods, so dense
that the sun only dappled the ground in spots. He bent low to
get under a thick vine covered in thorns. As he stood, he felt the
barbs of the thorns catch the back of his shirt.

"Damn it," he muttered to himself as he attempted to free
himself from the vine's grasp.

He pricked his finger on a thorn and anger coursed through
him. When he continued to push forward the thorny vine clung
to him like a needy child. Jefferson leaned forward and pressed
with his legs. The sound of ripping fabric filled the air as
Jefferson came free and stumbled forward through some
branches. He fell to his knees.

Wonder replaced Jefferson's anger as he found himself
staring at the crater in front of him. The trees and brush around
the five foot deep hole were scorched black.

Jefferson pushed himself to his feet. *What the hell?*

He looked up into the sky as if some clue would still remain
there, but all he saw were the snapped limbs on a few trees
where whatever it was had pushed its way through the tree tops.

Jefferson squatted down by the crater's edge. The bottom of
the crater was filled with a small puddle of gelatinous goo.

He grabbed a stick from nearby and stuck the tip in the goo.

The goo dripped off the stick like dirty oil. Jefferson dug around in the loose soil at the bottom of the crater hoping to find something large enough to make such a hole. He found nothing.

Jefferson's face grew perplexed. *Goo wouldn't make a crater.* That's when he noticed the trail leading away from the crater, but it wasn't a normal animal trail. It looked like someone had dragged a large rock across the ground but, ever so often in the dirt, there was something that resembled a snake trail. But even that was too thick and heavy to be a snake.

Jefferson let out a big sigh. There was nothing to do but to follow the trail. A guy who writes books about aliens and spaceships just can't walk away from something like this, even if there's a chance it leads to something horrible.

He stepped off the animal trail and pushed though even thicker parts of the woods. More thorny vines did a number on his shirt and scratched his skin, but he was too interested in the strange tracks to notice. He found places around the odd trail where something had marked up the trees as if a rope had wrapped around the base of the small trees leaving gashes in the bark. Jefferson tried to picture the animal that made this trail, but couldn't come up with anything. He picked up the pace and followed the trail to a large patch of blackberry vines that were weighed down with clusters of blackberries. He didn't even think about picking any though they had been his favorite as a kid.

Feathers coated the ground like someone had gotten into a serious pillow fight, but pillow fights don't leave small splatters of blood and bird gore spotting the ground.

"That's not good," he muttered.

He knelt and found more of the goo beneath the blackberry bushes.

The ditch-like trail ended, and turned into tracks the likes of which Jefferson had never seen. Whatever it was had left large circular indentations in the dirt, like a giant caterpillar had taken over from whatever had been dragging itself through the dirt.

Jefferson looked at the strange trail leading away and then back toward the farmhouse. He sighed and kept following the trail.

He followed the tracks to a patch of thick, low bushes about waist height. He lost the strange circular tracks but could see the broken branches in the bushes where something had moved through them.

He stepped into the bushes and felt his heart start to race as he realized whatever he was tracking could still be in the bushes. Still, he continued to follow the path back to the main trail and the grassy area he had been doing yoga earlier.

He walked to where he threw the dead squirrels, and saw a few circular tracks in the grass.

A branch snapped and he looked up quickly.

Mary stood there with big, brown eyes, still barefoot, looking like she didn't know whether to run or say something hurtful or say something hurtful and then run.

"Mary, right?" Jefferson asked.

Her brow knitted together in suspicion. "How you know my name?"

"Daisy told me."

"The game warden? Ugh, I don't like her. Make sense you two are friends."

"Did you take those squirrels?" Jefferson asked.

Mary just looked at him.

"I wouldn't be mad if you did."

"If I had a bunch of squirrels, I'd be off eatin' 'em now wouldn't I?"

"Looks like something beat you to them," Jefferson said. "I'm just not sure exactly what."

Mary looked mighty disappointed. "Well, thanks for nothing."

"I really wouldn't be here if I were you. Might not be safe," he told her.

Jefferson turned away and made to follow the trail in the soft dirt and leaves of the forest floor.

"Is that a threat?" Mary asked. "You threatening me? I ain't scared of you."

Jefferson stopped. "No, I'm not. I just don't want you to get hurt. Something...I just don't know if it's safe here. You should run home."

Jefferson moved to pick up the trail again.

"How come people say you're Big Beau's brother. Doesn't make sense."

Jefferson turned and gave the girl a frustrated look. "Clearly, one of us was adopted."

"I know that," Mary said. "I'm not a dummy. I meant that Big Beau was nice to me and Tom, even though we're some white trash that no one cares about, but you just take our squirrels and yell at us. Seems like if you and Beau were really brothers you'd be more like him, adopted or not."

"You shouldn't refer to yourself as white trash," said Jefferson. "It's your decision what you are. Try to remember that."

Jefferson tried to get back to following the trail, but Mary said, "I'm adopted too, sorta. I live with my uncle on account of my mama being in jail."

"Glen?"

Mary nodded.

"He take care of you?"

"Not really," Mary said. "He just lets us live there."

"I wouldn't expect much from him," said Jefferson.

"You know him?"

"Unfortunately, I do."

"You seem more like Glen, than Big Beau," said Mary. "You're both mean to me and Tom."

That stopped Jefferson in his tracks. He looked at Mary. He was about to yell at her to just go home, but he heard her stomach growl.

Jefferson looked at the strange tracks that led into the woods then back at Mary.

"Maybe," he said. "I'm not like Beau, but I'm certainly not

like Glen. I was about to go make some sandwiches...if you want some."

"Can I bring some back to Tom?

"As many as you can carry."

The girl skipped over to him on her bare feet and looked up at him as if to say, "what are we waiting for?"

Jefferson stuck a stick in the ground to mark the trail.

"What's that stick for?" asked Mary.

"I'm tracking something."

"You gonna kill it?"

"No. I just want to see what it is." Jefferson looked down at her feet. "You don't own any shoes?"

Mary nodded. "I do, but I don't like them. Make your feet all soft. My feet are tough. I can walk over briars and thorns no problem."

Jefferson looked down at her soiled feet. "Briars can't penetrate dirt that thick."

A while later, Jefferson started up the concrete stairs to the porch of the farmhouse.

Mary stopped a yard from the steps.

"I thought you wanted some sandwiches," he said.

"I ain't trying to get kidnapped."

"Fair enough," said Jefferson. "I'll bring the sandwiches to you."

"And, don't forget Tom. We'll need about eight sandwiches."

Jefferson nodded and walked into the house. Mary waited for the door to close behind him and ran for the barn.

Jefferson stood at the counter making as many sandwiches as he could. He didn't know what the kids liked so he kept it simple, just meat, cheese and bread. Beau had a large bag of unopened chips that he planned on giving her as well.

He glanced out the window that faced the barn to see Mary walking up to where Gray Man was grazing.

Jefferson threw open the window and yelled, "Hey, get away from that horse. He's crazy."

Mary looked toward the window and stuck out her tongue as she skipped toward Gray Man. The horse raised its head and galloped toward the girl, more like a happy dog than a horse. Jefferson felt his body tighten, but the horse stopped just before the girl and dropped to his front knees. The little girl swung onto his back and yelled, "Go, Gray Man go."

The horse hopped to his hooves and took off. The girl's tangled hair waved behind her like a flag.

Jefferson sighed and rubbed his temples. He stuffed the sandwiches in a bag, hoping that would lure the girl off the horse.

By the time Jefferson made it down the steps, Mary stood there with Gray Man casually eating grass behind her.

"Please don't ride the horse," said Jefferson. "He's dangerous."

Mary looked confused. "Gray Man? No way! He's always nice to me. Nicer than people for sure."

Jefferson didn't move too far into the yard with Gray Man nearby. He set the bag of sandwiches down. Mary reached inside and started eating the sandwich with the zeal of a pit-bull.

Jefferson moved toward Gray Man hoping to grab his bridle, but the horse's head came up and he chased Jefferson back to the steps of the farmhouse.

Mary laughed. "Gray Man don't like you none."

He ignored the girl and eased off the steps and reached for the horse's bridle again. Gray Man snapped at Jefferson's arm with his big horse teeth. Jefferson had to jump back onto the porch.

Mary laughed so hard she fell over in the grass. She eventually sat up.

"I guess he don't like niggers."

Jefferson looked at her. He wasn't mad, just in awe that a

little girl would say something so terrible so casually.

Mary felt him staring at her. "What?"

"Why would you say that?"

"What did I say?"

"Just now you called me..."

"A nigger. That just means black guy, and you're a black guy," she said.

Jefferson sighed. "That's not what it means. It's a horrible, ugly word. You shouldn't say it, ever."

"Well, I ain't trying to hurt your feelings."

Jefferson stared at her.

"So, sorry if I did," she went on. "You have to remember I'm just stupid, white-trash. I always say the wrong thing. Maybe that's why everyone hates me."

Jefferson said, "Don't say that about yourself either." He turned and looked at Gray Man. "Besides, Gray Man used to be my horse. I used to ride him everyday. He and I won our share of rodeos."

Mary laughed. "Now you're just telling stories."

"It's true," said Jefferson. "Gray Man's not prejudiced. He hates me in particular and I guess I deserve it."

The girl set the sandwiches down.

"Big Beau used to have a giant jar of pickles. If you let me go get one," she said. "I'll put Gray Man back in the field for you. Otherwise, he might bite off your ear and stomp you in the dirt."

Jefferson nodded.

Mary ran into the farmhouse and came back out a moment later eating a large pickle.

She walked to Gray Man and he dropped to his front knees for her.

"Hey, walk him, don't ride him," cautioned Jefferson.

She jumped on the horse's back and the horse stood tall.

"Don't try to boss me if you want to be friends. Yah, Gray Man."

She galloped away on Gray Man and rode him fast a few

times up and down the field. She got him to slow at the gate and slid off Gray Man. She walked back toward the farmhouse and closed the gate behind her.

She picked up the bag of sandwiches as she walked back toward the woods.

Mary waved to him.

"Thanks for the sandwiches, man."

"Hey, don't go in those woods. I'll give you a ride."

"Nah, I'm used to walking."

"No really. You shouldn't be in those woods alone."

"Why not?" she asked.

He didn't want to explain that something may have fallen from outer space.

"It's just not safe. Besides, it's trespassing."

"Nuh-uh, not now that we're friends."

"Well, friends give each other rides," said Jefferson. "Come on."

He walked to his rental car as Mary took off toward the woods.

Mary yelled over her shoulder, "You're trying to kidnap me."

"I'm not."

He thought to chase her, but it wasn't like he could drag her to the car. Besides, his testicles were just getting back to normal.

DEVOURER VS. DEVELOPER

Dan pulled his truck well off the road and into the high grass. He got out and went to the back of his truck and pulled out a large canvas bag filled with red and white "No Trespassing" signs and a hammer.

He walked to a fence and nailed one of the signs to a post. He threw the bag over the fence and climbed after it.

As he walked through the woods, he occasionally nailed up one of the signs on a tree.

When he found the fire pit, he paused and a look of disgust formed on his face as he realized he would have to pay someone to clean it up.

He mumbled under his breathe about "those damn kids". He pulled over one of the make-shift chairs carved out of a log and climbed on top of it to nail a sign out of reach of the teenagers.

He drove one nail home and drew back to drive another.

The thick shrubs around the clearing shook as something moved through them.

Dan peeked around the tree, but whatever it was had gone still.

He started hammering again. Bam. Bam. Bam.

An animal's piercing shriek came from the bushes. It was the sound of animal dying, and not pleasantly. Sucking sounds and the sounds of bones snapping followed.

He almost fell off his perch as he jumped back and raised the hammer. The brush swayed like an ocean in an angry storm.

Dan held the hammer high above his head like a weapon. "Yah, get out of here...animal."

The bushes became still, except for a slight rustle, then something large darted away through the foliage, but he couldn't see what it was through the thickness of the brush.

He sighed with relief and thought it was probably just a wild boar rooting around. Dan got up on the log and finished hammering in the sign. He stepped back and looked at it, as proud of himself as if he just put the finishing touches on the Sistine Chapel.

He turned and grabbed his bag of signs. That was when he saw the Devourer. He wasn't as scared as he should have been. It took his mind a long moment to figure out exactly what it was he was looking at.

It was as big as a blue ribbon cow, but its jellyfish-like flesh made it hard to tell just how big it was. It stood on a cluster of long, thick tentacles. The rest of its body was covered in tentacles of different length and thickness that were constantly in motion like a nest of snakes, but snakes don't pulsate with vibrant lights of their own.

Dan started to feel more sick than scared. Then, he saw various animals being rapidly dissolved in the strange, translucent flesh of the creature. He didn't need to be a xenobiologist to figure out what to do next.

He ran with no clear plan of where he was going.

One of the thicker, longer tentacles shot out like a striking cobra and wrapped itself around his ankle. It pulled the developer off his feet and back toward her body as easily as man might reel in a baby catfish. Dan flailed about trying to grab onto anything he could to stop his momentum, but his fingers just dug grooves in the soft earth and didn't slow him a bit.

He soon found himself beneath the Devourer and pinned to

the ground by the creature's weight. Its flesh smooth and hot against Dan's skin.

He could see his reflection in the creature's flesh as he said, "No. No. No."

He kept pleading as if something like this just wasn't supposed to happen, certainly not to him.

The Devourer didn't seem to care. She raised a few of her barbed tentacles and slammed them into Dan's torso. He screamed, making a sound not unlike that of the animal the Devourer had just killed in the brush, only louder.

The creature raised a second barbed tentacle above Dan's face. He screamed again. The tentacle went deep into Dan's neck. His body went limp as the Devourer's tentacles turned red at their base and the creature rapidly sucked in his cells. Dan's body collapsed in on itself. Tentacles wrapped around his shrinking body to squeeze the juice out of him. Dan's bones snapped as loud as thick branches.

The Devourer shook Dan's body something fierce as it tore what was left of him into pieces small enough to suck through her feeding tentacles. During this process, his head fell off and rolled a few feet away.

The Devourer absorbed the rest of the corpse and reached out a tentacle toward Dan's head that ended in a cluster as thin as spaghetti. The thin tentacles stretched into the decapitated head's ears and pushed past the eyeballs. The worm-like tentacles pulsated with light. Dan's eyes sprang open as if they looked back at the Devourer.

The Devourer dropped the head and danced around it, happy as a dog that's found a steak flavored tennis ball. She scooped the head back up almost lovingly and set it on the end of the tentacle that ended in the spaghetti-like appendages. The thin tentacles pushed into the ears and around the eyes and wrapped all around the head. As the tentacle rose into the air, the eyes came open. They seemed to look around from the expressionless face. The mouth on the severed head opened and closed.

The Devourer held the head high before it like a head on a spike as the thin tentacles around it pulsated with green and blue.

BRINGING MARY HOME

Jefferson was considering calling Ambrose about Mary, but he didn't think it would do any good. He was just about to call Daisy when a knock came at the door.

He looked out the glass to see Mary standing there and opened the door.

"You promise no kidnapping," she said.

"Yeah, I promise."

They walked to the rental car in silence and got in.

As Jefferson started to pull away, Mary said, "I guess nobody would want to kidnap me anyway. No one wants me."

Jefferson felt a lump in his throat. "I'm sure that's not true. I already like you, even though your feet are really dirty."

Mary held them up toward Jefferson. The bottoms where as black as a dog's paw. "I'll put them on you."

"Please, don't."

Mary laughed. "Thanks for saying someone would want me, but if they do I'd like to know where they are."

"Here," said Mary, pointing at the place where Jefferson should stop. "This is good right here. I'll have to sneak in the back so Glen don't steal Tom's sandwiches."

Jefferson pulled his car onto the side of the road. She opened the door before the car was fully stopped.

"Hey, be careful," Jefferson warned her.

Mary sighed and closed the door.

With the car fully stopped, Mary hopped out.

"Okay, bye."

Jefferson opened his door and looked over the roof of his car.

He said, "Hey, Mary. Really stay out of the woods, and, if Glen doesn't feed you or anything like that, you call Ambrose, I mean Sheriff Hill."

Mary laughed. "Man, I ain't got no phone."

She waved and ran into the woods. Jefferson sat for a long moment. He looked after where she had disappeared into the woods, but then drove back to the farmhouse.

GRAY MAN VS. DEVOURER

The Devourer moved through the woods fast and as smooth as a rushing river.

She came to an abrupt halt. The tentacle that held Dan's head peeked around a tree, the eyes of the severed head darting all around. The thin spaghetti-like endings encompassing the head rose and undulated, tasting the air.

The monster changed direction slightly and pressed itself close to the ground as it emerged from the woods and into the tall grass surrounding the four catfish pounds. It moved like a serpent for a hundred feet and raised Dan's head above the grass.

There, at the edge of the smallest catfish pond, Gray Man lowered his head to drink.

She slid toward the large stallion as silently as she could, but the horse heard the rustle of the dry grass. Gray Man's head came up and he took off for the trail.

The Devourer sprang out of the grass and shot a tentacle toward the horse. The tentacle wrapped around the fleeing horse's tail. The horse slowed from the weight of the creature but still pulled the thing behind it like some awful carriage. The Devourer lurched toward the horse just as it kicked backwards with both hooves, one hoof caught Dan's head in the jaw and sent the decapitated head flying through the air like a football. The other hoof landed into the base of the Devourer's body and sent it tumbling backwards. The tuft of hair it clung to came free from the horse's tail. The Devourer tumbled backwards like someone who had been giving their all in a tug of war when their opponent let go of the rope.

The Devourer tried to find purchase with its many tentacles but the mud around the pond was too slick.

It fell backwards into the catfish pond.

The Devourer's appendages flailed violently like a kid that doesn't know how to swim, causing the water to turn white, but it suddenly went still and drifted to the bottom of the murky water.

She sank all the way to the bottom of the deep pond and started to pulsate with red and orange flashes bright enough to light the murk. The Devourer reshaped itself, lifting its tentacles toward the surface as if it were trying to grasp the bit of sunlight penetrating the murk. The tentacle with the spaghetti-like endings rose the highest. It tracked the small dark shapes that swam around it. Thousands of catfish, literally tons of them. Food.

The Devourer started feeding, reaching out her tentacles and absorbing the catfish as easily as picking fruit.

Even the catfish soon realized a predator was in their midst and they tried to flee.

The surface of the pond became a writhing mass of catfish flesh, but they were just avoiding the inevitable. Their numbers were soon diminished to a few jumping catfish.

One catfish jumped onto the thin bank between two ponds. The fish snapped its body back and forth, slowly making its way toward the next catfish pond. It made it to the edge of the next pond with another flop and leapt for the water. A long tentacle shot out of the murk and caught the catfish before it could escape into the next pond. The tentacle threw the fish back toward the smallest pond as another tentacle shot from the water to catch the fish and consume it.

The water became still and placid, then several large tentacles emerged from the pond. The Devourer pulled itself onto the muddy bank between the two ponds. It was already decidedly larger, having added a ton of catfish flesh to its own mass.

It sank two tentacles into the next pond. Catfish rose to the surface. The Devourer slide its mass into the water and its bulk caused the pond to spill over its banks as if someone got into a bath tub that was too full.

GAME WARDEN/SOCIAL WORKER

Daisy pulled her big truck to a stop in front of Glen's house. Junk cars rusted in the yard, but the grass was so high that one could only see the roofs of the cars, giving the impression that their tops were rusting islands in a sea of green.

She felt sick to think that kids had to live like this. *Hell, maybe I should just take 'em. Certainly couldn't do worse.*

The game warden walked onto the porch, being careful not to step through one of the holes in the rotting wood.

She pulled open a tattered screen door and knocked loudly.

At first all she heard was silence, then she heard what sounded like twenty empty beer cans hitting the floor.

"Glen," she yelled, "I know you're in there. Open up. It's the game warden."

He yelled through the closed door, "Weren't me that spot-lighted those deer."

"It was you, but I'm not here about that. It's about Tom and Mary."

Daisy heard Glen's heavy footsteps stomp across the room to the door. She heard his weight shift as he paused at the door. She rested her hand on her pistol.

The door flew open to reveal Glen in a soiled undershirt and a pair of cut offs. The shirt wasn't long enough to contain his

135

belly that hung a good four inches below the bottom of the shirt.

Before Daisy could say anything, Glen said, "What did those lil' bastards do now?"

"Nothing. Geez, calm down. I'm just going around telling everyone with kids that the Balladeer farm isn't a place to play or hunt, especially out of season. There's going to be a lot of workers out there soon. I'm sure they would like it if bird shot wasn't raining down on them."

"They been huntin' back there?" Glen asked.

"Of course not, just tell them not to go back there."

"Those lil' ingrates don't listen. You'd think they would be grateful for me taking 'em in and all, but they ain't."

"Why thank you so much, Mr. Glen for taking those kids in out of the goodness of your heart, and, oh, that monthly check you get. From the looks those kids, they don't see much of that money," said Daisy.

"They promote you to social worker?"

"Just let them know and take better care of them, or I'll do something about that," she said.

"If that's all, you can get off my property."

Daisy tipped her hat. "Always a pleasure, Glen."

Glen eased toward her until his belly was almost touching her. "Could be a lot more pleasure if you want to come inside."

Daisy grimaced. "Now that doesn't sound appealing at all. Be like having one of those lion seals on top of me, but no way a lion seal would wear a shirt so soiled or be in such a need of bath."

Glen took a stepped back in his doorway. "One day, I'm going to show you just what it's like."

He slammed the door hard enough to shake the house.

GLEN'S AN ABUSIVE ASSHOLE

Glen leaned against the closed door, his face red with anger and embarrassment. He looked through a crack in the blinds and watched Daisy get in her truck and back out of the overgrown driveway. He dropped Sweet Darling with a thud, as he had been holding the homemade mace behind his back just in case she had tried to come inside and look around.

"Tom, Mary, get in here!" he bellowed.

No one answered him and the only sounds came from the poker game on the big screen.

Glen stomped though the house looking for the kids, but didn't find them.

He finally opened a metal door to a room that was filled with rows of marijuana plants with bright lights overhead. It was the only room in the house that wasn't filthy.

He looked down the aisle of growing plants. One of Mary's dirty feet stuck out from the row of pot plants.

"Mary, I see your foot. Come here."

The girl's face peeked out from behind the plants.

"Why ain't you come when I called you the first time?" Glen asked her.

She stepped into the aisle between all the marijuana plants.

"We playing hide and seek."

"I ain't playing. Get over here."

Mary hesitated.

"Come on. Get over here. You're only making it worse."

Mary walked slowly to him. When she was a step from him, he grabbed her upper arm and nearly yanked the small girl off her feet.

"What did I tell you and that boy about squirrel hunting?"

"You said not to."

"Why can't you listen? Lil' ungrateful bastards. I take you in. You have to listen. You have to be good. If the cops come here, I'll go to jail like your mama. They'll separate you and Tom. That's what you want?"

Mary stomped Glen's foot and yanked her arm free.

"Yeah, I want you to go to jail. Me and Tom can live in the woods. We don't need nobody. You just eat all our food. You're just a no good fat ass."

Mary stood there defiantly, staring up at the large man who easily out weighed her by three hundred pounds..

Glen undid his belt.

"I'm going to teach you to keep your mouth shut."

As he slide out his belt, Mary ran toward the back of the room, but he pushed her down and put his foot on her lower back to hold her in place.

"Get off me. Tom! Tom! Help!" she yelled.

"You think you're smart," said Glen. "I'm going to show you what happens to smart girls."

He raised the belt to whip her but before he could bring down the belt, a loud thud sounded through the room.

Glen swayed on his feet. The belt slid from his hand, then he fell forward like an oak tree to reveal Tom standing behind him holding the 4.10 shotgun by the barrel.

Glen lay on his stomach. The back of his head had been split open to reveal a line of red flesh beneath his thinning hair.

Mary stuck her head out from beneath Glen. "Tom, I'm getting squished."

Tom dropped the gun and ran to her. The kids rocked Glen

enough so Mary could squirm free from beneath him.

Mary looked at the gaping wound in the back of Glen's head. "He dead?"

"Hope so."

He pulled Mary to her feet with one hand and grabbed the shotgun with the other as he pulled her into the living room. Tom grabbed a green, army bag and started stuffing supplies into it.

When Mary just stood there, Tom said, "Steal all his groceries."

She ran to the fridge and yanked it open.

Mary reported, "There's just beer."

Tom said, "Never mind. I have enough shells to hunt."

Mary pushed all the beer out of the fridge and onto the kitchen floor. She ran and grabbed Sweet Darling. She started to smash all the beer.

"What are you doing?" asked Tom.

"Just in case he's still alive. He'll see this and die of heartache."

"Come on."

Mary gave another couple of whacks to the beer and started to run after Tom toward the back door. She stopped and looked back at the large TV and smirked. She raised Sweet Darling above her head and ran toward the TV and smashed the home-made mace into the screen. It shattered. Mary pulled the mace free and ran after Tom.

She stepped outside the house still holding Sweet Darling. Tom sat on a large, four wheeler.

"What was that noise?"

"You kilt Glen, I got his only friend."

The boy shook his head. "Get on."

Mary sat the weapon on the metal rack behind the backseat of the ATV and she and Tom sped off into the woods.

MARY SEES A MONSTER

Mary stuck her head out from behind Tom's shoulder as they sped down the wide trail. The wind pushed her tangled hair against her scalp. She smiled, happy as a dog with its head out the window.

Tom slowed as the trailed narrowed and they approached the catfish ponds.

Mary slapped his shoulder.

"Hey, don't slow down."

Tom motioned to the mud between the pond. "Got to."

Mary groaned in frustration as her hair fell back around her face.

"Well, ain't this boring."

Tom ignored her as he slowed the four wheeler to a crawl to navigate the muddy terrain between the third and forth ponds. Mary spun so her back was against Tom, hoping to get a glimpse of the big catfish that inhabited the ponds, or maybe a turtle.

Deep beneath the murk, streaks of light flashed like an electric storm was taking place beneath the water. She hopped on her knees on the back of the four wheeler and leaned out over the water as far as she could.

"Be still," said Tom.

Mary ignored him. She saw another flash of light, this time tinged with a reddish orange. The flash was bright enough to reveal a large tentacle moving through the water. Mary's eyes got big as an owl's who had just spied a fat mouse.

"Tom?"

"Not now. Concentrating," he said.

Mary said, "Seriously, go faster."

Tom got them through the rough, muddy section and gave the four-wheeler some gas. They soon picked up speed as they headed toward the wooded trail. Mary's hair flew in her face, but she pushed it back with one hand and kept her eyes on the pond.

The water seemed to swell, the Devourer, massive as a double wide trailer and covered in hundreds of long tentacles pulled itself out of the pond and onto the bank they had just passed and slipped into the fourth and largest ponds. The water of both ponds sloshed back and forth like they were stormy seas. The catfish fluttered to the surface of the larger pond.

She watched as thick tentacles broke the surface of the murk. The tips of the tentacles opened wide like blooming flowers and scooped up catfish from the thick masses fluttering on the surface of the pond.

Mary hadn't fell silent too much in her life but for a long moment she just stared, but it didn't last.

She turned back toward Tom. "Monster! I saw a monster, a big, freaking monster, eatin' all the catfish."

Tom just sped up and yelled back, "Ain't no monsters."

Mary said, "Yeah-huh, got a million snakes for arms, giant snakes, and they're like invisible."

Tom just ignored her.

Mary punched him in the side.

"Hey, now," he said.

"Tom, I saw it."

"How could you see something invisible?" he asked her.

"Not invisible, clear. You could see through it and it had lights."

"You're imagining."

Mary put her face against Tom's back and said softly, "Why don't you believe me?"

Tom didn't hear her over the engine of the four wheeler.

LET'S GET THIS PARTY STARTED

A powder-blue pick-up truck from the early eighties, still in fine shape, pulled into the grass in front of the defaced sign advertising the new subdivision. Though the sun had set, you could still read the sign because a big, full moon rose above the trees.

Anne used the gear shift on the steering column to put the truck in park.

She looked over at her two passengers. A wide shouldered young man sat in the middle, taking up most of the cab. He wore a tight t-shirt that showed off his efforts in the gym. Pearl sat by the window.

"We just have to wait on the others to get here," said Anne.

The young man stared down at Anne's long legs as her sun dress pooled around her thighs.

He looked up. "Huh?"

Anne smiled. "What's got your attention, City Boy?"

City Boy (called such as he had just moved from Los Angeles) said, "I guess I'm busted."

Anne shrugged.

"What did you say?" he asked.

"Don't like to repeat myself," said Anne.

"Even when someone is distracted by your beauty?" asked

City Boy.

Pearl crossed her arms by the window and rolled her eyes as she looked up at the moon.

"Even then," she said.

"So, this party is in the forest?"

"Right," answered Anne. "No one will bother us there."

"What about bears?" City Boy asked.

The two girls laughed.

"Wow, you really are a City Boy," Pearl said.

"I'm not frightened. I'm just curious," he said.

"No bears," Anne assured him. "The fiercest thing you're liable to see is a possum."

"Will those attack?" asked City Boy.

The girls laughed again.

"Only if you're a trashcan," said Pearl.

Anne patted his muscular leg.

"Don't you worry, City Boy. I'll protect you."

"I'm not worried. It's just I've never been to a party in the forest before."

"It's the woods, not the forest," said Pearl.

"What's the difference?"

The girls looked at each other, hoping the other would answer.

Pearl looked out of the window. "Look, here come the others."

A caravan of pick-up trucks pulled around them, many of which had passengers in their beds.

The young men riding in the back of the trucks jumped out wielding axes and sledge hammers. They attacked the large sign with a fury. It was like *Braveheart* but with rednecks.

Pearl pulled herself out of the truck window. "Hey, is that necessary?"

Brock, a thick, stocky young man, and the obvious leader of the band of redneck vandals, looked back over his shoulder.

"We're going to need wood for the fire," he said.

"I'm sure we could find some in the woods," said Pearl.

"After all, it's called the woods."

Brock shrugged. "Too late now. Be a waste to just leave it here."

Pearl slid back into the cab of the truck.

"Is vandalism part of every party?" asked City Boy.

"Mostly," said Anne.

"Maybe we should just go. I'm not sure I want to be part of this. I've got a football scholarship to think about."

"I kind of agree," said Pearl. "Not about the football scholarship, but hanging out with these guys. How fun could it be?"

City Boy went to say something else, but Anne put her hand on his thigh.

"Everyone just relax. I promise we're going to have an amazing night."

Pearl rolled her eyes again and looked out of the window. She knew that meant Anne aimed to have an amazing time.

The boys finished throwing the torn sign into the back of the trucks. Everyone moved to get in their trucks, but Brock stood on the bumper of his truck. "Hey, hey, everyone gather around."

People gathered around the front of the truck.

"Now, save the hollering for when we get deep in the woods," he said. "We gonna turn off our lights and ease past the farmhouse and to the trails. I don't want anyone revving your engines or peeling out or shit like that."

Another boy yelled from the crowd, "Why are we sneaking? What's that guy going to do?"

Brock looked down at the boy and gave him a look like he was stupid.

"Do you know who is in that farmhouse tonight? The Black-Redneck, that's who. We've all heard the stories. He fights five dudes at the same time and can shoot a fly in half with whatever is handy. Ain't no one tougher or meaner than the Black-Redneck."

Inside Anne's pick-up, City Boy looked at her with concern.

"This sounds really like a bad idea. The party is on Black-Redneck's property. He might shoot us."

Pearl said, "Nah, we met him. He's nice."

"Oh, Pearl thinks he's *real* nice," said Anne. "You want us to drop you off at the farmhouse?"

Pearl gave Anne a look that made her chuckle.

"You're not funny, Anne Taylor."

Anne nodded her head as if to say, "Oh, yes, I am," as she killed her lights and followed the other trucks.

TRESPASSERS WILL BE
TURNED TO SPACE ZOMBIES

Jefferson sat on his porch watching the moon move higher over the trees and the stars grow brighter in the sky. He had turned off the porch light so he could see the fireflies in the bushes that separated the front field from the long front yard. A slight breeze rustling the trees and crickets singing for girlfriends was the only thing that broke the silence.

He had forgotten how peaceful and beautiful the farm was at night. He was almost thinking he would keep a few acres for himself or maybe call Daisy for that cup of coffee, when he heard the low rumble of truck engines.

He sat there in the dark and watched a long caravan of pick-up trucks creep past the farmhouse. When the trucks came to a closed gate in the fences, boys from the back of the trucks hopped out and opened them and waved the trucks through. As the last of the trucks passed through the gate, the boys closed them and ran to jump in the back of a truck. The coordination with which they did this made it clear it was not the first time these guys had snuck onto someone's property.

Jefferson sighed and rubbed his temples. He remembered what ruined such beautiful nights as these on the farm - the people that surrounded it.

He turned on the porch light and went straight inside and dialed the phone

"Hello Ambrose," he said.

Ambrose frowned and paused the video of Miss Marple as he sat in his house in jeans and a t-shirt, obviously in for the evening.

"How did you get this number?"

"You gave it to me in the second grade."

"I would say nice of you to finally use it, but I know you must need something."

"I'm calling to report a crime."

"Please, tell me someone murdered you," Ambrose said.

"Just listen, this is serious. A parade of trucks just drove into the woods. They just ignored the "No Trespassing" signs. There must have been thirty big trucks, full of kids. It was like a redneck parade."

"Wow, that does sound serious," said Ambrose. "But I'm unfortunately in the middle of another murder investigation." He motioned toward his giant TV as Deputy Kirby sat on the floor drinking a beer and chuckling.

Deputy Kirby said loudly, "It's true. It's true."

Ambrose added, "I don't know how this one will ever get solved."

"You're lying. I dialed your house. Did you discover a body at your house?"

"That's a fine bit of deduction," said Ambrose. "I would deputize you to help with the investigation but you're an asshole."

"Ambrose, you don't have to like me, but minors are trespassing on my property, drinking and driving. I will not be responsible when one kills himself."

"Oh, calm down. They're just blowing off some steam, drinking some beer in the woods. Ain't nothing we didn't do a hundred times. As long as you don't run them off, they'll sleep it off in their trucks."

"Ambrose, You're the sheriff. I'm reporting a crime. You

have to..."

Ambrose said, "Get right on it."

He hung up.

"God, I do love hanging up on that dude. I bet he's so made he's yelling at the phone right now."

"Yeah, you really get to him," said Deputy Kirby, rolling his eyes.

"What's that mean?"

Deputy Kirby shrugged and went to the fridge. He reported, "We're out of beer."

"Go buy some more."

"Why buy beer when we can confiscate it?" asked Deputy Kirby.

"I already took off my uniform," said Ambrose.

"Aw, come on now. Just put on your tin star and let's go."

"You just want to see Anne Taylor."

"I want to do more than just see her," said Deputy Kirby.

"Kirby, am I going to have to arrest you for being a perv?"

"Come on. Some high school boy who doesn't know what he's doing is probably moving in on her at this second. Help me get all up inside that."

"Wow, shut up. I can't stand all the romance. Seriously, shut up. I've never seen this particular Miss Marple, and it will be watched in peace."

Deputy Kirby went to protest, but Ambrose held up a hand and continued, "And, if I do experience a peaceful viewing, maybe, just maybe, I'll be in the mood to run some kids out of the woods and steal their beer."

Deputy Kirby turned back to the television and remained silent.

AN UNDELIVERED LETTER

Back on the farm, Jefferson slammed the phone down almost hard enough to break it. He paced around the room for a bit and, if Ambrose had been there, it would have been the eighth grade all over again.

Jefferson took a deep breath and rubbed his temples. He picked up the phone and dialed.

"Hello, Daisy. Hi. I need your help."

He explained about the trespassers and Daisy assured him she was on her way, but that she wasn't rushing because she wasn't at his beck and call.

He had no sooner put down the phone when a loud knock came at the door. Jefferson knew it couldn't be Daisy, not unless she had been sitting at the end of the road again, and that would have been creepy.

He walked to the door thinking it was probably Old Ed, but he still looked out the window before opening the door.

All three of the large Tillman brothers stood shoulder to shoulder at the door wearing serious faces.

Jefferson didn't care if they wanted to fight. He pulled open the door.

"What?"

He looked at how large Baby Tillman had gotten and

thought maybe it would have been a better idea to leave the door locked.

Saul cleared his throat and pulled Jefferson's attention away from Baby Tillman. "You sold mama that big dresser earlier."

"Everything was sold as is," said Jefferson. "I can't take it back."

"Oh, you ain't getting back. She'd chase you with her shotgun if you tried."

The two other Tillman brothers smiled and nodded.

"She loves that dresser. Yep. She does," said Saul. Baby Tillman and the middle brother nodded in agreement.

"Well, I'm happy she's happy. You gents have a fine evening."

He tried to close the door, but Saul put out his ham-sized hand and stopped the door from closing.

"Don't be hasty," said Saul. "There was something hid in that dresser you probably didn't mean to sell."

"Whatever it is, keep it."

"We ain't keeping it, cause it ain't ours. It's yours. Besides, mama told us to bring it to you so you'll have to consider it brought."

Saul reached behind him and pulled out a tattered notebook from his back pocket. He held it out to Jefferson.

"Your brother wrote all this."

"You mean Beau?"

Saul held the notebook out a bit longer. When Jefferson made no move to take it, he sat it on the porch at Jefferson's feet.

"Read it and say he ain't your brother."

The big redneck turned away and walked off the porch. His brother Paul followed him, but Baby Tillman stood there and just looked at Jefferson. He reached out and placed his giant hand on Jefferson's shoulder.

"You let us know if you need anything," he said, then walked away as if he was trying not to cry.

Jefferson stared down at the tattered notebook on the porch

at his feet for a moment, then scooped it up and went back to where his laptop was on the floor. He slid down the wall and stared at it some more and considered never opening it.

But he was too curious. He opened it and saw the pages were filled with Beau's messy print. He flipped through the pages and soon realized it was the same letter written over and over as if someone was trying to get the words just right.

Jefferson flipped to the final entry and read.

THE LETTER

Dear Jefferson,

As you might guess I ain't the best writer, but I been thinking about the night you left over and over. I think the reason you left is probably because I'm not a great talker either. I said things all wrong and well, with you being a hot head and all, it didn't work out the way it should.

You know, I ain't sorry you left though. Not that I don't miss you something fierce, but you wouldn't have done what you done if you would have kept your ass in Picayune. I'm right proud of you for writing all those books, and though I ain't one to read much or at all because I like my shows better, I read all your books and even thought that shit was pretty cool.

Anyway, you did well and I'm sorry I didn't recognize you weren't me. Otherwise I wouldn't have taught you to be me, but remember you did ask, but you were just a little kid and I should of realized you had different interests. You were already into those space movies and shit, and, when I should have bought you some books about space or something, I put a gun in your hand, taught you how to shoot, ride a horse, throw a punch, and choke someone until their eyes popped out.

I ain't saying I'm old and wise, but I figure I did that because those were the only things I knew how to do, and, you see, I was never happier when I was teaching you stuff. I was never prouder when you were better than me at all of those things. Hell, you were better than anyone. And, in a very selfish way, I took credit for it in my head.

I said, "look at my brother. I taught him how to do all that shit."

When you came to me and asked me to teach you how to be a black redneck I said, "Hell yah" because there wasn't nothing else I could teach you. Hell, if you would have been raised by someone else besides me you could have been the next Shakespeare or some other guy that writes really good.

Anyway, I'm sorry you got a late start on what you really wanted to do because of me. But, I'm proud of you because even I couldn't stop you, being born in Picayune couldn't stop you.

I'm getting way off the subject. I wanted to talk to you about the night you left.

It's the truth that Pa Balladeer told everyone he took you in because he knew you could haul watermelons and work on the farm at some point, and he said that to anyone that would listen, so ain't no surprise it got back to you, but that ain't even half the story. That's just the beginning.

First, it wasn't his idea to take you in. The fact of the matter was he ain't had a choice.

Ma came home from work one day crying hard and said she was going to be bringing you home from the hospital soon as you were strong enough. Pa was against it, but it wasn't up for debate. It was the first time I ever heard Ma scream at him. I guess she was saving it for something she really wanted, and that something was you and that night was the first I heard I was going to have a little brother.

You can imagine my surprise when she brought home a black baby. I asked her if she had grabbed the wrong one, but she fussed me good. I got a look at you and even though you were a baby and supposed to be fat, I could see your ribs.

Ma said something like he's had a rough beginning, but you and me are going to see to it that's over. He's your brother now.

With the look that she gave me, I just said "Yes Ma'am."

She took you right to her room and for the first few days you did a lot of crying. Can't say it was a lot of fun to have you around at first, but after a few days she brought you out of her room and set you on the table. You sort of looked around and our eyes met and you smiled at me and giggled as if I was the funniest thing you had ever seen.

You crawled right across the table and came and sat in my lap while I was eating some cereal. You put your head on my chest and went right to sleep. And, even though I had agreed with ma you were my brother, it really wasn't until that moment that I meant it.

Ma came back in the room and saw me holding you and smiled.

I asked whats his name?

She said you ain't had one yet and I said we should name you Jefferson after my Great Granddad who was a general, and she said she liked it. I guess maybe I owe you another apology for naming you after a confederate general, but I meant well at the time.

I guess when you arrived we were all prejudice, not KKK prejudice, but, you know, the regular sort. But, having you around, you being in our family, cured us of that, even Pa.

You see it wasn't long before we all loved you and you can't be prejudice against something and love it at the same time, and prejudice is no match for love.

Hey, maybe that's the solution to all the hate in the world. Just make everybody trade babies. Then, everyone would love those babies so much they'd be cured of their hate. Well, probably a bad idea, but I bet it'd work.

Well, I'm getting off the subject again, what I wanted to say is that Ma took you in to help you, but it was you that ended up helping us. You got us over what little hate we had and made us better for it. So, don't be sore at Pa Balladeer. The man who told his friends he took in a black baby for free labor wasn't the same man that died when you were seven. You were just his son, same as me. Hell, some days he liked you better.

They died when you were seven. I hadn't seen you cry since you were a baby, but man did you cry for them. I was worried you were going to die too.

Some people came around after that and said they were going to take you to live with a family in Jackson on account of me being only 17, but I told them if anyone tried to take you I would shoot them dead in the yard. I know you won't think it's cool, but I was one hundred percent serious, and those people just seemed to drop it after that.

Now, I know you're upset with us. You always got mad easy, and you were the kind to stay mad, but I hope you will come to see me. I know you write your books under a new name. I know you want to forget your past. I know you would be embarrassed if your fancy writer friends knew you had a fat, redneck brother like me, but we are brothers, and if you ever need me you know I got your back.

Your bro,

Big Beau

PS. Oh, hey, if you ever want to come for a visit, you can come work on your books here. It's quiet and I won't bother you. Also, both Old Ed and Gray Man are still alive. They both have hurt feelings about you, but they'll get over it if you came around.

BIG BEAU'S GRAVE

Jefferson sat the notebook down at his side. His head sank into his hands, and he began crying. He hadn't cried since Ma and Pa Balladeer died, and he wept like he'd been saving it up all this time.

He jumped up and ran to the back door and out of the house. He sprinted across the yard and damn near hurdled the fences in his way. He kept running until he reached the back hill and charged right up it.

He stopped when he saw the fresh mound of dirt with the large tombstone that read, *Big Beau Balladeer-Everyone's Big Brother.*

Jefferson collapsed to his knees and started to cry some more. It's not a pleasant feeling to realize things ain't quite the way you imagined them and even a worse feeling to know it's too late to make it right.

Jefferson sobbed out, "I'm sorry, Beau. I'm sorry. Why didn't you mail that damn letter, you big asshole?"

He bowed his head and wept some more.

He felt something very large looming over him and looked up to see Gray Man standing over him.

"Go on. Bite me. Stomp me. I deserve it."

But, Gray Man didn't bite him. The horse lowered his large head and nudged Jefferson affectionately a few times before resting his head against Jefferson's shoulder.

PARTY IN THE WOODS

At first the teenagers kept their engines quiet, at least quiet for large trucks but, as they got deeper into the woods, they revved their engines and spun their tires, sending up plumes of dirt and dried leaves and forcing those in the back of the trucks to hang on tight.

The sound grew increasingly louder until they sounded like a herd of massive, metallic beasts.

Their headlights came on, and they would have scared the bejesus out of any small woodland critters as they sped down the trail, had the Devourer left any.

The trucks came to a sliding halt and lined up on the trail outside of the clearing that contained the fire pit.

The teenagers ran from the trucks and into the woods, carrying coolers of beer and torn bits of the sign. The coolers were arranged in a semicircle around the fire pit as the ruined sign got stacked and covered in gas.

A few of the young men handed out beers as Brock stood in front of the crowd on one of the logs.

"Everyone, shut up!" yelled Brock.

The crowd grew quiet, and Brock held up his beer.

"Death to Shady Pines!"

Everyone cheered. Brock downed his beer and roared like a caveman. One of Brock's friends handed him a flare gun. The crowd backed away as Brock turned and fired into the ruined sign that was wet with gas.

Whoosh!

The flames rose so quickly that they seemed to come into existence instantly and stretched to the lower branches of the surrounding trees. Brock staggered back from the heat and fell on his ass.

The crowd burst into laughter. Brock jumped up quickly.

He laughed. "Eyebrows are for pussies."

Some time later, the party went into full swing, and Anne sidled up to City Boy.

"Not your idea of a party?" she asked.

"It's interesting from an anthropological viewpoint," he said.

"You like anthropology?

"Sure," said City Boy. "And literature too. At the moment, I'm somehow reminded of *Lord of the Flies*."

"How about biology?" She eased closer. "You like that?"

City Boy said, "I'm curious where you're going with this."

"Just answer the question. You like biology or not?" she asked.

Before City Boy could answer, he yanked Anne toward him and spun her out of the way as two large boys crashed through the space she had been occupying and collapsed to the ground. The boys struggled against each other, trying to choke each other and land punches.

Anne looked back over her shoulder. "Thanks. Guess that could have been bad."

City Boy held the embrace.

"I think it worked out okay though, and, yes, I like biology a lot."

She pushed away from him and pulled him away from the crowd gathering around the two young men fighting on the ground.

"Are they really fighting?" City Boy asked.

"It's Mississippi," answered Anne. "Wouldn't be a party

without a fight."

He looked back, concerned.

"Don't worry. They'll be best friends in five minutes," said Anne.

City Boy stopped and watched the two young men roll around on the ground. They were both tiring but the fight was still raging. One bled profusely from his forehead.

"It seems serious. You think I should intervene? I'm much larger than them and could easily make them stop."

Anne grew frustrated with his continued interest in the fight.

"No. Now, do you want to see something interesting or not?

"Better even than the gladiatorial offering?"

"You're in Picayune," she said. "You can see a fight anytime you like, but, if you come with me, I'll show you some interesting biology."

"I'm coming with you. I have to admit I'm more than a little curious."

Anne ran to a paper bag filled with snacks and grabbed a large bag of chips. She then stole a flashlight from the side of a couple sitting near the fire. She pushed the chips into City Boy's hands, but kept the flashlight.

"Follow me and be sure to keep up."

She ran into the woods.

THE MYSTERY OF THE MISSING CATFISH

City Boy easily kept pace with Anne as she led the way through the woods with the flashlight.

"It's really okay for us to be out here?" he asked.

"Are you scared?"

"Yes. I don't want to get attacked by one of those possum things, or do they run in packs?"

Anne chuckled.

"And what about this Black Redneck character," he went on. "I don't want him displaying his marksmanship by shooting my ear off. I have great ears."

"Don't worry. I'll protect you," Anne said.

City Boy stopped and looked back in the direction of the party. The country music was barely a whisper through the trees at this distance.

Anne walked back to his side.

"Be brave. Fortune favors the bold."

City Boy smiled. "What kind of favors are we talking about?"

Anne shrugged and pointed in the direction of the party. "You won't find out going that way."

She ran on. City Boy followed, not looking back again. Anne's smile and her scent were like a siren's song. He was ready to throw himself against some rocks.

Anne emerged from the woods near the largest of the catfish ponds. City Boy came out of the woods right behind her and stopped as he took in the four large ponds and the fish sculpture on top of the tall pole.

"What's this place?" City Boy asked.

Anne grabbed his hand and pulled him the last ten yards through the high grass and nearly to the water's edge.

"Watch your step. It can be slippery at the edge."

City Boy took the flashlight from her hand and shined it all around.

"This is kind of neat. These are man-made for sure."

"Well, aren't you the quick one," said Anne.

He shined the flashlight up at the fish sculpture on top of the tall pole.

"That looks like those things people put on the back of their cars." His shoulders slumped and he turned to Anne. "Please tell me you didn't bring me out here to pray or something."

Anne raised an eyebrow. "You'll come to find that's not my thing, but this is Mississippi so don't go advertising that."

She snatched the flashlight away from him. "Now, crunch up those chips and throw them in the water."

"Huh?"

"Just do it. And you'll see something you haven't see before."

There should have been the sound of bullfrogs and the song of some night birds, but the area around the pond was silent, so when City-Boy pressed his hands against the bag and crushed the chips it seemed awfully loud and echoed across the water.

"Good," said Anne. "Now open it and toss the chips in the water."

"Is this an offering to some dark water-god?"

"Stop being silly and throw the damn chips," said Anne, moving her arm as if she was throwing an invisible Frisbee. "It ain't hard. Just try to spread the chips as much as you can."

City Boy eased toward the water until the tips of his sneakers were almost touching the brown water. He swung the open bag as hard as he could but held the bottom. The smashed chips flew out of the bag and rained down on the surface of the pond like greasy, little snow flakes that covered the brown water.

Nothing happened.

He watched the water for a moment, then looked back at Anne.

"Wow, that's something."

Anne said, "No."

She handed the flashlight to City Boy and knelt down at the edge of the pond. She splashed her hand on the water and wiggled her fingers in the murk.

"Come on, stupid catfish. You're making me look bad."

"Looks good to me," City Boy said.

Anne turned to find him shining the flashlight on the back of her thighs where her sundress had crept up just enough to reveal a bit of her white panties.

She stood quickly and explained, "Like a million catfish should have popped up and ate all those chips in a second."

"Maybe they gave up junk food?"

Anne raised an eyebrow at him.

"Shows how much you know. Catfish will eat anything, even other catfish."

City Boy said, "No excuses. You promised to show me something interesting, so let's see something interesting."

He shined the light up and down her body.

"You think it's that easy?" Anne asked.

He shrugged. "A deal's a deal. You said I would see some interesting biology."

He shined the light on her cleavage.

"I would be satisfied with a little anatomy."

Anne lurched forward and snatched the flashlight away from him and shined the light up and down his body.

"You take off your clothes first."

"Ah," said City Boy. "I get it now. You get me to strip down to my underwear and run off with my clothes, leaving me lost in the woods." He turned toward the trees. "You have some of your friends in the woods?"

"That's not my plan at all," she said. "I figure we start dating, and go away to college together, far from here, maybe someplace it snows. We'll have to take Pearl with us. She'd be lost without me. But, first things first, I have to see the goods."

She smirked and shined the light up and down his body. He gave her a skeptical look.

"Come on," she said. "At least the shirt. Let's see what you got."

"Fine, but you're next," he said.

"Sure, but I won't hesitate as much."

He grabbed the bottom of his shirt and pulled it over his head.

She shined the light over his defined pectoral and abdominal muscles.

"Quite acceptable," said Anne. "I like the way those hip bones stick out."

She sauntered to him and ran a hand over his bare chest as she handed him the flashlight.

"The product is good, but let me show you a thing or two about presentation."

Anne walked a few steps away from him as if she was a model on a runway. He turned to watch her. She flipped her hair and looked over her shoulder almost angrily at him.

She slowly bent over and let her dress ride up her thighs until her panties were about to show, then came back up slowly. She began to sway her hips back and forth as if she was listening to a slow beat only she could hear. Her hips incrementally gained speed like the pounding of City Boy's heart.

She pirouetted and spun so fast that her dress flared out to give City Boy a good look at her panties. She stopped and faced him and her hemline floated back to just above her knees. She gave him a look like a lioness would give a gazelle and took a step toward him. She let one thin strap of her dress fall, then the other. She spun her back to him again and her body moved snake-like as the dress slowly fell down to reveal a perfect back.

She looked back over her shoulder as if considering if he

were worthy of seeing more.

She turned toward him, holding her dress to her chest with an arm pressed against her breasts, then she held up her arms as if she was reaching up to touch the full moon. The dress slid down her body and pooled around her ankles.

City Boy's mouth fell open. There wasn't a thought in his head. Every bit of his brain became desire. He didn't think. He wanted to have a thousand hands to feel every inch of Anne's skin at once. He wanted this so much he forgot to use the hands that he had. The flashlight fell from his loose grip and rolled toward the pond.

He came out of his hypnotized state. "Shit."

Anne giggled as he chased the flashlight toward the pond.

PLOP! The flashlight fell in the water.

He didn't hesitate. His hand followed the flashlight into the murky water. He reached his arm almost to the shoulder.

"Got it."

There was a slight splash. Anne's laughter stopped suddenly. Colorful lights flickered from behind him and reflected on the surface of the pond as if someone had turned on the Christmas tree at Rockefeller Center.

City Boy paused as he studied the reflection in the water of the Devourer's large tentacle pulsating with color.

He jumped to his feet and turned.

Anne hung from the end of the large tentacle as the tip of the tentacle enveloped her head with it's Venus flytrap-like mouth.

The flashlight fell from City Boy's hand again.

Even though Anne's perfect body hung from the end of the tentacle, City Boy didn't find it sexy at all as Anne twitched at the end of the tentacle as if she were being electrocuted. The tentacle pulled Anne over the water, the tips of her toes streaking across the surface.

He stood there for a long second before he regained enough of his faculties to start backing away.

The Devourer's massive body rose out of the murk. Sending

a wave a of water before it that knocked him off of his feet.

City Boy pulled his head up and stared at the Devourer. The sight of the creature froze him. The multicolored bioluminescence suspended in clear, alien flesh was like staring into the uncaring universe. Only in this case, it was looking back.

As he regained his feet, a second tentacle shot from the water like an attacking sea serpent and closed over his head. It easily pulled the large, young man into the air and over the water to where he hung at Anne's side. Both he and Anne hung from the tentacles like strange fruit as their bodies twitched.

They eventually fell still as a clear, gelatinous goo ran down their bare chests.

The Devourer laid them gently on the bank of the pond, like a mother laying her babies down in a crib.

Anne and City Boy convulsed on the bank of the pond in a synchronized epilepsy as the goo covering their faces burned away their eyes and skin. The violent chemical process created a mist that rose from their faces.

The two once beautiful people fell still as the process revealed their skulls beneath clear alien flesh.

The Devourer pulled herself further out of the water and loomed over them, her bioluminescence pulsated rapidly.

The mask of goo covering their skulls responded to the Devourer's call. Filaments within the clear flesh slithered into their empty eye sockets as thin tendrils rose from their foreheads and reached in the direction of the Devourer. The goo formed openings around their mouths and the two newly formed space zombies gasped for air.

The filaments that reached into their brains from the empty eye sockets began to pulsate in time with the Devourer as they both sat up simultaneously. They stood and raised their arms toward her. The alien flesh on their faces pulsated in time with the Devourer.

The two teenagers, now space zombies, ran into the woods to do the Devourer's bidding.

The Devourer sank back into the murk of the pond.

DEAR PRUDENCE

Prudence and Wade sat well away from the others on a picnic blanket in a small clearing but close enough that they could still hear the music and the occasional whoop from someone displaying how much fun they were having.

Wade kissed Prudence tenderly, and she leaned into him. He kissed her with more urgency as his hands slid up her stomach to her breasts.

She pushed his hands away and looked at him like he had gone crazy.

"What?"

"I told you not to rush me," said Prudence.

"Rush you? We've been going steady since the seventh grade," said Wade. "I can't even touch a boob?"

"You'll have to wait."

"I've been waiting. You're the one being unreasonable."

Prudence got up and walked back toward the others.

"Aw, come on."

She didn't look back at him.

"PRUD-ence!" Wade yelled. "You sure living up to that name."

He watched her until she disappeared into the shadows, then stood and got a beer out of a small cooler. The sound of the beer can opening echoed through the small clearing. As he turned to sit back down, Wade saw her.

Anne Taylor stood just outside the clearing with her back to him in just her underwear.

Wade just stood there for a long moment, not believing what he was seeing, but liking it a great deal. He was sure it was Anne. Her long, golden hair hung to the middle of her back and her legs seemed impossibly long even though she was standing in between two tall pines.

"Anne?"

Wade took a soft step toward her as if he was trying to get closer to a butterfly he didn't want to scare away.

"Anne, what are you doing?" Wade asked, a bit louder.

She didn't turn. She motioned for him to follow and walked into the shadows.

She didn't have to motion twice. Wade scooped up the small lantern and walked quickly to catch up but, as he got within a step of her, Anne took off like a rabbit that had caught the scent of a fox.

Wade struggled to keep up and even lost sight of her, but he emerged from the woods to find her at the edge of the largest catfish pond. Her arms outstretched toward the water as if a lover would rise from the murk to embrace her.

Wade walked just behind her.

"I always did like you, Anne Taylor. Prettiest girl in the whole world."

He slowly stretched out a hand and rested it on her shoulder. Anne didn't move, even a little, so he leaned in and put his lips against her shoulder, feeling like a fox who had caught a rabbit.

He put his hand on her stomach and eased it upward to cup her breast. As he was enjoying the feel of the soft weight of her breast in his hand, his finger brushed against something slimy. He pulled his hand away and looked at his hand. A thick, clear fluid covered his finger.

"Girl, what's on you?"

Anne lowered her arms and turned.

Wade staggered back as he took in the clear alien flesh over

Anne's bare skull and the brightly flashing filaments running into her empty eye sockets like glowing worms entering a dark hole.

His mouth opened like he was going to scream as he staggered back, but all that came out was a weird stammering noise. He would have fallen on his ass, but he backed right into City Boy's thick chest. Wade spun and saw the same alien visage staring down at him. He lurched away from them, but City Boy grabbed him by his throat and slammed him to the ground. The two space zombies started to stomp him like they were initiating him into their gang.

When Wade went limp, City Boy yanked Wade to his knees by his hair and pulled his arms behind him as he put his foot between his shoulder blades.

Wade raised his head as streaks of light came from beneath the murk of the catfish pond. He stared in wonder at what seemed like a colorful electrical storm beneath the surface, then a large tentacle shot from the water and enveloped his head, and, just like that, Wade wasn't Wade anymore.

BELLE OF THE BALL

The teenagers arranged themselves into clusters around the fire pit like planets forming around a new star.

Belle was the core of one of these groups, her own popularity pulling the other girls around her.

Nearby, Brock lorded over his own circle of teenage boys as he retold tales of football glory.

Belle looked to Pauline, a tall, skinny girl of sixteen, and said, "I can't believe he's telling that story again."

Pauline chuckled and the other girls followed suit.

Antonia, a freckled face seventeen-year-old, said, "He has to tell that story once for every three beers he drinks."

Belle watched as Brock got down into a three point stance to act out the story.

She rolled her eyes. "Come on. Now, would be a good time to go for a pee."

Pauline nodded.

"Oh, let's," Antonia said. "I've been needing to go for an hour."

"Why didn't you?" asked Belle.

"I don't like the woods at night, not by myself."

Belle rolled her eyes again.

"There's nothing in these woods that could eat you."

"Or that would want to," Pauline added.

Belle walked toward the woods with the two girls following her.

Brock paused his story and yelled over the music, "Where you going?"

"Ladies room," said Belle. She looked at the other boys. "He ends up breaking the other quarterback's ribs and scoring the winning touchdown."

Brock threw down his beer and yelled, "God damn it, Belle! You ruined my story."

The girls laughed and ran into the woods.

When they made it to the small clearing surrounded by high bushes they were still laughing.

"It's too easy for me to push his buttons. I can't help myself," Belle said.

"God damn it, Belle," Pauline imitated Brock, making her voice ridiculously deep.

The girls started giggling some more.

"Stop, stop! I'm going to pee myself," said Antonia.

Belle stepped to the middle of the clearing and undid her belt. Antonia unsnapped the button on her jeans.

Belle looked at her and said, "Nope. You're on look out duty. Make sure none of those perverts followed us."

Antonia saluted and turned her back on the other girls.

"Just hurry up. I have to go *sooo* bad."

She scanned the shadows of the woods and saw a flash of colorful light. She rubbed her eyes and looked back to see only darkness.

As the other two girls started to pee, Antonia said, "Geez, you two sound like a couple of old mares. Did someone leave a bathtub running?"

The other girls didn't respond. It grew very quiet.

"Will you two hurry up? I'm about to spring a leak."

No response came from her friends.

Antonia got the sneaking suspicion the two other girls had

snuck off and left her alone.

She sighed and turned expecting to see an empty clearing, but found herself face to face with the space zombie formerly known as City Boy.

Her eyes teared up and her lips quivered. It was like her face was charging up to release an epic scream but, before she could pierce anyone's eardrums, Anne appeared behind her and cracked her in the back of the head with an elbow.

SEARCH PARTY

Brock looked around like he'd lost something as the young men around him continued to laugh and talk. "God damn, how long does it take to piss?" he interrupted.

"Man, they been gone a while," said one of the boys.

Brock motioned for some of the other football players to follow him, and four large guys followed him into the woods.

He yelled, "Belle! Belle!" He looked at the other guys. "Spread out."

The young men fanned out through the woods, yelling for the girls and getting no response.

As they neared the catfish ponds without seeing the girls, Brock's face took on a look of worry.

"God damn it, Belle," he yelled into the darkness. "You better not be messing with me. You better not be."

One by one, the guys emerged from the woods at various spots around the big catfish pond.

"Anybody see 'em?" asked Brock.

The other guys shrugged.

One of the guys shined his flashlight across the pond.

Belle floated face down in the brown water. Her thick curly locks spread out around her head.

Brock sprinted and launched himself into the water with three of the guys following closely behind him. They all swam toward Belle, disturbing the water something fierce.

Brock reached her first and grabbed a handful of her hair to pull her face out of the water.

"Belle! Baby!"

He yanked her head out of the water and stared for a long moment at the horrible, space zombie visage. He let out a high pitched scream and pushed away from her with his feet as he swam for the shore. The three other boys stopped swimming and treaded water, trying to figure out what was going on.

As Brock swam frantically toward the bank, a light appeared beneath his face in the murk and grew brighter until he could see that what used to be Belle was easily keeping up with him. She swam with her face toward the surface. The light of her face grew brighter as she rose toward him. She embraced him from below. There was a brief violent struggle that turned the water around them white, then Brock disappeared beneath the surface.

The three other boys swam for land. They almost made the bank, but long tentacles as thick as a full grown pine rose out of the water. The tips of the tentacles opened and enveloped their heads and pulled them into the air as their bodies convulsed. Another tentacle rose from the depths, holding Brock by his head.

The boy on the bank watched as his four friends hung from the tentacles. He thought of a band of robbers all meeting the hangman's noose at the same time, but it didn't exactly look like that with all the bright flashes of light making it seem like a rainbow colored electrical storm going on beneath the pond and rising up through the tentacles.

He started to back away slowly, hoping to avoid the notice of whatever was in the pond.

He wasn't aware of the group of space zombies that were sneaking up behind him.

SPACE ZOMBIES ATTACK

Pearl put down the beer she had been pretending to drink and looked around. Not only was Anne not back, but pretty much anyone who had stepped away from the fire pit had never returned.

A loud scream came from the woods. Pearl sprang to her feet, but the rest of the trespassers treated it like just another good-time holler.

"Anyone seen Anne?" she asked.

A boy with his arm around his girl near the fire said, "She left with the City Boy fella. Bet he's enjoying some country living."

His girl punched him playfully in the stomach. "Maybe it's her that is enjoying herself."

Pearl scanned the crowd. "And, where is everyone else?"

Everyone just kept drinking. Pearl leaned into the pick-up and killed the music that had been blaring from its open doors.

A few people complained and looked at her like she'd lost her mind, but she didn't care.

"Does it escape everyone that more than half of us are gone, but not one truck drove away?"

A short freshmen suggested, "It ain't strange for everyone to hook up." He high-fived one of his friends.

Pearl looked at the two guys and reminded them, "Not everyone."

She turned to the woods. With the music off she realized how quiet it was, not even an owl hooting.

As she stared into the darkness she saw a flicker of colorful light streak through the darkness. Then, from several different spots in the darkness, more flickers of light moved toward the party.

She looked back toward the others and said, "Something is definitely wrong."

One of the guys stepped to her side and watched the flickers of light grow brighter as they got closer.

The guy said, "Shit, Pearl. That's just some of the others trying to be funny and give us a scare. Nothing to pass out about."

"I'm not going to pass out," she said. "I did that one time in the seventh grade." She turned to the woods and yelled, "It's not funny, ya'll. Stop it. Ya'll?"

Everyone turned toward the sound of running footsteps. A second later, a seventeen-year-old guy, pulling an hysterical fifteen-year-old girl by the hand burst into the clearing.

Pearl nearly jumped out of her skin.

"Run!" screamed the guy. "Get to the trucks!"

The others just sat there watching as the guy ran toward his truck. A mass of space zombies appeared from the other side of the trucks and cut off his escape. They lurched onto the boy and gave him a fierce beating as another punched the hysterical girl. She fell flat on her back, and the space zombie picked her up and carried her back into the woods.

There was a moment of stillness like when you throw a ball in the air and it pauses ever so slightly at its apex before it comes crashing down, then it was all chaos and screaming.

The space zombies had them surrounded and outnumbered. Two or three space zombies attacked each of the people around the fire pit.

In all this mess, Pearl staggered into the woods. She swayed as if she had drank two six packs and struggled not to faint.

She spotted Anne with her back to her and, even though

Anne was just in her panties and some colorful things were sticking out of her hair, it didn't seem that odd in comparison. Pearl stumbled toward her friend.

"Anne, we have to go," Pearl said. "I want to go home. Something is bad wrong."

As she took another step closer, she realized Anne had another girl on the ground and had her foot pressed into the girl's throat.

"What? Why are you..."

Anne turned her head and looked straight at Pearl to reveal the gruesome, translucent, alien flesh that had replaced her beauty.

The crotch of Pearl's khaki shorts grew dark as she peed down her leg.

Anne took her foot off the unconscious girl's neck and charged Pearl with her arms outstretched toward her.

Pearl's legs collapsed beneath her, and she fainted into some bushes.

Anne paused her attack and stared down at the unconscious Pearl who appeared to be taking a nap in a cluster of bushes.

As Anne reached for Pearl, a girl ran by with a space zombie in pursuit. Anne turned and joined the chase into the darkness leaving Pearl laying in the bushes.

RED EYES

Jefferson stood on the steps of the porch looking toward the woods as Daisy pulled up in the large game warden's truck.

She jumped down from the truck and took a few steps toward Jefferson. She saw him staring toward the woods and looked in the same direction. It was so quiet they could hear the leaves rustle in the breeze.

"Wow, must be some party," she said.

Jefferson took a step toward her. "You missed it. Twenty minutes ago it was nothing but screaming."

"Screaming or hollering?"

"Hard to say at this distance," said Jefferson.

Daisy shrugged and walked back to her truck. She put down the tailgate and pulled out the ramp to lower her four wheeler to the ground.

Jefferson followed her. "Maybe you shouldn't go by yourself? You could make Ambrose go."

She didn't look back as she continued to lower the four wheeler.

"I'm serious," he said.

"I handle poachers with AK-47s and people that fish with dynamite. I think I'll be alright with some drunk teenagers," Daisy said without looking up.

"I'm coming with you," said Jefferson, taking a step toward

the four wheeler.

"You ain't," she said.

He stepped to her side.

"Look," said Jefferson. "I think they might have been screams, the bad kind. Not 'whoo, I'm having fun,' but 'argh, something dreadful is happening.'"

Daisy looked him in the eye. She opened her mouth to comment on what he said when she noticed his eyes.

"You been crying?" she asked.

Jefferson paused.

"Is that important?"

Daisy shook her head. "Geez, it ain't that bad here. You can go home soon and forget all about us, again. Nothing to get all weepy about."

"That's not why I was crying."

"So, you were crying," she said.

"Yes," said Jefferson, "My brother died. Things...thing were left unsaid, and it's all my fault."

"You called him your brother, not Beau."

Jefferson nodded.

"Good for you. Too bad you're just realizing it now."

Daisy jumped on her four wheeler and started it. Jefferson moved to get on with her.

"I told you. You ain't coming." She reached her hand down the blade that was strapped to her ankle for emphasis.

Jefferson took a step back. "I really think I should. This might sound crazy, but earlier I found this crater, and..."

"Forget it. You ain't coming. Having you there will just escalate things. I might as well bring Custer to a Pow Wow. Besides, I don't have a crush on you anymore, so just go inside and dry your eyes."

She put the four wheeler in gear.

Jefferson took another step forward.

"You're not listening to me. I really think there's something..."

Daisy gunned the four wheeler sending up a plume of dirt

that rained down on Jefferson as she sped away toward the woods.

SPACE CHURCH

The space zombies lined the bank of the large catfish pond as orderly as soldiers.

City Boy and Anne stood slightly in front of the others. Being that they were the Devourer's first children, the alien cells had consumed more of their flesh. One of Anne's arms was almost clear, showing the bone beneath, and the fingers of that arm had grown twice as long and into something more like tentacles than fingers, making it look like she was holding a squid.

A small group of space zombies dragged three beaten teenagers before the Devourer. Two were barely conscious, but the third pleaded and called out the names of friends that no longer existed.

The Devourer snatched them up by their heads and pulled them high into the air.

As the soon-to-be space zombies convulsed and kicked their feet, the other space zombies raised their arms in reverence and swayed as the filaments in their clear flesh throbbed with color.

The Devourer laid the three gently on the bank. They continued to convulse as the alien cells consumed their faces and clouds of steam rose from their faces like a hot cup of coffee brought out into the cold morning air. They soon sat up and joined the ranks of the others, mist still streaking from their faces.

With the fish symbol in the background, the Devourer lifted all of her tentacles toward the sky. Like some horrible flower in full bloom, she pulsated with a storm of bioluminescence.

The space zombies reached out to her and swayed back and forth like some kids at a Christian rock concert, the ones that get into it so much that it's disturbing, but these weren't kids anymore. As they held up their arms in worship, their faces pulsated to mimic their new god.

LONE SURVIVOR

Jefferson sat with his back against the wall in what had once been a living room. Now, it was just empty space. He stared off into space like a man who had a few things weighing on his mind and maybe a regret or two but, before he got to ruminate for very long, he heard the sound of urgent feet run up the steps to his porch, and the old porch squeaked as someone made double time toward the door. A fraction of a second later, someone pounded on the door.

Pearl's voice was distorted with distress as she screamed, "Open, open up. Mister...Mister Jefferson. Help!"

He sprang to his feet, got to the door, and cracked it open. Pearl squeezed through the crack and pushed past him into the hall. She kicked the door closed and locked it.

She backed into the hall a ways and sank down on the floor and started to cry.

Jefferson stared at her for a moment. She had twigs in her hair and was scratched up good on her bare arms and legs like she had sprinted through the woods without a care to the briars in her path. The crotch on her khaki shorts was stained dark.

Jefferson kept his distance. "Daisy...er...the game warden will be here in just a bit."

Pearl sobbed.

He knelt down by her side.

185

"Do you want me to call someone? Maybe your friend, Anne."

Pearl let out a big sob at the mention of Anne's name.

"Anne's a monster," she cried, her hands coming up to cover her face.

"So, you two had a fight?" asked Jefferson.

"No. I mean she's a monster," said Pearl. "She ain't got a face and some weird light where her eyes were." Pearl put her palms against the side of her head and wiggled her finger as she continued. "And, they all have worm thingies on their heads."

Jefferson stood up and took a step back.

"You kids have been eating the mushrooms."

"No way, Mr. Balladeer. I only had a bit of beer. You have to believe me. They're all monsters now."

Pearl saw Big Bang just sitting on the floor. Jefferson noticed her staring at the gun. When she went for the giant handgun, he stepped in front of her. He snatched it up and stuck it in the back of his pants.

"I don't think you're in any condition to be handling a gun," he said. "Have a seat. I'm going to call you ambulance."

"No, call the sheriff!" she insisted.

Jefferson said, "I've been trying to do that."

Pearl put her face in her hands and started to cry again.

Jefferson picked up the phone and put it to his ear. No dial tone.

He checked the wires to make sure everything was plugged in. Still, no dial tone.

He pulled out his cell phone in a hopeless attempt to look for a signal.

That's when the power went out and everything was plunged into darkness.

Pearl made a pathetic sound. "They're here. Oh no. They followed me. I don't want to be a monster."

Jefferson walked back into the hall. Even with the moonlight coming in from the door window, he could barely see.

"Calm down. It's just a power outage," he told her.

"No. They're going to make use like them. I don't want..."

The porch creaked with heavy steps. Pearl put her hand over her mouth and moved behind Jefferson.

"Who's there?" yelled Jefferson.

No response came, but someone tried to turn the door knob.

Jefferson didn't pull Big Bang but said, "I'm armed. I don't want any trouble."

The footsteps backed away from the door, and everything went silent.

BAM! Something big slammed into the door hard enough to shake the entire house. Pearl screamed and grabbed the back of Jefferson's shirt.

Jefferson's whole body went tense, but he wasn't one for taking a step back.

Whatever it was continued to throw itself against the door. Jefferson heard the wood of the door frame cracking.

One more violent crash and the door flew open.

Two space zombies stood shoulder to shoulder in the doorway. The clear, alien flesh pulsated with enough colorful lights to reveal the skull beneath the clear, alien flesh and to light up the distance between them and Jefferson.

Pearl released her grip on Jefferson's shirt as she fainted and fell to the floor with a thud.

The two space zombies charged and collided with Jefferson. He tripped over Pearl and went down on his back hard. One of the space zombies knelt over him and started to punch him as the other pulled Pearl's limp body down the hall and out of the house by her ankle.

On the fourth punch from the space zombie, Jefferson's face pulled into a snarl. He knocked the next blow away from his face and pulled his legs up between him and the space zombie. He kicked it in the chest with the heels of his boots. He felt the creature's ribs crack, and it staggered all the way to the door and had to grab onto the shattered door frame to keep from falling.

It pulled itself right back toward Jefferson and flailed toward him. Jefferson didn't really think. His hand just seemed to work of its own accord as it reached into the back of his jeans and pulled out Big Bang. He cocked the gun and pulled the trigger without really aiming and while the gun was still too close to his face.

BOOM! A length of flame came out of the barrel and the force of the blast spun the gun out of Jefferson's hand. His whole world hummed as if a flash grenade had gone off in his face. He rolled to his hands and knees, shook his head and crawled toward the gun. He shook his head again and, clearing the cobwebs, snatched up the gun and turned on one knee, holding the gun properly.

The space zombie laid sprawled in the hall way with a gaping hole torn from its torso. The bioluminescence pulsated dimly then faded to total darkness.

Jefferson stood and kicked it once to make sure it was dead. He shook his head again and ran out of the house.

The other space zombie had Pearl draped over her shoulder as it ran toward the woods.

Jefferson quickly gained on it with the burden of Pearl throwing off its gait.

"Stop! Hey, stop."

The space zombie slowed and turned. It dropped Pearl to the grass and looked in Jefferson's direction as its face flickered with reds and orange.

Jefferson stopped. His hand squeezed the grip of the large gun. His thumb stretched out and pulled the hammer back on the large pistol, but he didn't raise the weapon.

"Whatever you are...we don't have to be...."

The space zombie charged him, its face flashing like a strobe light and its arms outstretched.

He raised Big Bang and held it with both hands. As the space zombie sprinted toward him, he looked down the long, dark barrel. He used the light from the creature's own face to sight the weapon. He let the space zombie get two steps from him and pulled the trigger. Boom!

The creature's head exploded in a rain of gelatinous flesh and skull fragments. Its body took a few more steps before it collapsed at Jefferson's boots.

Jefferson scanned the area. He didn't see any other flickers of light in the surrounding darkness. He stuck the still hot gun in the back of his pants and ran to Pearl's side.

"Young lady, are you okay?"

Pearl tried to get up but was still too out of it. Jefferson yanked her to her feet and threw her over his shoulder in a fireman's carry as he ran back toward the farmhouse.

He stopped at his rental car and threw Pearl in the back seat, jumped in the driver's seat and turned the key. Nothing.

He hopped out of the car and noticed the hood was slightly ajar. Pulling it open, he discovered the torn wires. The car wasn't going anywhere.

Jefferson paused for a long moment. His shoulders slumped as he realized whatever the monsters were they had the intelligence to cut off any means of easy escape.

He ran back to his rental car and pulled Pearl out by her hand. She'd recovered enough to could run on her own.

Pearl made a high-pitched gasp as he lead her past the dead space zombie in the hall.

She muttered something about it being Joey Daniels.

Jefferson tried to close the door, but the frame was destroyed. He grabbed the space zombie by the shirt and threw it against the door to keep anything from just walking in.

"Stay here. I'm going to get the lights back on."

"You're going out there?" asked Pearl. "Why? Don't leave me."

"I'll be right back," he said.

"Why do you want the lights on?"

"Because, those monsters turned them off and I want to get a better look at that thing in the hallway. See what we're up against."

Steven Roy

Pearl urged him not to go, but he ran to the back door. He looked for any sign of bioluminescence in the darkness. Seeing none, he opened the door and sprinted toward a large shed.

SECOND CONTACT

Tom twisted the throttle open as the four wheeler barreled down the trail.

Mary stood on the back of the seat and clung to Tom's shirt to keep from falling off as the speed pushed her tangled hair flat.

"Mary, sit down right," he said for the hundredth time.

She ignored him and leaned out farther from the seat.

"Mary!"

"We're not the type of kids that get to be safe," she yelled back.

Tom was just as persistent as Mary was stubborn.

"Sit down. Ain't safe."

"You just go faster," she screamed over the engine.

"You ornery," Tom said.

She poked him in the side. "Faster, I said, faster."

He shook his head. "Ain't safe."

While the two argued at high speed, something curious was happening just a short distance away.

The long fingers on Shorty's armored hand twitched. He reached up with a long arm, grabbed the scorched sheet of tin that had been covering him and tossed it aside. He sat up, but stayed there for a moment as if he was too tired to get up, but he reached up a long arm to grab a branch and pull himself to his feet.

He staggered into the woods, occasionally leaning on a tree to keep himself upright. The inside of his armor echoed with warnings that he was too injured to be moving around. He stepped on to the trail and grunted the override to shut off the alarms. With the alarms off he heard the roar of an engine.

BAM! The four wheeler collided with Shorty and knocked him flat. It rolled over him and teetered onto two wheels. Mary went flying. Tom purposely threw himself clear of the four wheeler as it flipped.

He let his momentum carry him to his feet. He scanned the area for Mary but didn't see her.

"Mary!"

She sat up from the tall grass at the side of the trail. Briars clung to her hair and clothes.

"I fell in some briars."

Tom ran to her side and began pulling the briars free.

She held up an arm that looked like it had lost a fight to twenty cats.

"Stupid briars, got me good."

Her eyes started to well up with tears.

"Be tough now," said Tom.

Mary yanked an arm free of some briars and wiped her eyes.

"Tom, everyone knows I'm the toughest. Just got some dirt in my eye when I fell is all."

He grabbed her by the shirt and pulled her to her feet. Some briars clung to the back of her shirt as if they still wanted her, but Tom ripped them away with his bare hands.

As he picked some twigs and leaves out of her hair, Mary looked around him and stared at the shiny, black form laying on the trail.

She pointed at Shorty.

"Am I imagining again. Maybe, I hit my head?"

Tom glanced over his shoulder and nearly jumped out of his

boots. He ran to where the shotgun laid in the briars and snatched it up. He pressed the stock to his shoulder and raised the barrel as he approached Shorty cautiously.

Mary walked past him and right up to Shorty. She leaned over him.

"Mary!"

She paid him no mind and leaned in closer. His armor reflected back her face and the moon like a still pool of water. She put her bare foot on Shorty's chest and gave him a few hard pushes. He didn't move.

Mary looked over her shoulder. "Tom, what is it?"

He walked to her side and poked Shorty with the barrel of his shotgun.

TINK-TINK.

Tom lowered his weapon.

"It's a robot."

"Coooool," said Mary. "Can we keep it?"

"Hell yeah, we're keeping it," said Tom.

He slung the shotgun over his shoulder and squatted down by the "robot". The kids tried to pick Shorty up but he was way too heavy.

Mary stood up. "We can't just leave him here. Someone will steal our robot for sure."

"We ain't leaving it," said Tom, looking back at the four wheeler's metal rack, which had a length of logging chain coiled around it.

He rarely smiled, but one formed on his face.

A short while later, Tom and Mary sped down the trail again. Mary sat properly as she held on to Tom with both hands. She turned her head and looked behind them.

The chain wrapped around Shorty's thick torso as the kids pulled him down the trail after them.

MACHETE

Jefferson pulled open the shed door, raised Big Bang and swept the room. The shed was empty, besides the water pump, a large generator, and several black, metal barrels of fuel along the wall.

He left the door open so the light from the full moon could stream into the shed. He stepped to the side of the generator and gave it a crank. The generator sputtered to life. A few seconds later the lights overhead flickered to life. He checked the fuel gauge on the generator and saw that it was almost full.

Jefferson looked around the shed. The walls were covered with tools.

Good thing I forgot about this place. I would have sold all this stuff, even the generator.

As he scanned the tools, his eyes fell on a long machete in a green, canvas scabbard. He pulled it down and pulled the blade out of its sheath. The black metal blade looked more like medieval weaponry than something you would cut weeds with. Jefferson smiled knowing that is exactly what had made Big Beau purchase it. He attached the scabbard to his belt and ran back toward the farmhouse.

By the time he made it to the back door, Pearl had turned on every light in the house. He turned the knob to the back door and found it locked.

He banged on the door.

"Young lady, it's me. Open up."

Pearl peeked out of the window and opened the door.

"Didn't know if you were coming back."

Jefferson ignored her as he marched toward the space-zombie holding the broken door in place with its weight.

He leaned over it, staring at the strange alien flesh that covered the skull. It was like someone had stuck a skull inside a large jellyfish and it had started to eat the rest of the human flesh.

Pearl came up behind him and leaned over his shoulder for a glance before recoiling.

She sobbed.

"That's Joey alright."

"Not anymore," said Jefferson.

Pearl backed a bit deeper into the hall but kept Jefferson in sight.

He ripped open the thing's shirt to examine the gaping wound that Big Bang had torn in its chest.

"This is amazing. This...life form seems not only to take over its host, but to also highjack the circulatory system. Kill the host body and you kill it. At least, I hope it's dead and not dormant."

Jefferson stood. He turned his attention to Pearl.

"You might not want to watch this."

Jefferson pulled the machete and faced the dead space zombie. As he raised the blade, Pearl scurried away.

In a few whacks, the head rolled to the floor.

He turned to Pearl who had backed all the way to the end of the hall.

"I had to be sure," he said.

Pearl nodded.

"You said all your friends were...changed?"

"Yes, sir."

"How?"

Pearl shrugged. "That I can't say."

"You had to have seen something."

Pearl shook her head. "I've always...I have fainting spells if I get scared," she explained.

"You didn't see one of these things spit or inject something into one of your friends? Bite them?"

"I don't think so. They would just beat everyone up and drag them away."

Jefferson's face lit up. He figured it wasn't *somewhere* they dragged the other teenagers but to *something*.

"Where did they drag them?

"Glad I didn't find out," said Pearl. "Everyone who did looks like that." She pointed at what used to be Joey.

"Oh no," said Jefferson, running toward the back door.

He looked over his shoulder at Pearl and stopped.

"You should get up in the attic. Pull the ladder up after you."

"What? Where are you going now?"

"I sent Daisy out there," said Jefferson. "I'm going to go get her."

"It's too far. You'll never make it on foot."

"I'm not going on foot, at least not on my own."

HORSE AND RIDER

The lights in the barn flickered on. All the stalls were empty except for one.

Gray Man's ears twitched, and he picked up his head and looked to the opening of the barn. A second later, Jefferson sprinted into the barn.

He opened Gray Man's stall and led him out. He quickly bridled the horse and gathered his saddle that was made from black leather and silver with the words "Black Redneck" embossed into the leather. He swung the saddle up toward Gray Man's back, but the horse spun out of the way.

Jefferson lowered the saddle. "I thought we made up?"

Gray Man stomped his front hooves.

"Look, we have to go save Daisy," said Jefferson.

He tried to place the saddle on the horse's back again, but Gray Man spun away from him.

Jefferson groaned in frustration. He put the saddle down and approached the horse. He scratched the horse's ears.

Gray Man moved closer to Jefferson.

"Fine. I got no right to ask for your help, but I need to you to carry me like you used to, and if you help, I won't sell you."

The horse walked around Jefferson until he was alongside the saddle and stopped. He picked up the saddle and set it on the horse's back. Gray Man stayed as still as a statue while

197

Jefferson buckled the saddle into place.

He put his boot in the stirrup and grabbed the saddle horn.

"Okay, please don't buck me off."

Jefferson swung onto the horse. It had been more than a decade since he had sat atop Gray Man, but he could feel the horse's desire to run.

He loosened the reins. "Go, Gray Man! Go!"

Gray Man raised his front hooves into the air and sprang forward, charging out of the barn and toward danger.

SEXY GAME WARDEN VS. SPACE ZOMBIES

Daisy stopped her four wheeler next to Anne's powder blue pickup. When she turned off the engine, the woods were so quiet she could hear the crackle of the coals that gave off an orange glow through the trees.

She hopped off the four wheeler and scanned the forest, seeing only trees and shadows.

As she walked toward the fire pit, her hand rested on the handle of her nine millimeter handgun.

In the clearing she saw the remnants of the sign laying next to the fire pit. She threw a few small pieces of sign on the coals, and they burst into flames, giving her a bit more light to investigate the area.

There were tracks everywhere and a few places where she saw the parallel impressions of feet being dragged through the dirt. She knelt by a beer can on the ground. She turned it upside down and a stream of beer came out.

She went to a cooler and flipped open the lid. She shined her light inside. Full cans of beer floated in the melting ice.

What could have happened that was so bad that teenagers would abandon coolers full of beer?

Daisy stood and scanned the woods with her light. Her other hand stayed on her gun.

She shined the light slowly across the trees and didn't even realize she was holding her breath.

Through the woods she saw a long, smooth leg sticking out from behind a tree.

Even though her back was to Daisy and she was obscured by a low hanging branch, there was only one girl in Picayune with legs that long.

"Anne Taylor, I know you ain't running around the woods in just your panties."

Anne didn't respond. She slipped behind a tree and disappeared into the shadows.

"Anne, you get back here. I know your mama."

The game warden eased closer to the tree line.

Anne stepped from behind the trees about twenty yards away from where Daisy stood. This time she was facing Daisy but still obscured by the shadows.

"What's that on your face? Are you kids having a rave?"

Anne didn't answer. She charged.

As Zombie Anne got closer, Daisy got a better look and pulled her gun.

The game warden felt her heart begin to pound. "Stop!"

Daisy focused so intently on Anne that she didn't even see the flickers of light growing brighter from the woods behind her.

Bam! Daisy fired and blew a chunk out of the tree just to the side of Anne's head, but the space zombie didn't even flinch as she kept running, even though the blast sent splinters into her face.

Anne grew ever closer. Daisy could see the light in her face and the skull beneath the alien flesh, which had eaten enough away that she could see Anne's collar bones and the top of her ribs.

That's no mask. She took aim to put one in the creature's chest.

Before she could pull the trigger, two space zombies crashed into her from behind like a couple of linebackers. Daisy would have screamed but the weight of one of the zombies came down on her hard and pushed the air out of her lungs. Her gun flew from her hands.

She laid there for just a moment, then started to fight the space zombies with everything she had. She kicked one off of her and rolled to her knees, snatching up her gun in the process. As one of the space zombies jumped to its feet, she put a bullet into its ear and it sank to the loose soil. Daisy jumped to her feet and backed away as she filled the second space zombie with a spray of bullets, but it kept coming forward and crashed into her again.

She pushed the dead space zombie off of her and got to her hands and knees. She heard charging steps and looked up to see Anne's foot blur toward her head.

GLEN WAKES UP

About the same time Daisy was getting knocked out by Anne's heel smashing into her temple, Glen moaned and turned on his side. He moaned louder and his hand came up slowly to feel the wound on the back of his head. He winced and pushed himself to a sitting position. "I'm going to kill those lil' bastards. Gonna kill 'em."

He got slowly to his feet, wobbly as a newborn calf, and staggered into the living room. He saw all his beer and giant TV smashed up. He stared at the TV for a long moment and looked as if he might cry, then he picked up a mostly empty bottle of whisky and used it to wash down some prescription painkillers.

He steadied himself and gingerly touched the back of his head. He winced again and picked up one of the few undamaged beers off the floor. He downed one and dropped the empty on the floor.

"Damn beer is warm," he muttered. But that didn't stop him from picking up another beer and opening it.

Glen stomped over to the door and looked around like he lost something. He stopped and threw what was left of his beer across the room where it smashed into a wall.

"Goddamn it!" he yelled. "They stole Sweet Darling."

His big belly bounced as he trotted to the back door still wearing his cut-offs. As he slipped on his boots, he thought of ways to dispose of Tom and Mary but still get the check and the extra food stamps. He stepped out onto the back steps and froze, staring at the empty place that used to contain his four wheeler.

He cursed and stomped the ground, but he soon got winded and leaned against the back of the house. His head sank in defeat for a moment, but then it raised and he walked to a rusty shed and disappeared inside.

The sound of a high pitched engine came from the shed and a second later Glen came riding out on a dirt bike meant for a little kid. He looked like a gorilla on a tricycle. The engine of the small dirt bike whined in effort to pull Glen's great bulk as he rode off into the woods at about five miles an hour.

Even Glen could follow the trail left by the big four wheeler, and they led him all the way to the catfish ponds. He stopped for a moment, noticing that there was an awful lot of mud between the two ponds, as if they had recently overflowed their banks. He thought that was odd because there hadn't been any rain for a couple of weeks. He drove the bike forward and just to the edge of the large pond. He wondered if the tiny bike could carry him through the mud when he saw something like a blue and red lightning storm streak beneath the murk of the largest pond. Glen leaned over the pond and the colorful flashes came again, bright enough to reveal the tentacles of some giant horror just below the surface.

Glen was a lot of things, but curious or brave wasn't one of them.

With one hand holding the handle bars and another holding the back seat, Glen stood up, lifting the tires of the little dirt bike off the ground. He turned in the opposite direction and sat the bike back down.

He had every intention to ride home when a group of space zombies stepped out of the darkness to block his path.

Glen turned the throttle of the little bike wide open. The small engine whined like a million mosquitos, but the best the small bike could do was to carry Glen toward the space zombies at a leisurely pace. The space zombies had time to look at each other before they flailed at Glen and knocked him off the bike.

Glen fell hard in the mud with the space zombies on top of him and the bike kept on going until it fell over into some weeds.

The space zombies kicked and punched Glen as he curled into the fetal position. Two of them grabbed his arms and attempted to drag him back to the pond, but their feet came out from underneath them in the mud. They stood, flickering as more space zombies clustered around Glen and dragged him to the edge of the pond. They were like some ants dragging a grass hopper back to the nest.

The Devourer rose out of the pond, sending a wave of brown water before her.

Glen stared up at the towering monstrosity and started to blubber.

"Please, please don't eat me!" screamed Glen. "Baby-Jesus, help me. Help!"

The Devourer pulled up a long tentacle. The tip opened like a mouth dripping with a clear, gelatinous fluid. The open end of the tentacle slipped right over Glen's head and pulled him into the air as if he weighed nothing.

Glen's legs twitched and his fat belly jiggled as he convulsed. It was as if he were being electrocuted.

Soon, the Devourer laid the fat man gently on the bank. Glen's face burned off as the alien cells quickly ate it away. He sat up and his clear face pulsated with light as he stretched out his arms toward the Devourer.

And, just like that Glen went from being the biggest asshole in Picayune to being the biggest space zombie.

DAISY AIN'T DEAD YET

About the time Glen rose to his feet as the fattest of all space zombies, Daisy's eyes flickered open, and she realized she was draped over the shoulder of a large space zombie as it marched down the trail.

Her first instinct was to flail around like a fish on a hook, but she fought down her fear and lay as still as she could while she looked around to survey the situation.

As far as she could tell, there was only the one space zombie. She reached slowly to her pant leg and touched the handle of the large knife strapped to her ankle. As silently as she could, she unsnapped the strip of leather holding the blade in place.

The space zombie stopped at the sound. Daisy pulled the blade and rose up, leaning as far back as she could to see its face. With her free hand she grabbed the space zombie's neck and drove the blade into the creature's eye to the hilt. Its legs buckled and it fell to its knees.

Daisy twisted her blade and kicked the dying creature in the chest. It fell back in an awkward position. As the lights in its face dimmed to darkness, she took off down the trail at a full sprint. She ran toward her four wheeler, only glancing over her shoulder to make sure that the thing she stabbed in the eye didn't get up.

She ran until she saw her four wheeler and only had a brief

moment to feel relief before she saw more flickers of colorful light coming from the shadows of the trees. Four space zombies emerged from the woods and charged right at her.

Daisy's plan changed quickly from getting to the four wheeler to simply running like hell.

As a space zombie tried to tackle her, she side-stepped it, then sprinted right between the three others. The time she spent playing football with boys had finally paid off as she ran full out away from the space zombies, who turned and gave chase.

Daisy kept herself in fine shape, but she could only sprint for so long. The space zombies didn't seem to get tired.

Her legs started to burn, and she knew it wouldn't be that long before they overtook her. By that time she wouldn't be able to put up much of a fight. She dug her boots into the trail and stopped so quickly one of the zombies ran right by her. Daisy swung her blade at the creature's neck and felt the serrated blade dig into the strange flesh. The space zombie staggered a few more steps and crumbled to the ground as the remaining three encircled her.

"Come on then!"

The space zombies obliged her. They flickered in unison and charged all at once. Daisy slammed her blade into the forehead of the space zombie in front of her. Its body went limp with the hilt sticking out its skull like a unicorn's horn, but its momentum still carried the monster's weight into her, knocking her off her feet.

Daisy struggled to get her blade free and get back to her feet, but the other space zombies piled on. One of them raised its fist and slammed it down toward her face. As she moved her head out of the way of a space zombie's punch, she swore she heard the pounding of galloping hooves coming down the trail, but she figured it must be her heart about to explode.

As one space zombie pinned her down, another stood and raised its leg to stomp her in the face but, before the blow could land, a lasso fell around the standing space zombie's neck and tightened. It flew backwards and landed hard on its back before being dragged down the trail.

The remaining space zombie jumped off of Daisy and turned. The spaghetti-like tendrils on top of its head waved violently as it tracked the large, gray horse dragging the other space zombie down the trail. The horse turned sharply and charged back toward them. The space zombie charged toward the horse.

Bad idea. Jefferson leaned in the saddle and swung his machete.

The blade bit into the space zombie's neck and its head flipped end over end. The lights in the space zombie's face went dark before it hit the ground and rolled into the bushes.

Daisy got to her feet as Jefferson slid off his horse and decapitated the space zombie he'd been dragging.

He swung back onto Gray Man and rode to Daisy's side. She put her boot on the side of the space zombie's face and twisted her blade free.

She knelt to catch her breath, feeling like she was going to throw up.

Jefferson said, "Are you okay?"

Daisy managed between gasps for air, "I think...I think...my crush on you is officially back on."

Jefferson held out his hand to pull her into the saddle, but she walked past Gray Man.

"I have to get my gun and my four wheeler."

She stopped as she saw a few strange lights flicker from the woods around the fire pit.

"On second thought, I'll just buy another gun."

She grabbed Jefferson's outstretched hand, and he pulled her into the saddle behind him. She clung to him tightly. Jefferson could feel her heart pounding against his back.

"Glad you're okay, Daisy."

"I'm glad you came to get me."

Jefferson didn't answer her. He spoke to Gray Man instead. "Yah, Gray Man. Go."

Gray Man took off and charged back toward the farmhouse.

FORT AWESOME

Fort Awesome rested in an isolated part of the woods and, though it was fifteen feet high and twice as long, it was surrounded by a wall of large oak trees that made it hard to find if you didn't know just where to look.

The walls were constructed of old tires and mud. The roof was old sheets of tin with another layer of dirt stacked on top.

But the door was the truly unique part. It was made from an old, rusted VW van that made it seem like the van was embedded in a small hill. Moss and lichen had grown over the entire thing, making it look like it had been there for a thousand years, though every bit of it was built by Tom and Mary - mostly Tom. The place lived up to its name.

Tom and Mary pulled up in front of Fort Awesome, dragging Shorty behind them.

The boy jumped off the four wheeler and lit an oil lantern that hung from a tree branch.

He opened the side door of the van to reveal that the other side of it had been cut away and opened into the interior of Fort Awesome.

Old seats pulled from junk cars lay around a cast iron pot-bellied stove that rested in the middle of the fort.

Tom carried the lantern as he jumped back on the four wheeler and drove right inside pulling Shorty with them.

He jumped off and hung the lantern from the ceiling. As Mary lit two other lanterns, Tom went to the van door and slid it closed. And, just like that, they were hidden in Fort Awesome.

Tom sighed and collapsed into an old car seat.

Mary knelt by Shorty and tried to shake him awake.

"Get up, lazy robot. Get up. Your master wants a sandwich."

When Shorty didn't respond, Mary groaned in frustration and walked to the back seat of a Lincoln Continental and let herself collapse onto it.

"Just our luck to find an old, busted robot," she said. "Think you can fix it?"

Tom got up and brought Mary a dirty jar of peanut butter.

She opened it, but there were only a couple of spoonfuls inside.

She smiled. "I'm not hungry. I ate sandwiches earlier. You take it."

"Your stomach growled. I'll just go to the catfish pond and..."

"No! Don't!" cried Mary.

"You worried about monsters?"

"No," said Mary. "Maybe. You just can't go there."

"We have to eat."

Mary held up the jar and said, "This is plenty."

"It ain't," said Tom.

He collapsed back into an old car seat and put his head into his hands.

Mary walked over and put her small hand on his shoulder.

"It'll be okay?"

"How you figure?"

Mary had to think about it for a bit.

"When our robot wakes up, he'll make us food and beat up people we don't like. Did you see how long his arms are? He'll punch 'em from across the room."

"We're on our own."

"Not-uh, you'll see. I can tell he's a good robot."

She went back to Shorty's side and held a canteen of water to his faceplate.

"What are you doing?" asked Tom. "Everyone knows robots drink gas."

"Well, I forgot."

ATTACK ON FORT AWESOME

A small group of space zombies moved through the woods just outside the large oak trees that formed a natural wall around Fort Awesome. They would have crept right by, but they heard Mary's high-pitched screech as the van door slid open and a bit of light came from the gap in the door.

"Don't you leave this fort, Tom!" Mary screamed.

"Fine, I won't go." The van door slid shut with a loud bang, and the space zombies faces flickered with the same blue-green colors and moved toward Fort Awesome.

Tom sighed and plopped down on a bucket seat torn from an abandoned wreck. He put his face in his hands briefly, then looked up to see Mary going through the red wagon where they kept the comic books and novels they had stolen.

Shorty laid behind the four wheeler as if he were passed out drunk.

Tom got up and grabbed a well-read Kung fu novel and collapsed back into his chair.

"Why do you think those older kids were screaming?" Mary asked.

Tom didn't look up from the novel. "Don't know. Don't care."

"I bet they got drunk and went crazy like Glen."

She drank some water out of a canteen and staggered around, mumbling loudly. She dropped into what had been the backseat of a Lincoln and pretended to pass out.

Tom still didn't look up from his book.

"Hey, we have any picture stories about robots?" asked Mary.

"Nope."

Mary picked up a crumpled legal pad and some worn crayons from the red wagon.

"I'm going to make my own."

As Mary started using the last inch of a black crayon to draw Shorty, the handle of the van door turned as if someone was trying to open it from the other side.

Tom jumped to his feet and grabbed the shotgun. He snuck to the door and tried to peer out of the dirty window.

"Glen, we know it's you. Best get out of here," said Mary.

Loud steps came from outside as someone walked over leaves and branches without making any attempt to be quiet.

Tom looked at Mary and held a finger over his lips.

"Last time you got the back of the gun!" Mary yelled. "This time you'll get the front."

The wall of tires just to the side of Mary exploded inward as two space zombies smashed their way into the fort, creating a cloud of dust.

An avalanche of tires buried Shorty where he laid on the floor.

Mary screamed loud. Tom spun and paused for just a few seconds at the sight of two space zombies, then he pulled the trigger. Boom! A space zombie staggered backward and fell as the shotgun blast hit him in the gut.

Tom tried to take aim at the other through the cloud of dust, but it already had Mary by her ankle and lifted her into the air as she kicked at it with her other foot.

"Put her down!" screamed Tom.

The space zombie ignored him. Tom ran toward it but, before he could get there, Shorty rose out of the fallen tires with enough force that it sent a few radials flying.

The long, vibrating blade emerged from his wrist and hummed like a thousand angry hornets, distorting the air around it. He swung and the space zombie holding the girl fell to the floor in two sections.

Mary kicked the dead hands off of her ankles and scurried back against the wall. Shorty turned toward Tom holding up the vibrating blade. The two stared at each other, but then the blade disappeared inside the alien's armor. Shorty swayed on his feet. Mary hopped up and ran to his side.

"Good job, Robot," she said.

Shorty dropped face first into a pile of tires, then bounced back into the red wagon and on top of the comics.

Tom ran to the hole in the wall and held up the shotgun. He saw a fat space zombie disappear behind the oak trees before he could shoot. Tom moved back inside.

Mary and Tom just stared at each other as the dust settled around them.

The gut-shot space zombie sat up quickly. Mary jumped back, but Tom shot it in the face with hardly a look and knocked it back flat on the floor.

Mary ran across the room and punched Tom in the arm. "What's that for?"

"For lying! You said there weren't no monsters."

"Ain't supposed to be."

"Stupid monsters broke our wall, but our robot saved us," said Mary.

She went to Shorty's side and tried to shake him awake. "Wake up. Come on. Wake up."

She looked at Tom. "What's wrong with it?"

Tom shrugged. "Low batteries?"

"Well, let's go get some batteries. I bet he can eat them and get real strong. I bet he can eat four car batteries and that's just a snack."

"Let's just go. That thing'll be back."

Tom took the chain from around Shorty's chest and used it

to secure the red wagon to the back of the four wheeler. His shoulders slumped.

"What's your problem?" Mary asked.

"Where are we supposed to go?

"Balladeer farm."

"That guy?"

"Yeah. I didn't tell you but he's my friend now."

"What?"

"That's where I got the sandwiches," she said. "I guess he's okay."

"Well, we ain't got nowhere else to go."

He handed her the shotgun. It was much too big for her and she had to hold the stock under her arm to reach the trigger.

"You keep watch. I drive," said Tom.

"If some monsters come around, I'll shoot 'em in the damn face."

Tom nodded and leapt onto the four wheeler.

Mary ran and opened the van door and ran back and climbed on top of Shorty's armored chest. She faced away from Tom so no monsters could sneak up on them.

"Best hang on," he said.

ESCAPE FROM FORT AWESOME

The four wheeler shot out of Fort Awesome with the red wagon in tow behind it.

Tom guided the machine through a narrow gap between the oaks and onto a narrow animal trail. The branches on either side of the trail slapped against them as Tom slowed to make his way down the winding trail.

"Faster!" Mary yelled.

Tom looked over his shoulder. "Monsters?"

"No, but they gonna just walk up to us with you going this slow."

Tom turned back around. "Just keep watch."

Mary stared into the darkness. "Just hurry."

Tom got them through the short cut and emerged onto the main trail.

"Okay," said Mary. "Now, go faster. Gun it."

Tom turned the throttle and the engine roared. Mary's tangled hair was pushed into her face. As she pushed the hair out of her eyes, the four wheeler hit a large bump in the trail. Tom barely felt the bump on the four wheeler, but the red wagon wasn't designed for these speeds or terrain.

The bump jarred Shorty into a seated position, throwing Mary off his chest and straight up into the air. By the time she came down, the red wagon had moved on without her. She landed on her belly on the trail with the shotgun underneath her.

The blow knocked the wind clear out of her, so she laid there gasping like a catfish out of water.

By the time she sat up, Tom was too far away to hear her over the roar of the four wheeler.

She tried to yell anyway, "Tom! Tom! You dummy!"

Mary almost started to cry. She was used to getting left behind, but not by Tom. But she wiped her eyes, got to her feet, and plucked the leaves and twigs out of her hair.

She picked up the shotgun and walked after the fading sound of the four wheeler with the gun on her shoulder as if she were a tiny soldier.

The pounding of large feet came from behind her on the trail. She turned and saw the lights of a space zombie growing brighter as it ran toward her. In just a second more, she could see from the creature's giant belly and poor choice of attire that it used to be Glen.

Mary planted the butt of the shotgun in the dirt and pointed the barrel at Zombie Glen. She pulled the trigger.

The flash of the blast lit up the trail, and the shot hit the creature in the thigh, causing it to fall face-first onto the trail. It pounced right back up and hobbled toward Mary, dragging the shot up leg behind it.

The little girl struggled to pump the shotgun again, but Zombie Glen made it to her before she could pull the trigger. Zombie Glen swatted the gun away and landed a clubbing blow to the side of Mary's head.

She staggered back and fell at the edge of the woods. Zombie Glen's leg poured blood as he shuffled toward her like a traditional zombie.

Mary pushed herself up to her elbows and looked straight at the approaching horror.

"I thought a monster would hit harder than that," she said.

Zombie Glen charged her. She rolled to her feet and ran down the trail. Even with the injured leg, he gained on her. Just as he was about to grab her, she ducked off the trail and into some thick woods, using her small size to her advantage as she slipped under some low hanging vines.

The creature tried to push through the vines and branches that blocked its way, but he soon lost her and just stood there, waiting.

Zombie Glen didn't have to wait long before he heard the sound of an approaching four wheeler. The creature turned back toward the trail. Seconds later, the four wheeler skidded to a stop on the trail. Tom stood up on the seat.

"Mary! Mary! Where are you?"

Zombie Glen charged toward the trail. Tom turned toward the rustle in the woods too late. Zombie Glen crashed into him and knocked him off the four wheeler. Tom landed hard with Glen's more than significant weight on top of him. Tom threw a flurry of punches that landed on the side of the creature's head but, if it hurt the creature, it didn't show.

Zombie Glen rose up and punched the boy right in the mouth. Tom's lip split, and his body fell limp.

Like an ant bringing food back to the nest, Zombie Glen grabbed Tom's pant leg and started dragging him toward the catfish ponds.

The creature made it about ten yards, when something small stepped out onto the trail about twenty yards ahead of him and blocked its path. It was Mary, holding the shotgun.

"Ain't never liked you, Glen, and now it's okay to shoot you 'cause you a monster."

Zombie Glen dropped Tom's leg and charged toward her. Mary used the ground to aim the shotgun again. This time going for the head. Boom! The shot went too high and the force of the blast staggered Mary backwards and ripped the shotgun out of her hands.

With the gun out of reach and Zombie Glen bearing down on her, she ran for the woods. This time she wasn't fast enough. As she ducked into the woods Zombie Glen reached into the brush and pulled Mary out by her hair.

Mary fought like a cat trying not to get a bath, all pissed off and scratching.

Zombie Glen lifted her over his head and slammed her down on the trail. For the second time in less than thirty minutes, the wind got knocked out of Mary.

As Zombie Glen reached to pick her up, he didn't see Tom running toward him with Sweet Darling held high. Tom smashed the homemade mace into the side of Glen's knee, bending it in the wrong direction.

Tom jumped back and ducked as Glen turned and swung at him. The fat zombie tried to lurch toward Tom, but his damaged knee wasn't able to bear his excessive weight, and Zombie Glen belly-flopped onto the trail and kept crawling toward Tom.

Tom jumped forward and landed on Glen's back, like one of those guys at Sea-World riding a killer whale. From there he rained down blows to the back of the creature's head. Zombie Glen rolled over onto his back. Tom jumped off and kept his balance and continued to strike the creature in the face with the club. The creature covered its face with his arms. Tom struck down again, and the creature grabbed onto Sweet Darling and wouldn't let go.

As he and Tom were locked in a tug-o-war over the weapon, Mary got to her feet and grabbed the shotgun. She ran to the fray and started slamming the stock of the gun into Zombie Glen's face over and over.

The creature reached for the gun. This allowed Tom to twist Sweet Darling free. He drew way back and brought the weapon down hard. Splat! Sweet Darling sank into the creature's forehead. Before the bioluminescence started to fade, the kids could see the skull was cracked. Tom twisted Sweet Darling free from the alien flesh. Mary kept slamming the butt of the gun into its face.

"Die, fatty, die!" she yelled.

Tom collapsed to his knees, out of breath. Mary followed suit and dropped the shotgun. She looked like she was about to cry, but held it in.

"Tom?" she asked.

"Yeah."

"Glen turned into a monster."

Tom shook his head. "Always was one"

The boy pulled her to her feet. They walked hand in hand back to the four wheeler.

Shorty still laid in the red wagon as if he was taking a nap.

"Stupid Robot," said Mary. "You're supposed to kill monsters so we ain't got to."

She climbed back on top of Shorty and looked into his mirrored faceplate. It reflected back the stars above.

"Stupid, lazy robot."

A GIRL NAMED PEARL

Pearl sat in the dark in the corner of the attic. She heard the buzz of the four wheeler's engine and made her way quietly to a small, slated window.

She recognized Tom driving the large ATV and Mary riding behind in the red wagon as they rode through the lower field toward the farmhouse.

"Hey! Hey! Get out of there!"

The kids didn't hear her over the roar of the engine.

Pearl took a deep breath and ran to the folded ladder that led to the hallway. She pulled up the hatchway and checked the hallway. Seeing no monsters with glowing faces and visible skulls, she lowered the ladder and ran down the hallway. She froze when she saw the decapitated space zombie holding the door closed with its weight.

Her lip quivered, and she placed her hand on the wall to steady herself.

Damn it. Don't pass out. Help those kids.

Pearl took a deep breath and held it as she grabbed the pant leg of the deceased space zombie and gave it a tug toward the hall. Its back thudded against the wooden floor.

Pearl made a disgusted noise and leapt over the corpse and onto the porch.

By the time she got to the steps, Tom and Mary were already

in the front yard and driving toward the house.

Pearl waved at them frantically.

Tom waved back as if he was just saying hey.

As he got a bit closer, Pearl yelled, "Hurry up and get in here! There's..."

"Monsters," yelled Mary, "Yeah, we know."

Tom pulled right up to the steps and Mary added, "We done kilt three."

Pearl's eyes widened as she noticed Mary was sitting on a strange, creature clad in black armor.

"Ah, what's that you're sitting on?"

"My robot."

Tom turned and gave Mary a look.

"*Our* robot," she corrected herself.

Mary hopped down. She and Tom struggled to pull the red wagon up the steps of the porch.

"No way. You're not bringing...whatever that thing is inside."

"It's good at killing those monsters," Mary said.

Pearl rushed to grab the edge of the wagon and pulled as hard as she could.

THE DEVOURER FEEDS HER KIDS

City Boy and Anne led two cows to the edge of the large, catfish pond. The alien flesh had grown farther down their bodies revealing most of their ribcages and spines. The new alien flesh had replaced most of the muscle and skin of their upper bodies but left some of the major arteries suspended in the clear flesh like purplish tubes that connected to the heart and lungs.

Spots of bioluminescence and colorful filaments shone over their bodies as if the alien flesh contained its own galaxy.

The Devourer rose out of the pond and stretched to a height even with the tallest trees. The many tentacles of the Devourer undulated as the giant creature loomed over the two cows.

The two bovines mooed and pulled away from the pond, but Anne and City Boy dug their feet into the mud and tried to hold the animals in place, but the two frightened cows were too strong for them and began to pull the two space zombies through the mud.

The Devourer shot out two massive tentacles that wrapped around each cow and raised them high into the air before smashing them down hard enough to shatter their bones.

The Devourer continued to slam the cattle into the ground and trees as if they were rag dolls, then dropped the broken carcasses to the edge of the pond.

City Boy and Anne rushed forward and removed the animals' harnesses as the Devourer raised two tentacles that ended in clear barbs. The monster slammed the barbs downward, deep into the abdomen of the cows.

Horrible sucking noises came from the two corpses. The flesh of the animals moved through the tentacles, a red river of gore rushing toward the Devourer's core. The base of the thick tentacles went pink as the cow cells pooled there.

Zombie Anne and City Boy fell to their knees, arms outstretched toward the Devourer as she fed. They began to pulsate with green and yellow light as more tentacles stretched out from the towering creature and ripped the cows into chunks that were swallowed whole by the tentacles that ended in the snake-like maws.

At the base of the Devourer's large tentacles, the gore that had once been the two cows bubbled and the monster's flesh turned mostly clear as the cow cells assimilated into the Devourer.

The massive monster held her feeding tentacles high and expelled a steam-like vapor.

Anne and City Boy began to flicker rapidly. The Devourer lowered the barb-like ending of the tentacle over their upturned faces. Both space zombies leapt up to grab the tentacles. They opened their mouths impossibly wide and let the barb go down their throats like a pair of sword swallowers.

The clear flesh of the tentacle contracted and expanded like a beating heart. The combination of cow and alien cells flowed down the tentacle and down the open throats of the two space zombies. Their torsos began to expand like balloons on the end of a faucet.

The tentacle stopped contracting and the flow of sustenance stopped. Anne and City Boy flickered green, but the Devourer threw them to the muddy bank and sank back into the pond.

Both space zombies tried to stand, but they fell back into the mud and convulsed as if in great pain. They pulsated with points of white light as a viscous fluid within their swollen torso exuded from their clear flesh. The goo ran down their bodies and consumed the remaining human flesh so fast that steam rose from their bodies.

Anne tried to stand again and lurched to her knees.

The alien cells ran over her arms and body, reshaping her rapidly. Her breasts lengthened into forward facing tentacles. Her arms stretched into long, thick tentacles. The clear flesh grew down her body replacing any human cell in its path.

As Anne grew larger, her skeleton pulled inward and floated uselessly in the transparent flesh.

More tentacles sprouted from her sides and undulated like clear worms emerging from clear earth.

A moment later, Anne stood on strange new legs. The beginning of a barb formed at the tip of her longest tentacle. The only feminine thing about her now was the pair of lacy panties that still floated within the clear flesh.

She turned to face City Boy who had been similarly transformed. They intertwined their new tentacles and touched each other the way an animal might touch its own reflection in a mirror.

Anne ran one of her fore-tentacles over City Boy's torso. Deep within his stomach a cluster of pulsating fibers twisted together like a nest of vipers.

She pressed a tentacle to her own stomach where the same organ twisted into existence in her own body.

City-Boy and Anne flickered a golden color and space zombies of varying transformation levels fell in behind them. They both ran into the woods in opposite directions with space zombies following behind.

FARMHOUSE MEET UP

Pearl pushed the red wagon as Tom and Mary pulled Shorty into the living room. The long arms of the whatever was in the red wagon dragged on the wooden floor as Pearl was careful not to let her hands touch the black armor.

Once they parked Shorty in the corner, Pearl stood straight and said, "If this thing wakes up, I don't know what I'm going to do."

Mary stared at the dark stain on Pearl's crotch. "You pee yourself?"

Pearl blushed. "I spilled a drink."

"Whatever you were drinking sure smells like pee."

"I think we have bigger problems," said Pearl.

Mary looked at Tom. "This one peed her panties."

"Just leave it," Tom said.

Mary smirked at Pearl and asked, "Hey, Pee-Pee-Panties, where's that guy?"

"Mr. Jefferson? He probably ain't coming back, not as himself anyway. He went into the woods..."

The porch squeaked with footsteps and a clip-clop sound grew louder as something large approached the door.

Pearl backed against the wall and went pale.

Tom snatched up the shotgun and stood in the hallway. Mary tried to shake Shorty awake.

"Get up," she whispered. "Monsters are here. Sounds like a big one. Turn on. Turn on."

She pressed her index finger all over Shorty's armor hoping to find the power switch.

"God, ya'll. They're...they're.." said Pearl.

Mary looked over her shoulder. "Keep it together over there and hush up."

She gave up on Shorty and picked up Sweet Darling. She stood behind Tom and held the homemade mace like a batter ready to hit one over the fence.

The door swung open. Tom almost pulled the trigger, but pointed the barrel at the ceiling and then lowered his gun.

Daisy stood in the doorway. "Tom, how are you?"

"Been better."

"Mary, always good to see you," she said.

"I don't like no game warden," said Mary. "You'll probably tell us it ain't monster season and we just 'spose to get ate."

"Nope. It's always monster season."

Mary pointed at the clear gore on Sweet Darling. "We done kilt three."

"I think you mean you've killed three," said Daisy.

Mary sneered at Daisy, but when Jefferson lead Gray Man into the hallway, she smiled and ran up to him.

"You were right. Something is in those woods, a big monster and some people-monsters too. Gray Man likes you now?"

Jefferson said, "We like each other. I'm glad you're not..."

"Monster food. Yeah, us too."

Mary ran toward the living room. "Come see our robot."

Jefferson and Mary stood in the hallway.

"Great. Now we have little kids to look out for."

"At least they're not little monsters," said Daisy.

Mary leaned back into the hallway. "Well, come look at the robot already."

"Well, at least Tom's not a little monster," Daisy said.

Jefferson and Daisy walked into the living room. Gray Man stayed at Jefferson's heels.

Jefferson froze when he saw the black-clad figure lying in the red wagon with the long arms stretched out on the floor.

"What is that?" asked Jefferson.

"Done told you, it's our robot," said Mary.

Jefferson looked at Tom. The boy shrugged. "Kills monsters."

"You saw it kill the...monsters?" asked Jefferson.

Tom nodded. "Has a sword in his arm."

"He cuts the monsters in half." Mary imitated the buzzing noise the vibrating blade makes and swung her arm.

Jefferson moved a bit closer and leaned over Shorty. He tried to look past the mirror shield of the helmet, but only saw his reflection.

"I'm not convinced this is a robot."

"How do we know it won't cut us in half?" asked Daisy.

"He won't," said Mary. "He's one of the good ones."

"I hope so," said Jefferson. "But we have to be certain." He stepped to Gray Man's side and grabbed a coil of rope from the saddle and moved toward Shorty.

SMALL TOWN COPS

The credits for Miss Marple rolled on the big screen. Ambrose started to nod off in his recliner.

"Really, this is how our Saturday night is going to end," said Deputy Kirby. "Falling asleep in some recliners like some old men watching their mystery shows?"

Ambrose sat up in the recliner and rubbed his eyes.

"I would love for my Saturday night to end like that. It's what I call pleasantly boring."

"Come on," said Kirby. "Let's go break up that party."

"You just want to see Anne Taylor."

"Yeah, I do."

"If we go out there, you're not going to do anything I'll have to arrest you for. Like handcuff her and feel her up."

"I'm offended. I'd never do something like that. At least not until we been dating for a while and we have an established safe word."

Ambrose held up a hand. "I've heard enough."

"I can tell Anne really likes me."

"She likes you when she's talking her way out of a ticket."

"No, she likes likes me, and isn't it our duty to stop trespassers?"

Ambrose stood. "Like you care about that."

"Okay, you're right. I just want to get inside Anne."

"Fine, we're going to go out there and break up this party. Call Leon and tell him to bring the big truck."

Kirby did a fist pump like he had just thrown the winning touch down in the Superbowl.

"Don't get excited," said Ambrose. "We're going to ask Anne if she really likes you, and, if she says no, you're not going to bother her again. Agreed?"

"Well, she might get shy in front of you."

"Anne Taylor is not shy. Do we agree or not?"

"Fine," said Kirby.

THE WAY TO OLD ED'S

Jefferson stood from tying up Shorty to the red wagon. He looked in the direction of Old Ed's place.

Daisy put a hand on his shoulder. "You're worried about him."

"He probably doesn't even know what's going on. He goes to bed at seven-thirty."

"Go get him," said Daisy.

"And leave you alone?"

"I strike you as incapable?"

"Not at all, but if you ever saw a horror movie, you know not to separate. Strength in numbers."

"Old Ed would make one more. I also have Tom and Mary. More importantly, Tom has a shotgun."

Jefferson looked to Tom. "Tom, how many shells you have left?"

"Five, sir. But, three of those are birdshot."

Jefferson looked back to Daisy.

"Well, we can't just leave Old Ed," she said.

Jefferson unbuckled the gun belt that held Big Bang and held it out to Daisy.

"You can't go out there without a gun."

"I don't plan on fighting and making a lot of noise. I'll get

Old Ed and rush back here. Besides, I have my machete and Gray Man to run them over if they get in my way."

Daisy took the gun belt and pulled Big Bang out of the holster. Her hand looked like a baby's compared to the giant handgun. She looked at the picture of Big Beau painted on the handle and chuckled.

"Your brother sure was something."

"If he was here, those monsters would already all be dead." He smiled and looked at her holding the gun.

"You'll want to use both hands if you have to shoot that canon."

"I might have figured that one out on my own," she said.

Jefferson smiled and led Gray Man toward the door. Daisy grabbed his shoulder and stepped close behind him.

She whispered, "You be quick, Jefferson Balladeer."

Jefferson turned to face her. "I promise I will be. You still owe me a cup of coffee."

Pearl stepped up to them.

"You're leaving us? Again?"

"I have to go get Old Ed. Besides, he'll have a lot of guns. A lot."

GOING NEXT DOOR

As soon as he got Gray Man down the concrete steps, Jefferson swung into the saddle and loosened his grip on the reins so the horse could move freely and of its own volition.

"Go! Let's go."

The old, gray stallion didn't need any more encouragement and took off across the yard, cutting hoof-sized divots out of the front yard.

They were soon at the first wooden fence, and Jefferson rode down it until he found the gate. He slid off the horse and worked at untangling the chain that held it closed.

Gray Man turned in the other direction and galloped away toward the farmhouse. Jefferson stood straight and looked for any threats that the horse might have noticed. When he didn't see any, he yelled for Gray Man.

"No, come back!"

Gray Man ran until he was a good sixty yards away before turning back toward Jefferson. The horse stomped his front hooves before standing up on his back legs and springing forward. In a few seconds Gray Man was at a full sprint, charging right toward Jefferson.

"We don't really have time to play."

Gray Man kept charging toward Jefferson and covered the distance in seconds. The horse was ten yards away and wasn't slowing. Jefferson held his hands up as if that would slow the horse. Just before the horse crashed into him Jefferson dropped down low. Gray Man leapt and sailed right over both him and the fence as if he was as light as a gazelle.

Jefferson turned in time to see Gray Man land and make a quick turn. The horse held his head and tail high as he pranced up and down the fence line.

Jefferson climbed the fence and sat on the top of it. "Show off," he said.

Gray Man stopped in front of Jefferson, but moved his hooves up and down as if he couldn't wait to run.

Jefferson slid into the saddle and patted Gray Man's neck.

He grabbed the reins. "Fine, we won't stop for anything. Yah!"

BATTLE AT OLD ED'S

With Gray Man bounding over the fences, it didn't take them long to speed through the fields and emerge from a cornfield and onto Ed's property.

A small wooden house sat in the middle of a large field surrounded by gardens of everything from avocados to zucchini. A modest barn stood at the edge of the property in the shadows of the tall pines that marked the tree line.

As they neared Old Ed's house, strange flickers of colorful light came from within the barn.

Jefferson rode Gray Man to the front of the house, then dismounted. He led the horse close against the house and leaned out to take another look at the barn. More flickers of light came from the barn, but he wanted to get a better look.

Jefferson looked back at Gray Man and whispered, "Down, down Gray Man. Play dead."

The horse lowered itself to the ground and rolled over to his side, even closing his eyes.

Jefferson rubbed the horse's belly and then took off, sneaking down the side of the house and staying in the shadows. Gray Man raised his head and opened one of his eyes to watch.

He got to the back corner of the house and studied the darkness around the barn.

City Boy, now a full-on monstrosity more alien than human, carried three goats. The animals screamed bloody murder as the creature held them wrapped in its tentacle arms. Another space zombie appeared leading a cow, then two more emerged struggling to lead a large mare that fought them every step of the way as it kicked and bit at them. The horse knocked one of the space zombies to the ground and took off, pulling the other off his feet and dragging it through a patch of watermelons. The space zombie let go of the horse but jumped to his feet to find the other space zombie at his side. The two creatures ran side by side after the horse.

Ka-Pow! A rifle report came from the roof of Old Ed's house. Jefferson almost jumped out of his skin.

Ka-Pow! Another bullet threw up a cloud of dust a yard behind one of the space zombie's heals.

The two monsters turned from running after the horse and charged toward Old Ed's house.

More shots rang out from the roof, but they just threw up dirt around the space zombies. Most of the shots weren't even close to them.

Jefferson backed away from the house to see Old Ed on the roof, on one knee, taking aim at the space zombies.

Before Old Ed could waste another bullet, Jefferson cleared his throat. Old Ed whipped the gun toward him, but lowered it when he saw Jefferson.

"Eyes ain't what they used to be."

Jefferson held out his hand for the rifle. He looked over his shoulder to see the space zombies getting closer. He splayed out his hand more urgently.

Old Ed dropped the rifle off the roof.

Jefferson jumped up and snatched the rifle out of the air and spun.

The first space zombie wasn't three steps away.

Ka-Pow! The bullet struck the space zombie in the center of the face, sending a splatter of clear alien flesh in all directions as the creature crumpled.

The second space zombie leapt at him. Jefferson rolled out of the way and came up on one knee with the rifle on his shoulder.

Before the space zombie's feet hit the ground, Ka-Pow, the front of its head splattered clear alien flesh as the bullet exited the front of its head.

Jefferson spun back toward the barn. City Boy dropped the goats and ran toward Jefferson as the third space zombie sprinted toward the woods. Jefferson ran to the fence and steadied the rifle on the top of a fence post. He took careful aim and pulled the trigger. As the shot from the rifle echoed through the trees, the space zombie crumpled at the tree line.

With the last of the normal space zombies down, Jefferson turned his attention back to City Boy. The giant creature ran right at him.

Jefferson's instincts told him to run back to Gray Man and ride away as fast as he could, but he forced those thoughts away, took a deep breath and took careful aim. Jefferson fired rapidly, blowing chunks of alien flesh off City Boy's head. The monstrosity fell, but lurched back up and sprinted toward the woods.

Jefferson remained calm and continued to aim before each shot. Through the clear globe of alien flesh that was now City Boy's head, a skull floated like a fly caught in amber.

Ka-Pow! The bullet struck City Boy right where the vertebrae hung from the back of the skull. A chunk of clear flesh and shattered skull flew out the front of City Boy's head. The large creature's momentum carried him a few more steps before he fell in the field and slid to a stop in the loose soil.

City Boy lay there for a moment, then started to try to get to his feet like a boxer who couldn't accept that he had lost the fight.

Jefferson tried to fire again, but the rifle clicked empty.

He looked back where Gray Man laid on the ground and whistled, loudly.

Gray Man sprang to his hooves and charged toward where

he stood at the fence. Jefferson swung into the saddle as the horse ran past him. Just as he got situated in the saddle, the horse sprang over the fence and continued to charge toward where the monster struggled to stand.

Jefferson pulled the machete and held the blade high like a charging Buffalo Soldier.

Just as City Boy stumbled to his feet, Jefferson rode past and swung the machete. The blade sliced easily through the alien flesh and chopped off the top of the large space zombie's head. It fell face-first into some cantaloupes and the lights in the monster's face dimmed to darkness.

Jefferson pulled the reins to his left and Gray Man spun in a circle as his rider scanned the area for more colored lights. When all he saw was darkness, he slid off Gray Man and shined his light on the alien hulk.

A tattered pair of jeans were beneath the alien flesh, as were human bones that seem to float uselessly in the jellyfish like flesh. The limbs had grown longer than the bones could possibly support because they had become much more like tentacles than human appendages.

Jefferson stopped the light in the middle of the creature, just above the tattered belt line of the jeans. A strange cluster of colorful tendrils were coiled like twisted nerve fibers as some brown covering formed over it.

Jefferson heard a swoosh and looked behind him to see Old Ed had set one of the space zombies on fire and was limping toward the other one carrying a large can of gas.

"What are you trying to do? Have a conversation?" Old Ed yelled.

"I'm trying to understand how they work," said Jefferson.

"They die when you shoot 'em. What else you need to know?"

Jefferson turned his attention back to City Boy.

A lot.

He knew this had once been a person, but it had transformed..was transforming..but into what? And where did it come from? Jefferson imagined finding that crater in the woods wasn't a coincidence.

As Jefferson studied the long tentacle-arm of the creature, he didn't notice the flicker of light coming from the creature's midsection. He chopped down with his machete and severed the tip of the creatures arm-tentacle.

City Boy sprang up and wrapped a strange squid-like hand around Jefferson's neck and lifted him into the air until his boots dangled five feet above the ground. Jefferson felt like his head was about to pop off, but he swung the machete at the creature's arm. One of the creature's smaller tentacles caught his wrist. Jefferson knew he wasn't going to be conscious much longer.

A second later, he hit the ground hard and, as the blood flowed back into his brain, he realized the machete hilt was still in his hand. He jumped to his feet to see City Boy struggling to get to his feet. Jefferson ran toward it and slammed the machete right into the strange organ in the center of its torso.

A bright flash of light went through the creature's body. A wild swing from a tentacle hit Jefferson across the chest and knocked him onto his back. Jefferson rolled to his feet, but City Boy staggered back and fell flat on his back and didn't move.

Jefferson moved slowly toward the fallen monster and pulled his machete free, stabbing down into the strange organ a few more times for good measure.

Old Ed appeared at his side and poured gas over City Boy.

"Well, now you know, it doesn't like you."

Jefferson rubbed his neck. "How did I get free?"

"Your horse kicked the shit out of it."

Jefferson looked to Gray Man who held his head and tail high, like a warhorse out of one of those King Arthur stories.

Old Ed put his hand on Jefferson's shoulder. "It's good to have friends, 'specially the kind that will fight a monster for you, even after you abandoned them for years."

Jefferson nodded and walked to Gray Man and scratched his ears.

SWOOSH! The field grew noticeably brighter as flames consumed the monster's bulk.

"Smells like burnt sugar," said Jefferson.

"Maybe they're made out of candy," said Old Ed. "Stop talking nonsense and see if you can get my mare back."

Jefferson swung on to Gray Man and a moment later was leading the mare back to Old Ed.

Old Ed swung onto the horse bareback and they rode back toward Old Ed's house.

"What exactly were you doing on the roof?" asked Jefferson.

"Some coons have been pilfering my melons. I was going to take 'em out tonight."

Jefferson smiled.

"Something funny?"

"With shooting like yours, raccoons have never been safer."

Old Ed frowned. "I see you're still a smart-ass."

"Speaking of shooting, I was hoping you could loan me an arsenal of weapons. Then we can get back to my place. Daisy and some kids..."

"You just left 'em?"

"I had to come see about you."

"And some guns."

It was Jefferson's turn to frown.

"Wouldn't need to borrow any if you hadn't sold all yours."

"Right, I should have known there would have been some sort of alien-monster invasion. How silly of me."

"A man shouldn't be without a gun," said Old Ed. "How would he protect himself and his?"

"Actually, statistics show you're much more likely to shoot yourself than an intruder. Having a gun in your home makes you less safe."

Old Ed looked at him with a raised eyebrow. "But, you're in need of some weapons?"

"Yes, I am."

Old Ed nudged his horse with his heels and trotted over to the chicken coop.

"What are you doing?" asked Jefferson.

"Getting your guns."

Old Ed slid off the mare. He knelt down and brushed some dirt away and uncovered a hidden door. He pulled it open to reveal a large, green duffle bag. He hefted the duffle up with some effort and a grunt. He stood slowly and lowered the bag onto the grass. Old Ed placed his hand on his lower back.

Jefferson looked from the bag and back to Old Ed.

"What? You never know when the government is gonna come for your guns."

"Right, people with Apache Helicopters and drones with Hell-Fire missiles are so very concerned about your shotgun collection."

Old Ed almost smiled. "Lot more 'an shotguns in there."

Jefferson slid off Gray Man and grabbed the duffle. Even for him it wasn't easy to lift, but Gray Man didn't seem to mind when he draped the duffle over the horse's shoulders.

Jefferson swung back into the saddle. "Let's go."

"You get back to Daisy and those kids. I'm gonna go be Paul Revere," said Old Ed.

"You sure that's a..."

"It's a horrible idea. Probably get my old ass killed, but I have to warn folks. Go on, now."

"See you later then."

"I reckon nothing's for sure."

They nodded and rode off in different directions.

Jefferson looked back over his shoulder to see Old Ed riding away, then galloped to his side.

"I guess it's a good thing you taught me to shoot and ride."

"I reckon that's true tonight."

"You keep safe, Old Ed."

"You too, son. Now get before some monster eats those kids."

Jefferson turned Gray Man and galloped back toward the farmhouse.

MONSTER ANNE VS. MOTOR VEHICLES

Monster Anne stretched out her long tentacle-arms and grabbed the sides of two trees as she ran. She jumped and pulled upward with her tentacles. This propelled her body over a large patch of briars and lowered her to the ground. She kept running as the small anemone-like tendrils waved back and forth on top of the orb that had once been Anne's face.

Anne slid to a stop, sending up a spray of dried leaves. The tendrils on top of her head swayed back and forth and leaned to her left. Anne sprinted away in that direction and soon came to a large ditch that ran alongside a two lane stretch of blacktop. She lowered herself in the ditch and pulsated with light blue.

A few moments later, three space zombies of varying transformation emerged from the woods and ran to her side. They laid down by Anne's side and huddled amongst her tentacles.

They waited there like a pack of lions lying in wait for some unsuspecting gazelles to come along. They didn't have to wait long.

The hum of tires soon came from a distance. Anne pulsated orange and the least transformed of the space zombies stood and walked into the road, then turned his back to the approaching vehicle.

A new model VW bug slowed to a stop. The window slid

down with the burr of an electric motor. A curly headed girl pulled herself out of the window and sat on the door with her legs still dangling in the car.

"Larry! You're going to get yourself ran over. Then who's going to kick field goals on Friday nights?"

Larry turned to reveal that his face had been eaten away by alien flesh.

The curly headed girl made a sound like a frightened mouse and slipped back into her car. She put the car in drive and slammed the accelerator to the floor. The tires spun on the blacktop, sending up smoke as Anne crashed into the side of the car with enough force to knock the car onto two wheels and to shatter both side windows.

The blow knocked the curly headed girl almost into the passenger's seat and her foot slipped off the gas. The car rolled forward slowly. Anne ripped off the driver's side door. She wrapped a tentacle around the curly headed girl's thighs and slung her to the edge of the blacktop where she landed hard and rolled to a stop at the feet of a waiting space zombie. The space zombie scooped up the barely conscious girl and ran into the woods with her draped over its shoulder.

Anne pulled the car to a full stop and began to slam her tentacles into the car, bending metal and shattering glass. Monster Anne pulled the trashed vehicle to the center of the black top and with a bit of effort flipped the car onto its side.

The tendrils on Anne's head waved violently. A second later, the headlights of a very large truck appeared as the hum of the large tires grew louder.

Anne tried to hide behind the overturned VW, but whoever drove must have seen her because the truck engine roared as it sped up.

"Larry" stepped into the road with his back to the big truck, but the truck didn't slow and ran right over him, splattering the space zombie on the road. The big truck swerved to avoid the wrecked VW, but still clipped its bumper. That didn't slow the truck, but it spun the VW violently. Anne leapt straight into the air and avoided getting hit by the wreck.

She hit the ground running after the truck as it sped away, but it was soon clear even she wasn't going to catch it. She slowed and flickered with red and orange.

The truck drove another hundred yards and then slid to a halt on the side of the road. The two people in the truck got out. One was a male, the other female. They both had rifles.

As they got a bit closer, they raised their rifles and fired. Anne ran and jumped back behind the wrecked VW. The remaining space zombie in the woods started to charge at the two with the rifles, but Anne flickered and the zombie stopped in its tracks, then it ran parallel to the road, staying hidden well within the woods as it moved toward the truck.

One of the kids with the rifles yelled, "Shoot the gas tank!"

A hail of bullets struck the underside of the VW. Anne took off toward the woods.

The rednecks ran after Anne, shooting the whole time. Bullets whizzed by Anne or threw up bit of asphalt, but none of the bullets hit the large monster.

Anne leapt with her legs and tentacle arms which made it look a bit like she was pole vaulting into the woods.

The two rednecks' boots echoed as they ran down the blacktop.

One yelled, "Did you see that thing? Must be some alien. If we catch it, we'll be rich."

"Yeah, I saw it. Where did it go?"

"Into the woods," said one as he stepped over and examined the crushed space zombie in the road.

He laughed. "Well, we got this one good."

Anne hid behind a large oak tree and dimmed her bioluminescence as much as possible to a deep purple. She reached her tentacles upward toward the boughs of the trees above her and pulled herself high into the trees, suspending herself there like a giant, tentacle-ly spider.

Back on the road the two rednecks tried to peer into the woods.

"I don't see it no more."

"You go run it out of there and I'll shoot it," the girl said.

"Me, why me?"

"You're faster, and it was your idea to stop."

"We should go tell daddy."

"It'll be in the next county by then or back in space."

The boy didn't move.

"Well, go on," said the girl. "Let's kill this thing."

The boy shook his head but jogged into the woods. He looked for tracks but the trees were too close together and didn't allow enough moonlight for him to track the creature. He walked until he was out of sight of his sister and sat down with his back against a tree.

Multiple tentacles lowered toward the boy at the same time. One wrapped gently around the barrel of the rifle as the others dropped behind him. Simultaneously, a tentacle ripped the weapon away as another tentacle slid around the boy's neck and yanked him into the trees. The boy's boots kicked as he clawed at the tentacle around his neck, but it was too tight for him to make a sound.

Anne let him kick until he drooped, unconscious, and let the boy fall to the ground. Monster Anne lowered herself to the ground and wrapped the boy's body almost completely in one of her longer tentacles and carried him behind her as she moved through the woods toward the truck.

The girl on the road with the rifle yelled, "Harry! Harry! Harold Johnson!" No response came.

She saw a few flickers of light in the woods and started to run toward the truck. "I'll get Daddy!" she yelled back over her shoulder.

The girl ran with the rifle in one hand and jumped in the still open door of the truck. She threw the rifle in the passenger's seat and went to turn the key when she noticed a strange light in the rearview mirror. She looked up to see a space zombie's face staring back at her.

She screamed as the space zombie lunged at her, but she kicked and punched her way free and fell backwards out of the truck. She jumped up to run, but froze in her tracks. Her eyes got as big as the moon hanging over the trees.

Anne stood just to the side of the truck, holding her brother behind her wrapped up in a tentacle.

The girl screamed again and tried to run down the white line of the black top, but Anne whipped out a long tentacle and wrapped it around the girl's body, pinning her arms to her side and lifting her into the air.

As Anne moved back toward the woods the girl screamed as loud as she could and struggled against Anne's grip. Anne didn't seem to mind.

The girl started to plead through heavy sobs. "I'm sorry we shot at you. It was his idea. Please we're sorry. I don't want to go to space."

If Anne heard the girl's pleas, she made no indication that she did as she rushed toward the catfish ponds.

WHAT'S IN THE BAG?

Jefferson led Gray Man up the concrete steps of the porch. His hand wrapped around the door handle, but he paused before opening it.

"Hey, it's me!" he yelled. "Tell that kid not to shoot."

The door opened. Tom looked up at Jefferson, then looked around him as if something was missing.

"Old Ed?"

"He's fine. He went to warn everyone else."

The boy nodded and pulled the door open wide.

Daisy rushed into the hall and leapt into Jefferson's arms.

"I was getting worried about you," she said. "We heard all the shooting. Geez, your neck."

"It's okay. Just got choked a little by a big monster, but things aren't good out there."

Mary walked into the hallway.

"I hope you killed that monster for choking you like that. Why are you two hugging? Better kill all the monsters before ya'll start planning a wedding."

Daisy released her embrace and turned to Mary.

"I'm just glad he's okay," she said.

"And, you love him," said Mary.

As Daisy's face turned bright red, Jefferson said, "I brought guns."

Jefferson led Gray Man into the house and pulled the duffle bag off the horse's back. He dropped it on the floor, the metal of the guns clicking together like a bag full of lead pipes.

Everyone circled around the bag as Jefferson unzipped it.

"Holy crap!" screamed Mary.

"Young Lady, you watch your language," Daisy said.

She leaned over and looked in the bag. "I don't think most of this is legal."

"Normally, I'm against any sort of gun ownership, especially assault weapons, but I have to say I'm glad Old Ed disagrees."

"I'll take the grenades," Mary said.

She reached for one of the grenades that looked like a small, metal pineapple. Jefferson grabbed her wrist.

"You can't have a grenade. You're six."

"But I'm good at throwing stuff. They always let me be pitcher at recess, and I strike 'em out. Tell 'em Tom."

Tom nodded. "She's pretty good."

"Sorry, six year olds don't get grenades," said Jefferson.

Mary yanked her hand free and stomped over to where Shorty laid in the red wagon. She sat down, leaning against the wagon and looking away from everyone.

Jefferson extended an AK-47 toward Tom. "I heard you can shoot."

"I'm okay," said Tom.

"Good. You're on the roof. I want you to keep them off the generator. We keep our lights on and put theirs out."

Tom nodded as he took the gun and gathered extra clips of ammo.

"The rest of you can hide in the attic," said Jefferson.

"And you?" asked Daisy.

"I'll hold the house until the cavalry arrives."

"Not by yourself," Daisy insisted.

Daisy handed Big Bang back to Jefferson and picked up one of the AK-47s. She slung a high-tech shotgun over her shoulder and filled her empty holster with a nine-millimeter Berretta.

"I ain't going in the attic," said Mary.

She stood up and continued, "I can fight monsters too. I already kilt some. Tell 'em Tom."

Tom pushed a full clip into the rifle. "Listen to Mr. Balladeer."

Mary groaned in frustration.

She jabbed a finger in Pearl's direction. "Great! I'm in the attic with her. What's she going to do if monsters get in the attic? Drown 'em?"

Pearl packed up the food on the table. "Don't be so mean, Mary. Come on. We'll have all the sandwiches."

"I don't want no dumb sandwiches. I already got a stomach ache 'cause I ate too many pickles."

"Be nice," Tom told her.

Mary frowned, folded her arms, and sat back down on the edge of the red wagon.

"When my robot wakes up, nobody is gonna tell me what to do. Ya'll be taking orders from me."

Shorty's head came up and his head scanned the area. He rocked to his feet, throwing Mary to the floor.

He stood straight, still tied to the red wagon. Shorty pushed his long arms away from his body. The pressure folded the red wagon in half, then the ropes grew taunt and snapped as easily as silly string.

Mary jumped to her feet. "You're awake."

She ran to Shorty and hugged him around the thick waist, her arms unable to reach around his torso.

"Mary! NO!" Daisy cried.

They all raised their weapons and pointed them at Shorty.

"He ain't gonna hurt nothin'," said Mary.

"Mary, back away from it slowly," Jefferson said.

He holstered Big Bang and showed Shorty his empty hands and motioned for the others to do the same.

"We are no threat to you. Do you understand me?"

Shorty mimicked Jefferson's hand gesture with his own large four-fingered hands, then he snatched up Mary and held her against his chest.

"See, I told you. He likes me. My..."

The thin clusters of snake-like wires emerged from Shorty's helmet and jabbed into various places on Mary's head.

Pearl fainted.

The others raised their weapons, but Shorty pressed Mary against his chest and held the small girl up as if she was a shield.

"Let her go, robot!" yelled Tom.

Jefferson said, "Just put her down."

Tom started to sneak around to the side to get a shot a Shorty's head.

Mary's head popped up, but her eyes were still rolled back in her head. Her eyelids flickered like a humming bird's wings, but she looked right at Tom and pointed.

"Wait, dummy. He...shows...me...everything."

A few heartbeats later, the wires withdrew from Mary's scalp. Small trickles of blood stained her blonde hair and dripped down her forehead. She slumped forward as if she had passed out, but Shorty continued to use her as a shield.

Mary slowly lifted her head and blinked her eyes.

"Those guns ain't going to do much against his armor, but they'll kill me just fine."

Tom continued to hold his gun pointed at Shorty's head.

"Tom, he's a good guy. Get that gun off him."

Tom said, "How I know he ain't took over your brain?"

"You wouldn't know cause you're a dummy. Now, lower your gun."

Tom looked at Jefferson. "Seems like her." He lowered his gun.

With all the guns pointing toward the floor, Shorty placed Mary on the floor. She sat there for a long moment as if she was lost in deep thought.

Daisy said, "Mary?"

"Kid, what just happened?" asked Jefferson.

"Ya'll, the universe is really big. It's really big, so big and scary."

Daisy said, "Mary, you come to me now. Just step..."

"Hush!" said Mary, "Im thinking on some stuff."

They all just stood there. Everyone stared at Shorty, but he turned to the side to avoid direct eye contact.

Mary finally looked up at Tom. "He ain't no Robot. He's a alien-person from space, from very, very, very, very, very far away."

"He told you that."

"Showed me," explained Mary. "Showed me all sorts of stuff. I'm waaaay smarter than all of you now."

Mary sprang to her feet and ran to the crushed red wagon. She grabbed her tattered legal pad and a worn black crayon. She waved everyone over to the table and they all gathered around, including Shorty.

She pushed the drawing tablet and crayon to Shorty.

"I know what those monsters are. They're like zombies but from space."

"Space zombies," said Tom.

"Yeah, but the real problem is the big mama, because she's so mean and wants to eat the whole world."

Shorty drew rapidly and held up a crayon sketch of a full-grown Devourer.

Mary said, "That's her. That's the big mama. Man, she ugly, but look here, we have to kill all those space zombies cause they's gonna be a new mama. Well, not a new mama but the same mama in a different place. Understand?"

Everyone shook their heads no.

Shorty drew rapidly then held up a picture of a humanoid and the various stages as it transformed into a Devourer.

"It don't work like no animal here. It's like it plants seeds of itself in us but it turns into her."

"Like a genet."

Everyone looked at Jefferson.

"Like bamboo, or some fungi," he explained. "They seem to be different life forms but are actually clones. The largest life form on earth at the moment is a group of trees like this."

Mary looked at Jefferson. "Yeah, it's something like that.

'Cept we the dirt it grows in."

Mary ran toward the hallway. "Everyone follow me."

She ran to where the dead space zombie laid. She leaned down and picked up the severed head.

"See how its face is all ate away?" she said. "That's the little bits of the mama eatin' the lil bits of us." She looked up searching for the words. "It's like a piggy-back ride, but just the rider eats the other person until there's only the rider. Understand?"

Jefferson said, "I've seen this. The big one that chocked me wouldn't die when I shot it, even in the head. It had this thing forming in its stomach. It didn't die until I stabbed it there."

Mary pointed at Jefferson. "Right! That's where the hard place grows. When they are like this," Mary pointed at the dead zombie, "they still need a ride. We can just shoot 'em, but, as they get bigger and more like the mama, they'll get harder to kill, but, if they get old enough, they'll grow their own hard place in the middle and that would be very bad."

"How do we kill it at the...big mama stage?" asked Jefferson.

"We ain't gonna kill a big mama. Ain't nothin' on Eart' strong enough to crack that shell."

"Then how are we going to kill...the big-mama?" he asked.

Mary pointed at Shorty. "We got something ain't from Eart'. And, he's got one thing left that can kill the big mama, but we have to help him kill all her babies 'fore they is mamas."

Shorty took the cylinder off his back and twisted off the cap. A few mechanical beetle-like robots, the size of fists, scampered out and then back into the cylinder.

Mary looked at Tom. "Those are monster killing robots."

Jefferson nodded his head in the direction of Shorty. "He can't call reinforcements? They could bring more than one of these weapons."

"By the time they got here everything on Eart' will be ate already, and a lot of his suit is broke and he's hurt underneath." She looked at Tom. "He keeps falling asleep so his suit can repair his body. Cool, huh?"

Tom nodded.

"Please tell me he showed you a plan," Jefferson said.

"Yeah," said Mary, "We attack 'em."

"With two kids and a girl who gets the vapors. That's the plan?"

"There's me," said Daisy.

"Ain't no time to wait," said Mary. "We can't let the babies grow up, and we can't let them get too many monsters. Have to kill 'em or they have a hard place in their bellies and we won't be able to kill 'em."

Jefferson said, "Fine."

He moved to the bag of weapons and grabbed an elephant gun and an AK-47 and slung them both over his shoulder. He motioned for Shorty to follow him toward the backdoor.

Daisy walked after them. "I'm coming."

"No," said Jefferson. "You have to keep Mary safe. If something happens to us, she's the only one that knows anything about the...space zombies."

"I'm not letting you go alone," said Daisy. "We just started hanging out. I'm not going to let some monsters kill you."

"As much as I appreciate that thought, this isn't about just you and me. It's about saving the world, and you'll just have to keep Mary safe."

Daisy nodded. "What are you going to do?"

"I'm going to burn it, burn it all."

Jefferson clicked his tongue. Gray Man walked toward him Shorty hesitated but Mary waved him to follow.

"Go on. Follow him. Kill those monsters."

Shorty stepped behind Jefferson and followed at his heels.

Jefferson got nearly to the door when Daisy ran toward him.

"Wait!" Daisy yelled.

She ran to Jefferson and stepped close to him.

Daisy said, "I'm going to need you to come back. I haven't given up on you falling in love with me. I'm just stubborn like that."

Jefferson smiled and nodded.

"Now," she said. "I know you went away and became all self-actualized, but you forget about that. As soon as you step out that door you kill anything that stands against you. You become the guy who people tell stories about. Be the Black Redneck."

Jefferson motioned toward the living room. "My horse just took a shit in my living room. I've got redneck covered."

He turned to leave, but Daisy held his arm. She held his old worn cowboy hat in her hands and fixed it on his head, tightening the string beneath his chin..

"There that's better. You can't die now. Not even space zombies can kill the Black Redneck."

She grabbed the collar of his shirt and kissed him on the mouth.

Mary stomped to Daisy's side. "Hey! Monsters outside are getting bigger. Do gross, kissy stuff later."

Jefferson looked up and tipped his hat at Mary. The girl smiled.

"I want you to come back too."

"Yes, ma'am."

He gave Daisy one more look. and said, "Don't worry. These things are going to be sorry they ever stepped foot in Picayune. You know how I feel about trespassers."

YOU CAN'T TRUST ALIENS

Jefferson led Shorty to the shed that housed the generator and the large barrels of diesel. He walked straight to one of the large barrels of gas and used a hand pump to fill a smaller container.

Shorty walked to one of the barrels. He studied it for a moment, then wrapped one of his long arms around it and lifted it onto his shoulder as if it weighed nothing.

Jefferson stopped and stared.

"Is that suit augmented or are you just that damn strong?"

The armored alien held the barrel in place as he squatted down and scooped up a second barrel onto his other shoulder.

Shorty stared at Jefferson as if to say, "Where do you want it?"

"This way," said Jefferson.

Jefferson led Gray Man and Shorty to a small gate in the fence that opened onto one of the side fields.

As Jefferson took the time to open the gate, Shorty set the barrels down against the fence line.

"No, we need those to set the woods on fire," said Jefferson.

He pulled out a lighter and showed Shorty the flame and motioned toward the woods. As the flame was reflected in Shorty's faceplate, the alien stood as still as a black iron sculpture.

"Come on. Help me," Jefferson said.

He wrapped his arms around one of the barrels and tried to lift it to no avail. As Jefferson stood, Shorty struck out with a fast, open-palmed strike to the back of his skull. The blow crumpled the back of Jefferson's hat as he slid to his knees and leaned against the barrels, totally unconscious.

Shorty snatched him up and threw him over an armored shoulder. The short, thick alien grabbed Gray Man's reins and walked through the field toward the woods.

Shorty stopped at the tree-line and let Jefferson slide roughly to the ground. The alien tied Gray Man's reins to a small tree. He stepped back to Jefferson and knelt by his side. Shorty unscrewed the ending of the black cylinder and held it open at Jefferson's neck. A black, mechanical snake about a foot long slithered out and wrapped around Jefferson's neck like a tight onyx chocker.

Shorty resealed the cylinder and pulled all of Jefferson's weapons away, even the machete. The armored alien ran a few steps away and fired Big Bang into the air, then he ran into the woods, leaving Jefferson and Gray Man totally helpless.

As Jefferson laid there totally unconscious, bright flickers of light moved toward them from the shadows.

CAPRIOLE!

The tips of his boots marked parallel furrows in the mud as two space zombies dragged the unconscious Jefferson toward the catfish ponds. Just behind them, two more space zombies led Gray Man by his bridle.

The big horse hadn't given them much trouble on the walk to the catfish ponds as he wanted to go where Jefferson went but, once they got before the Devourer, Gray Man dug his hooves into the mud and refused to get any closer (friendship has its limits).

Several of the other space zombies came around and helped gain control of the large horse.

In the surrounding area, space zombies along all ranges of transformation had collected all manner of livestock to be food and captured people to be conscripted in the space zombie army. The whole area looked like some otherworldly festival lit by the pulsating lights of the Devourer and her minions.

Jefferson's head came up slowly as he woke. He looked around as if in a dream. His eyes fell on the Devourer as she pulled a screaming redneck into the air by his head.

He dug his boots into the ground and hip-tossed one of the zombies, then kicked the other in the knee and put an elbow to the side of its head.

"Capriole! Capriole!" Jefferson yelled to Gray Man.

Gray Man rose up on his hind legs. He clubbed a few space zombies with his front hooves before rocking back down to all fours, jumping into the air, and kicking backwards. He caught two space zombies in the chest and sent them flying through the air.

Gray Man spun free of the one remaining space zombies that clung to his saddle.

Jefferson ran toward his horse and got his hand on the saddle horn when a large tentacle wrapped around his chest, pulling him off his feet and high into the air.

"Yah, Gray Man! Go!" yelled Jefferson.

The horse took off, but no rider was in the saddle. Jefferson turned his head to look at what was holding him and saw something beyond dreadful.

AMBROSE ARRIVES

Tom knelt on top of the farmhouse roof, scanning the darkness for any flicker of light through the scope of the rifle. He checked the front yard and then the large field in front of that.

Bright flickers of blue and red light came from the road that led to the farmhouse from the blacktop.

That's a big one.

He swallowed hard and flicked the safety off on his AK-47.

A second later, a look of relief washed across his face and he chuckled at himself as he realized the lights were from Ambrose's cruiser and the Sheriffs department's big, four wheel drive truck running with their lights on, but no sirens.

Tom stood on the roof, waving his arms as they drove across the bottom of the front yard about a hundred yards away, then headed for the open lower gate.

"Hey! Hey! Stop! Hey!" Tom yelled.

The sheriff vehicles kept heading quickly toward the open gate and the trails beyond them.

Tom shrugged as if to say, "Can't be helped," and raised his weapon.

He aimed carefully in front of Ambrose's cruiser and opened up a spray of automatic gun fire that peppered the ground in front of the car and blew up dust.

The cruiser slammed on its brakes and the big four wheel drive didn't have time to stop before it plowed into the back of the car.

Ambrose and the two deputies rolled out of their vehicles and took cover on the other side of them.

"Sheriff Hill. It's me, Tom."

Ambrose stood up and holstered his weapon.

"Did you just shoot at us with a machine gun?" screamed Ambrose.

"No, sir. I shot in front of you."

"Still, you have to admit that's unusual."

Tom was never one for words and struggled to find the ones to explain the night's events. Luckily, before he had to mention space zombies and armored aliens, Daisy, with Mary at her heels, stepped out onto the porch and the screen door squeaked open.

"Ambrose!" Daisy yelled. "You get up here."

"Can't. We're going to break up that party."

"Ambrose!" she screamed. "Get in here."

A short while later, Ambrose and his two deputies examined the severed head of the space zombie on the table.

"Wouldn't believe it if it wasn't staring back at me with its creepy, empty eye sockets," said Ambrose.

"You don't know the half of it," said Mary. "But no time to explain. You need to take yourself and these two and go help Jefferson and the good alien kill space zombies."

Ambrose looked at Daisy. "So, she's in charge?"

"The alien, the one that might be friendly, injected her brain with vast knowledge of the universe. She's our subject matter expert on space zombies."

"Yeah, I'm the expert leader," Said Mary. "So, you get some decent guns and head out. It if glows, shoot it in the face."

Ambrose stood straight and decided he was still in charge. "Daisy, you'll take the kids and fall back to the station. Get the state police out here, the national guard, whoever will come."

Daisy nodded and grabbed Mary's hand.

"Don't mention aliens," Ambrose added. "Tell them Al-Queda is out here in the woods. That'll get us the fire power needed."

Mary pulled her hand free from Daisy. "No. I have to stay here and tell everyone what to do."

"You know, a general is never on the front lines," said Daisy.

"What's that mean?"

"It means you can boss people around over the radio."

"Good idea."

Deputy Kirby noticed Pearl staring off into space and looking like she wanted to be anywhere but the farmhouse.

"Pearl, is Anne still out there?"

Some tears rolled down Pearl's face. She shook her head and walked away after the others.

Deputy Kirby moved to follow her, but Ambrose grabbed his arm.

"Hey. You're with me. I'm going to need you to put your ridiculous obsessions aside for just a moment. We have a bit of a situation. Let's check out these weapons."

BATTLE AT THE CATFISH PONDS

The large, tentacled horror that had once been the most beautiful girl in town held Jefferson high off the ground with one tentacle and pulsated with red and orange.

He stayed still and stared down at her since struggling to break free hadn't worked out at all. He knew it had been a girl because he could see what was left of a pair of panties floating on the skeleton within the mass of clear flesh. Worse still, the skeleton curled inward around the brain-sized core that had formed in the middle of her gut like some grotesque fetus.

Shit. A new mama.

Anne lifted him higher and out over the pond by elongating her tentacle. Jefferson felt like a cricket on the end of a cane pool.

The Devourer leaned over toward Jefferson like a small building, a tower of tentacles. A large tentacle rose out of the water and wrapped around Jefferson, taking him from Anne. The Devourer pulsated with green.

Jefferson decided it was time for some more futile struggling, but futile it was. The Devourer took the offering from Anne and raised Jefferson thirty feet over the catfish pond. He gave up on the struggling, but the Devourer raised another tentacle out of the water. The tip was the shape of a snake head, a giant snake. It swayed back and forth like a cobra listening to a flute, then the tip opened slowly like a blooming flower. A clear gelatinous goo dripped from the strange maw. The open end of the tentacle eased toward Jefferson.

"No!" Jefferson yelled. "I'll kill you. I swear. I'll kill all your kind."

The tentacle kept easing toward him, but Jefferson didn't turn away, and he didn't stop struggling though the tentacle holding him wrapped so tightly around him it felt like he was being crushed. The open tentacle loomed over Jefferson. Some of the goo dripped onto his hat as the tentacle eased down to swallow his head.

Then, Jefferson felt the black cord that Shorty had put around his neck come to life. It spun around his neck and sprang into the open tentacle. The tentacle snapped closed, like a little kid who had swallowed a fly. The cord moved through the clear flesh of the Devourer like a mechanical eel swimming through water.

The Devourer dropped Jefferson. He fell thirty feet into the murky water of the pond as the Devourer thrashed around and tore at its own flesh.

Jefferson emerged from the water and gasped for air. The pond water was like that of a stormy sea as the Devourer thrashed around. Jefferson used the waves to get himself to the bank and pulled himself out of the water. He turned and looked back. The tiny black cord swam to the Devourer's core and started to drill inside it.

Jefferson rolled out of the way of a thrashing tentacle, which left a large impression in the mud where he had been a second before. He pushed himself to his feet and ran. The space zombies that stood on the bank of the pond were so distracted by the Devourer's rage that they didn't even seem to notice.

Anne took a step to chase after Jefferson, but small, black, mechanical beetles ran out of the woods and toward the Devourer like a plague of robotic insects. She paused to watch the small, black machines as they flailed on to the Devourer. They scurried all over her, getting close as they could to the core before burrowing into the clear flesh-like ticks on a hound dog. After they embedded themselves into the translucent flesh, they started to emit a fluid that turned the Devourer a bright green. The cord stood straight out from the core like an antennae.

The Devourer stopped thrashing around. She reached out her tentacles and touched Anne gently with the tips. Anne leaned into the embrace like a child toward its mother. The Devourer suddenly yanked Anne high into the air and threw her into the woods hard enough that she broke through the limbs that blocked her path as she sailed deep into the trees.

Jefferson looked back over his shoulder when he reached the tree line. He watched as the small, black machines poured some type of chemical into the Devourer. The thing that had been around his neck was tiny compared to the Core, but it was too bright to look at. He didn't know exactly what was going to happen, but he thought it would be a good idea to get the hell out of there.

He ran down the trail as fast as he could with water and mud sloshing in his boots. As he weighed whether to take the time to dump them out or not, he heard heavy steps behind him and turned expecting to see Monster Anne bearing down on him, but it was a much more welcome sight - Gray Man.

The large horse easily caught up and slowed down when he was alongside Jefferson. He grabbed the saddle horn and leapt onto the horse.

It is good to have friends

"Yah, Gray Man. Go!" yelled Jefferson.

Back at the catfish ponds, the mechanical beetles continued to pour chemicals into the Devourer. The black cord stopped drilling and stood up straight from the core like an antennae. The green mist within the flesh surrounded the core and the end of the black cord glowed bright, then sparked.

Kabooooom! The chemicals the little robots had emitted ignited and the Devourer's flesh vaporized, sending a column of bright energy straight into the air.

A rush of air pulled the trees toward the catfish pond. Even the surrounding space zombies were pulled toward their creator, then the explosion came, a violent one. Everything was thrown in the opposite direction as a wave of energy pushed out, and the surrounding trees were ripped out of the ground.

Jefferson felt the heat on the back of his neck and looked down to see his shadow painted on the trail as if the sun was high overhead.

"Damn it. Go, Gray Man. Go!"

Jefferson glanced over his shoulder to see flames rolling toward them. He guided Gray Man down a narrow trail. The way was blocked by a thick, fallen oak tree. Jefferson looked over his shoulder to see the flames reaching out toward them. He didn't slow.

"Yah, Gray Man! Over it. Yah."

Gray Man dug his hooves into the trail and increased his speed. He leapt, barely clearing the obstacle as his back hooves scraped off some of the bark.

They landed on the other side of the fallen oak. Jefferson slid out of the saddle and pulled Gray Man to the ground.

"Easy. Down. Play dead."

Gray Man let Jefferson pull him down. The horse laid still on his side. Jefferson leaned over the horse's head to protect him as the flames shot over the top of them.

After a moment, the intense heat passed. Jefferson released Gray Man and they both got to their feet. Jefferson realized the brim of his hat was afire and beat it out against the fallen oak. Then he hugged Gray Man around his thick neck.

"Thanks for coming back for me."

Shorty stepped out of the smoldering woods and walked toward them. Jefferson glared at the armored alien, but Shorty didn't stop to stare back. He walked past and dropped all of

Jefferson's weapons at his feet without breaking stride as he headed toward the catfish ponds.

Jefferson snatched up his weapons and strapped them all on and returned Big Bang to its holster.

"Hey! Hey!"

Shorty stopped and turned.

"You're an asshole," said Jefferson.

Shorty pointed toward the catfish ponds and disappeared into the smoke.

MISSION ACCOMPLISHED

As Daisy loaded the kids into the back of the cruiser, Ambrose and his two deputies stepped off the porch looking as if they were ready for war.

Deputy Kirby ran toward the big four-wheel drive.

"Come on!" he yelled. "We have to save Anne."

The other two didn't rush.

Daisy and Ambrose looked at each other.

"You shoot whatever needs shooting."

"Shooting stuff is my speciality," he said.

"And.."

"Yeah, yeah, I'll bring back Jefferson. Wasn't it always me that went to save his ass?"

Mary stuck her head out of the back of the cruiser.

"Don't shoot my alien. You'll know its him because he doesn't glow. He looks like a fat, black robot."

Deputy Kirby pounded on the side of the truck from the driver's seat.

"Let's go. Got to save Anne."

The earth trembled. They all turned toward the woods. A flame shot straight up into the air with such intensity that it seemed a giant rocket pointing toward the Earth fired its engines. The brightness of the flames created a temporary daytime and painted long shadows of everyone that stood in the yard.

"Look away. Look away. It'll burn out your eyes," said Mary.

Everyone turned their heads from the light until they felt the warmth of it replaced by the darkness again. A second later a breeze as hot as the air coming out of a hair dryer pressed the grass of the lawn flat and swayed the trees

They slowly looked up to see Mary climb out of the open window and start to do what looked like a really bad touchdown dance.

"They got her! They got her! Big Mama's dead. That mean monster got deep fried."

Everyone just stared at Mary.

"Well, that's that," she said. "Let's go get some sandwiches."

She walked toward the farmhouse, leaving everyone standing there looking after her.

Ambrose looked after Mary. "What just happened? Mary?"

Mary stopped and turned around. "The mama just got burnt up, and the babies can't live without a mama to tell 'em what do do."

"What is this kid talking about?" asked Ambrose.

"Come on! Anne's out there." yelled Kirby.

Pearl finally yelled back, "Anne's gone!"

Ambrose turned to Kirby. "Just wait. I'm not..."

Deputy Kirby pulled his head back into the big truck. The large tires of the truck spun on the grass for a second until they caught and sent the truck speeding toward the trail with the lights flashing.

Daisy stepped next to Ambrose. "Guess he got tired of waiting."

THE OLD QUEEN IS DEAD.
ALL HAIL THE NEW QUEEN.

Monster Anne wrapped her tentacles around smoldering trees and pulled herself upright. Spots of her own translucent flesh were charred black but, as she took a step toward the ponds, the damaged flesh fell away to be replaced with new flesh.

The same could not be said for all the other space zombies. They lay scattered all around, some of them still on fire. Anne walked on her big, strange monster legs to the edge of the catfish pond. The sides of the pond still glowed with heat, not a drop of water was left, and a thick fog hung over the pond. Monster Anne leaned over the edge of the pond. The core of the Devourer laid at the bottom of the pond, cracked and dry as an old pecan someone had stepped on.

Anne slammed her tentacles into the ground and flickered with red and orange. She became a bioluminescent tornado of tentacles and rage as she slammed her tentacles into the ground and ripped large branches from trees to smash them to splinters on the trunks. She threw a large branch into the air and let all her tentacles collapse to the ground.

With her tantrum over, she stood and walked to the prostrate space zombies littered around the catfish pond. She poked them with the end of her tentacles. When they didn't respond, she tried to set them on their feet, but they collapsed back to the ground like marionettes whose strings had been cut.

Anne gave up on this tactic and began to flicker with yellows, greens, and blues in rapid succession. One by one the space zombies that weren't damaged beyond repair flickered in response and got to their feet.

The fifteen or so space zombies were in various stages of transformation, but they held up their arms or tentacles in reverence and swayed. They clustered around Anne the way boys used to crowd around her when she was a girl. The old queen was dead but the space zombies celebrated their new queen. Anne didn't get long to celebrate her coronation.

Shorty stepped out of the mist. Anne flickered with enough red and orange to make it look like she was burning from within. Her tentacles fluttered. The space zombies gathered around as Anne turned toward him.

The long, vibrating blade emerged from Shorty's wrist and he took one of his space kung fu postures with his blade raised high and vibrating so fast that it distorted the air around it.

The space zombies flickered in time with Anne and took up a formation in front of her, with the newest space zombies in front. They charged toward Shorty, but some were just hobbling forward, as damaged as they were.

Shorty stepped out of the way of the fastest space zombie and took off its head as it ran by. On the back swing, Shorty cut another space-zombie in half at the hips. He did a black-belt-theatre-jump-spin and three more space zombies fell headless.

But numbers matter in a fight, and there were a lot of space zombies. One of the larger, more transformed zombies grabbed Shorty's blade-arm as other space zombies collided into him and brought him to the mud. Even Shorty couldn't push the large space zombies off of him.

Anne started to lumber toward him now that he was safely pinned to the ground. She stood over him and raised her large tentacles to strike.

Boom! One of the space zombie's holding down Shorty's blade-arm flew backwards as a spray of goo came out the side of its head.

Boom! A second, large space zombie holding down Shorty fell over with a hole in its gut where its core had been forming.

Anne turned her attention from Shorty. Jefferson sat on Gray Man with a smoking rifle. Jefferson fired again. The last of the space zombies holding down Shorty's blade arm flew backwards and tumbled across the ground.

With his blade free, Shorty hacked like a madman at the surrounding space zombies. As they backed away, he rolled to his feet and backed out of Anne's range. Two large space zombies backed to Anne's side, but Jefferson knew right where to shoot them.

Boom! Boom! They both fell dead with holes torn in their guts.

Anne stood in the center of her destroyed army and flickered red again. Her tentacles undulated rapidly in a rage.

Shorty took a step toward her with his blade raised high. Anne's monstrous image reflected in his mirrored visor.

Jefferson nudged Gray Man, and they galloped to flank the monster.

It was Anne's turn to back away.

"I said NO TRESPASSING!"

He opened fire. The bullets staggered her backward. Shorty charged her.

Anne turned and took off into the woods.

Both Shorty and Jefferson pursued her. Even though Gray Man galloped hard, Jefferson still fired his rifle, blowing chunks out of the clear flesh of Anne's body.

Jefferson reloaded the gun as he rode. He looked down in surprise to see Shorty had dropped to all fours and passed them up with a motion that was somewhere in between a greyhound and a gorilla.

Jefferson shook his head and turned his attention back to Anne, taking aim at her core.

Anne lurched into the woods, using her tentacles to swing like a giant monkey through the trees. Jefferson had to pull up Gray Man as the woods were too thick for a horse to follow, but Shorty plowed right into the thick, using his blade to cut a path through briars and branches.

Jefferson watched to try to determine which way they were going. "Damn it."

After a few seconds of watching the flickers of red coming from the shadows, he realized Anne was headed for the main trail.

"Gray Man. Go. Yah." He was determined to cut her off.

Shorty pursued Anne with a great deal of speed and agility, but Anne wasn't exactly slow. The flickers of light she gave off were soon barely in view, like a lightning strike far off on the horizon, then everything went dark.

Shorty kept sprinting after her and emerged into a small clearing. He slid to a halt and scanned the area. He couldn't see any marks on the trees where Anne might have passed. He grew still and listened. A bright flicker came from the darkness. A large object blurred out of the shadows toward Shorty's head. He ducked and rolled out of the way as a log sailed over where he had just been standing and hit a tree hard enough to knock it askew.

Anne charged into the clearing. Shorty didn't give an inch. She swung a tentacle at his head. He moved beneath it and sliced the tentacle off as close to the root as possible, but she had a lot more tentacles. She knocked him flat and he slid across the grass of the clearing. Before he could crash into the surrounding trees, she grabbed his ankle and whipped him into a large tree. Even though the collision with the tree was violent, he sliced down at his ankle and severed the tentacle, coming inches away from cutting off his own foot.

He flew free and crashed into some bushes. Anne stomped toward him as he rolled slowly to his feet. Just as Anne got there, he buried the vibrating blade in the dirt, sending up a cloud of dust that drove Anne back.

When the cloud of dust cleared, Shorty was gone. Anne turned back to the clearing. The tendrils on her head waving frantically. As she took a step into the clearing, Shorty sprung from the trees and landed on her back.

Shorty rode her as she spun and rolled trying to get him off of her. He clung tightly and cut a circle of flesh out of her back. She reached back with a tentacle to try to get him, but he cut the tentacles away. He cut another chuck of flesh out of her back and slammed his outstretched hand into the hole, reaching for the brain-sized core floating in her clear flesh. Just as his fingers were about to reach the core, a tentacle wrapped around his torso and jerked him roughly backwards. She slammed him into the trees and the ground over and over until he was as limp as a rag doll. She threw him to the middle of the clearing where he rolled to a stop, face down. She jumped on his back over and over driving him into the soil.

She stepped back. Shorty didn't move. He laid half buried in the dirt.

Anne straddled him and pulled his arms back until his armor finally gave and his arms bent in the wrong direction. Gaps formed in the armor where Anne had twisted his arms. A strange scream came from beneath the armor and Shorty's head collapsed back into the dirt as Anne raised her tentacles in victory.

She tried to slam a barbed tentacle into Shorty but couldn't penetrate the armor. She smashed the armored alien a few more times then stepped to the tentacles and chucks of flesh Shorty had cut away and began to suck it back inside herself.

Jefferson rode hard down the trail, then pulled Gray Man to a stop. He listened but he didn't hear a thing. He began to think maybe he might have missed them, but then he saw a bright flicker of light from the darkness. He held up his rifle.

"Come on. I have something for you."

A shadowy figure flew out of the woods and tumbled across the trail. Jefferson stared down at the torn suit of armor with the arms flopping around uselessly as Shorty slid to a halt just in front of Gray Man's hooves.

"Uh-oh."

A great deal of vibrant reds pulsated from the woods. The lights grew brighter as the sound of snapping branches grew louder.

Jefferson turned Gray Man away from the woods. "Go. Go, Gray Man. Yah!"

Gray Man didn't need much encouragement. He took off as as Anne exploded from the woods and onto the trail in a hail of scattered leaves.

Jefferson looked over his shoulder as Anne charged after them.

She made up the distance between them in a matter of a few strange strides.

Jefferson yelled, "Faster, Gray Man."

Anne started to elongate tentacles toward them.

Jefferson looked back over his shoulder. "Seriously, Gray Man faster. You're going to let some monster run you down."

Gray Man dug a little deeper and moved a bit ahead of the outstretched tentacles.

Jefferson looked ahead to see the flashing lights of the big four-wheel drive coming around the bend in the trail and the sound of the large engine growling through the darkness.

Jefferson knew he was on a collision course with the truck but couldn't slow with Anne reaching out for Gray Man's hooves.

"Come on, old man, faster."

Gray Man dug in and pulled a bit away from the monstrosity reaching for them.

The big truck came around the corner and Jefferson thought for sure the truck would smash into them from the side, but Gray Man leapt, sailing over the hood of the truck. Anne was not so lucky. The big truck smashed into her side as she reached for jumping horse.

The collision bent the front of the truck into a crumpled V as it came to an abrupt halt. Anne's body bent and slapped onto the hood and shattered the windshield before being thrown in the other direction and into a cluster of small trees.

Jefferson pulled Gray Man to a halt and turned, but he saw the strange lights pulsating from the woods. He shot at the creature a few times, hoping it would give chase to him again and rode away as fast as he could.

Deputy Kirby pushed himself off of the airbag and tried to open the door. When it wouldn't open, he laid down on the seat and kicked the door with both heels until it finally flew open. He staggered out and fell to his knees.

Anne rose from the bushes, flickering red. Deputy Kirby didn't have time to think. He rolled beneath the truck and held his breath, hoping whatever the giant thing was hadn't seen him.

The creature's tentacles moved along the side of the truck and paused. Kirby's eyes got big as he stared at the strange, bioluminescent flesh. Anne stood there a moment longer, then moved down the trail.

Kirby let out a sigh of relief.

The truck groaned as it was lifted into the air and thrown down the trail. Deputy Kirby laid on his back staring into the pulsating bioluminescence surrounding her core. The flickering light washed Kirby's pale skin in a series of colors. He was too scared to do anything but let his mouth fall open.

Anne raised a barbed tentacle and slammed it into Deputy Kirby's chest. Anne sucked the deputy's organs through the tentacle. The rest of his body was torn to bits and consumed, bones and all.

As Anne walked away, Deputy's Kirby's skull floated in Anne's alien flesh not far from the tattered panties that slowly dissolved in the alien flesh.

FAMILY

Gray Man emerged from the woods. Jefferson charged up the slight incline of the side field. They didn't slow down at the fences but sailed right over them. Gray Man galloped to just in front of everyone before Jefferson gave the reins a tug and looked down at them.

"Get those kids out of here. Where's Mary?"

Mary yelled from the front steps of the porch, "I'm over here!"

Jefferson slid off Gray Man and looked toward the girl.

"You have to get out of here. It's coming."

"But I saw the big fire."

Jefferson shrugged. "New mama."

Mary's shoulders slumped. "Oh."

She left the large jar of pickles on the steps and ran toward Jefferson.

He opened the back door of the cruiser. No one moved.

"No, really. A tentacled horror is headed this way, so move."

Pearl jumped into the back of the cruiser, and Tom followed.

Mary stood at the open door. "My alien is dead, huh?"

"Come on, Mary. I'll tell you what happened later."

"You can't kill it, not anymore."

"Thanks for the encouragement," said Jefferson.

"The hard thing can't be destroyed, but its body can be.

Then, you can trap the hard thing."

"Sounds easy."

Mary nodded and got in the back of the cruiser. He closed the door behind her.

Daisy stepped to Jefferson's side and put her hand on his shoulder.

"I wish there were time to say more," he said. "If I live, I'll be sure to say it, and I hope you'll listen, but for now, I'm going to need you to get in this car and drive away really fast."

Daisy embraced him and kissed him hard on the mouth. Jefferson's arms wrapped around her, and he returned the kiss.

"Oh. My. God," Said Deputy Leon.

Daisy broke the kiss and glared at Leon.

"Get over it. It's the twenty-first century."

"I'm not worried about that. I'm worried about *that*."

Deputy Leon turned toward the woods. His arm came up slowly and he pointed to the tree line beyond the side field. Anne stood at the edge of the field, pulsating red and orange.

"Go!" Jefferson yelled.

Daisy jumped behind the steering wheel and floored it as Jefferson and Ambrose opened fire on Anne.

Anne charged through the side field as bullets tore chucks from her clear flesh. When she came to the fence, she smashed her tentacles down in front of her and shattered the wooden beams blocking her path. At first, Anne charged right at Jefferson, but then she turned and charged toward the cruiser. She caught up to it just as it was turning onto the dirt road at the end of the front yard.

Anne crashed her bulk into the side of the cruiser and, with an added push from her tentacles, flipped it over on its side as if it were a toy car.

The monster started to pound the car with her tentacles. The flashing sirens died as glass shattered and metal bent. She pulled off the back door and sent it flying at Ambrose who had to dive out of the way. As she reached inside, a hail of bullets smashed into her, blowing chunks out of her translucent flesh.

She turned from the cruiser and charged toward Deputy Leon. He let loose a high-pitched scream that any little girl would have been proud of before dropping his gun and running. He didn't get far. Anne pounced on him from behind and pinned him to the ground with her weight. A thick tentacle that ended in a barb rose high into the air and slammed down into the screaming deputy right between his shoulder blades with a sickening crunch. Anne sucked in his internal organs as easily as if they were made from Jell-O.

Ambrose stepped closer and released shotgun blasts in rapid succession. The blasts actually seemed to push Anne back, and one of her smaller tentacles fell to the yard, flopping around like a fish out of water. When the shotgun clicked empty, Ambrose dropped it and pulled the two nine-millimeters on his hip and opened fire.

The monster charged right into the bullets and swung a tentacle at Ambrose. He rolled out of the way and came up firing only to be struck in the chest by another tentacle. He tumbled across the yard like a piece of trash caught in a hurricane and landed in an awkward position. He didn't get up. Anne stomped toward where he laid in the grass.

"Hey! Hey!" Jefferson screamed.

The tendrils on Anne's head leaned toward Jefferson, then she turned to face him. At the sight of Jefferson she started to flicker red.

He backed away from her as she moved forward.

"Come on. I'm very tasty. Follow me."

Anne stopped. Her tentacles waved as she pulsated a deep crimson.

"So, you remember me. That's right. I'm the one that killed your mama."

Anne charged him. He fired the elephant rifle over and over. The large weapon blew chucks out of her translucent flesh but she hardly slowed. She whipped a cluster of tentacles toward him. Just before the tentacle pounded into him, Gray Man appeared at his side and shoved Jefferson out of the way with a push of his long snout. The blow meant for Jefferson hit Gray Man in the shoulder and knocked the horse flat.

Before the horse could regain its feet, a long tentacle stretched out from the monster and wrapped around one of the horse's legs. The tentacle pulled the horse across the lawn toward Anne.

A machete blade came down and sliced the tentacle in half. Jefferson stood over Gray Man protectively. He glared at Anne.

"No one eats my horse."

Anne charged. Jefferson set his feet and pulled Big Bang. He didn't have time to aim.

Kaboom! The bullet left the barrel, penetrated the translucent flesh, and slammed against the core.

Anne staggered backward. Her bioluminescence flickered and went dark as she fell to the side.

Jefferson almost smirked.

"You're not eating anything else on this planet. Not even a gnat."

The overturned cruiser creaked. Daisy and Tom climbed out of the torn door and stood on the side of the car as they pulled Mary and Pearl out of the wreck. Jefferson waved for them to run to the house.

Anne lurched to her feet and tried to make for Jefferson. Kaboom! Jefferson shot her in the stomach and made another direct hit to her core. The creature fell to the front yard and pulled herself away from Jefferson like a squid trying to pull itself back to the ocean. The bullets from Big Bang may not have been able to penetrate Anne's core, but it was enough to disorient her.

Jefferson looked over his shoulder to see Pearl and Mary make it inside the farmhouse as Tom and Daisy pulled Ambrose across the yard by his arms.

As he turned to face the creature, Anne pushed herself up onto her tentacles like a boxer trying to make the ten count. Jefferson stepped a bit closer. Kaboom! Again the bullet ricocheted off the core and knocked her flat.

Jefferson looked at Big Bang. "Where do you think you're going? Haven't you heard? We don't like strangers around these parts, not ones that eat us."

Anne rolled to her back and pointed the tentacle with the frayed end right at Jefferson. She pulsated a blood red.

"You don't scare me," he said.

He pulled the trigger on Big Bang. Click. It was empty.

"Okay, now I'm a bit scared."

Jefferson ran back to a rifle laying in the grass. He checked the clip to see it was almost full and popped it back into the rifle.

Anne was already upright. She charged Jefferson. He fired the rifle, but the spray of bullets barely slowed her in her enraged state. In two seconds she was going to be on top of him.

Out of the corner of Jefferson's eye, he saw a small object fly just past his head, something about the size of a fist. The object hit Anne in the torso and fell to the ground. Anne stopped and loomed over the metal object. It looked like a small, metal pineapple.

Jefferson had time to think. *"Grenade!"*

He dove to the ground. Boom! The force of the blast took Anne off her feet and carved a small crater in the front yard.

As dirt rained down, Jefferson looked behind him to see Mary holding another grenade. She shrugged and smirked. Daisy and Tom ran to his side and took up positions on either side of him. They pulled Jefferson to his feet and shoved a fresh AK-47 into his hands. Tom nodded at Jefferson. Jefferson looked over at Daisy and she smiled like there was no place she'd rather be.

Jefferson glanced at each of them and thought, *"It's good to have friends but family is even better."*

"Okay, shoot the legs and its snake-arms, so it can't run or fight," said Mary.

"You heard her," said Jefferson.

Anne got to her feet. Her chest tentacles hung in tatters from the grenade blast.

"Fire! Kill that bitch!" yelled Mary.

The three of them opened fire. Anne jostled back and forth, but she was tough. She sprinted toward the broken fence and the bullets didn't seem like they were going to stop her. Luckily, Mary had another grenade and a hell of an arm.

They all heard Mary grunt, and the grenade landed a yard in front of Anne. It detonated just as she was stepping over it.

Anne just laid there for a bit, then started dragging herself toward the fence, leaving one of her larger legs behind, but her flesh was already twisting and reforming.

"Now what?" asked Jefferson.

"I need more gray-nades," said Mary.

Jefferson pulled his machete and took a step toward the creature.

Daisy grabbed his arm.

"Are you crazy?"

Jefferson said, "It's hurt."

"That doesn't make animals safer to be around. It has more than enough arms left to kill you."

"We can't let it reshape itself and run. This will just start all over. I'm going to go cut it's heart, or whatever, out of its chest."

He turned from Daisy and studied Anne. The tattered flesh grew together as she reshaped herself into something that could run and fight.

Tom sprayed her again with his AK-47, but didn't do much to slow the reformation process.

"If you go over there, you'll just become part of it," said Daisy.

Jefferson turned back to Daisy. "I have to try to do something."

"Wait! Do you hear that?"

The sound of truck engines, a lot of them, came from the end of the dirt road. In a moment they could see the headlights coming down the dirt road through the gaps in the trees. The trucks soon pulled into the yard. The beds of the pickups were loaded with fully armed rednecks. For the first time in the history of the universe, a black guy felt relief at such a sight.

Jefferson motioned for the trucks to form a perimeter around Anne. Old Ed realized what he wanted and yelled instructions from the back of one of the trucks until the pickups had Anne encircled.

The army of rednecks fell silent. Their eyes grew wide as they stared at the strange creature remolding itself.

Mary climbed unnoticed on the hood of one of the trucks and then on to the top of one of the cabs.

"Hey, it's very mean and eats people. Probably already ate some people you know. Shoot it! Fire!"

That was all the encouragement they needed. The rednecks opened fire. The storm of bullets tore away the alien flesh and severed tentacles.

Jefferson spotted the barrels of gas left at the fence line. He motioned for the three big Tillman brothers to follow him and together they carried the barrel of gas toward Anne.

"Hold yer fire!" yelled Old Ed. "Damn it. Hold your fire!"

Smoke hung in the air like a fog. Others noticed Jefferson and the brothers struggling with the barrels of diesel and helped them dump the two barrels onto what was left of Anne.

As the diesel spread around Anne in a large puddle, everyone backed away.

Old Ed yelled, "Burn it!"

The trucks backed away as Old Ed pulled a flare gun out and shot into the tattered remains of the monster.

Whoosh! Flames shot into the air and everyone felt the rush of heat on their faces.

Jefferson slid down against one of the trucks in exhaustion.

Before he could even take the time to wipe the sweat off his brow, Mary appeared at his side and tugged at his sleeve.

"Now, you know that ain't gonna kill it, not the hard thing. We have to trap it."

Jefferson sighed and stood. "Trap it in what?"

Mary thought, then snapped her fingers and ran toward the farmhouse.

Jefferson turned and watched the alien flesh burn with a blue flame and the smell of sugar burning.

Suddenly, a ball of fire shot out of the burning mess like a small meteor. It flew over the heads of the surrounding rednecks like a low flying comet.

"Don't let that get away!" Jefferson yelled.

He ran after the flaming core like an outfielder chasing one that's going into the stands. The core landed in the side field and rolled in the grass, extinguishing itself and going dark.

Jefferson yelled over his shoulder, "Light! Get some light over here. It's getting away."

A few rednecks ran to their trucks and emerged with big flashlights. They came sprinting into the field waving their lights around.

Jefferson got to where the core had landed. The grass was scorched black, but no tracks led away from the area, not one that he could see. He closed his eyes as he calmed his mind and tried to put himself in the mind of the creature. His eyes popped open.

"The tree line," he said. "Watch the tree line!"

Two trucks pulled into the field and turned on their fog lights, lighting the area bright enough to play a football game.

Jefferson spotted inch-worm like movement at the tree line as Anne's core pulled itself along. He sprinted toward the core just as it was about to disappear into some thick briars. Jefferson was faster. The heel of his boot came down on the core, again and again. He stomped his heal into the core until it was pressed into the ground like an overgrown seed.

"Die. Damn it. Just die."

Mary ran to his side holding the large jar of pickles above her head. She sighed and opened the jar and dumped out the remaining content on the ground.

"Hate to waste pickles, but it can't be helped."

She looked up at Jefferson and watched him stomp the core.

Mary said, "That ain't gonna work. Can't kill it with a boot."

Jefferson stepped back. Mary placed the large jar over the fist-sized core and used the lid of the jar to push it inside before screwing on the top.

The young core's internal tentacles emerged and slapped against the glass, but the glass held.

Mary held up the jar to the gathering crowd.

"Ya'll look. We saved the Eart'."

The rednecks cheered and picked Mary up as she held the jar high.

"Well, it was mostly Jefferson, but we helped."

Old Ed walked over to Jefferson as the crowd carried Mary away.

"Hard to imagine a thing that looks like a big turd caused all this trouble," the old man said.

Jefferson sat down in the field. "Thanks for coming, bringing all the help."

"Just being neighborly. Besides, you did all the hard work. Guess you might have saved Picayune, hell, the world."

Jefferson held out his hand and they shook.

"Speaking of neighbors. I've been thinking about keeping the old farm, but I did sort of sign it away already."

"Well, I saw Dan's truck on the side of the road, but no Dan," said Old Ed.

"Oh," said Jefferson, "Just as well. It would have broken his heart when I told him I didn't want to sell."

"I reckon he would have preferred to have his heart broken than what happened to him."

"Yeah, you're probably right."

Jefferson looked up as if he suddenly remembered something. He sprinted away. He ran all the way back to the front yard until he saw Gray Man still laying on his side with his eyes closed. Jefferson slowed as he made it to the horse's side and collapsed to his knees. He put his hand on Gray Man's neck.

"I'm sorry I left you. You were the best horse a man could

ever have, more than I deserved."

Jefferson's head sank to his chest and his eyes grew blurry with tears.

Gray Man cracked one of his eyes and raised his head slightly. Jefferson looked up. The horse closed his eye and lowered his head.

Jefferson stood up and chuckled. "I know you're faking. Get up."

Gray Man cracked his eye and peeked at Jefferson.

"Yes. I saw you. Now, get up."

The big horse rocked to his hooves and stood. Jefferson walked around the horse checking him for injuries. He had a few scratches, but considering the night that could be considered a great success.

Daisy walked to his side.

"Gray Man okay?"

"Yeah, few scratches. How's Ambrose?" he asked.

"Busted ribs and his brain is rattled. He'll be alright, but I don't know if his pride will ever recover with you saving the world without him."

Jefferson smiled. "*We* saved the world. Us and those kids."

Daisy took a step closer. "Yeah, looks like we made it."

"We did," said Jefferson. "And, if you're still carrying a torch for me, seems like a night for big fires."

"Fires need to be kindled, Jefferson Balladeer."

"Oh, I happen to be a great kindler."

He moved to kiss Daisy, but Mary pushed between them.

"Hey, game warden, you think you can make some more sandwiches? Saving the world made me hungry, and you did a pretty good job last time."

Daisy took Mary's hand. "I think we can manage that."

She started to lead Mary away, but the girl stopped after a few steps and looked back at Jefferson. She looked at him for a long moment, then stretched out her hand toward him.

Jefferson smiled and took her little hand. "Don't worry. I'm going to see you get all the sandwiches you want from this point forward."

"And ice cream?"

"A reasonable amount of ice cream," Daisy said.

As they walked to the farmhouse, Mary started to cry.

"Why are you crying?" Jefferson asked her.

Mary shook her head. She was too choked up to speak.

"The monster's trapped," he said. "You don't need to be afraid."

"I'm not afraid. I just ain't used to people being so nice is all."

Jefferson smiled down at her and then looked up at Daisy. "You two ladies will just have to get used to it."

EPILOGUE

LOCATION: Balladeer Farm

TIME: One year later

efferson laid a platter of scrambled eggs next to a pile of biscuits and a plate of bacon. Tom walked silently into the room and put out four plates on the big table.

"Thanks, Tom."

The boy nodded and sat in his place. His hair had been cut in a modern style and combed neatly. His clothes looked more like he had escaped a Banana Republic catalogue than a Mark Twain novel.

Mary stomped into the room. Her hair was still wild, but it was much longer and clean as her new, stylish clothes.

Daisy walked in buttoning up her uniform and sat next to Jefferson. "Thanks for breakfast."

"No problem."

Mary started to eat and everyone joined in.

"Hey," Daisy said. "I know you probably wanted to write today, but Ambrose texted me and asked if you would mind helping him at the sheriff's office."

"When is he going to hire some deputies?"

"The last two got eaten. People aren't lining up for that job."

"Sure," said Jefferson.

Daisy smiled. "I'll make it up to you."

Mary said, "Come on, not in front of the children. I'm trying to eat my breakfast."

Jefferson stood. "Come on, Tom. I'll drop you at school."

Tom cleaned his plate and stood.

"Have fun at school, sucker," said Mary.

"Mary, it's not like you earned your vast knowledge of the universe," said Daisy. "You were just lucky and got it injected in your brain."

Mary smiled and tapped the side of her head. "That's right, vast knowledge."

Jefferson kissed Daisy and tussled Mary's hair. He pointed at Mary.

"Stay out of trouble, or I will arrest you."

Mary saluted as Jefferson walked out with Tom at his heels.

Daisy stood and buttoned her uniform.

"I can trust you to get to your teacher on your own?"

"Yes, ma'am."

"No exploring, not on your own, and, if you take your dirt bike, wear your helmet and boots."

"Wait, let me write this all down. It's a lot to remember."

Daisy gave her a glare. "Alright, smartie."

As Daisy started toward the hall, Mary got up and ran to her side and hugged her. "You be careful, too."

Daisy saluted. "Yes ma'am."

As Daisy drove off in her truck, Mary came out of the farmhouse wearing a small backpack. She put on her matte black helmet and got on a small dirt bike. She kick-started the engine and drove off recklessly.

Mary drove to the catfish ponds and coasted to a stop. The

fish sculpture had been distorted and twisted as if tentacles were reaching toward the sky from the top of the pole.

She walked to the edge of the first pond. The water was crystal clear and she could see all the different fish swimming in the water. The heat of the blast that killed the Devourer had turned the side of the pond into something that resembled brown glass. Mary studied the fish that swam its depths. An alarm on Mary's watch beeped. She ran to her dirt bike and took off.

A short while later, Mary parked her bike in front of Fort Awesome. The fort had been rebuilt better than ever and the area around it had been cleared and planted with fruit trees. The fort itself was three times bigger. It looked like a grass covered hill with an old VW van embedded in the side. Mary often like to imagine it was a giant, green monster eating a van.

She opened the van door and stepped inside.

The inside of Fort Awesome was pristine as any lab. Strange lights gave an orangish hue to the room. Shorty's broken armor hung from the wall.

"Teacher, I brought biscuits," she said.

There was no answer, so she sat her backpack down on the floor and ran to the middle of the large room.

A circular glass enclosure took up a good four feet of the room and stood eight feet high. Mary skipped over to it and put her hands and face against the thick glass.

Inside, Anne's core swam in the water. The fist-sized core was surrounded by just enough clear alien flesh to make a strange squid-like creature. Anne swam to the bottom of the enclosure where there were piles of plastic letters. With her many arms, Anne held up the letters to read, "Hi Mary."

Mary waved back through the glass.

Anne arranged the letters quickly with her tentacles on the bottom of the enclosure to read "Let me out. I'm nice."

Mary shook her head and stuck out her tongue.

Anne sprang from the bottom of the tank and slammed her

tentacles against the glass hard enough to startle Mary.

"See, you ain't nice. You want to eat everything."

Anne swam back to the letters and held up letters that read, "I'm Anne."

"You're Monster Anne."

A strange reflection appeared in the glass behind Mary. The creature had mottled orange and white scales that covered his long, thick arms. He stood on two short, stocky legs.

Mary turned and bowed low. "Hello teacher."

"Mary, lovely to see you," said Shorty with a very gruff voice and a bit of a Mississippi accent.

The girl ran to her backpack and extended it to Shorty.

"I brought biscuits."

"Why, thank you. Those are my favorite."

He extended his long arm and took the bag of biscuits out of her backpack. He emptied the bag directly in his mouth and seemed to inhale the six biscuits so fast it would make a pit bull seem like a dainty eater.

"Tell the Balladeers their biscuits are absolutely decadent."

"I'll let them know."

"How is everyone?" Shorty asked.

"Jefferson is still mad he's got to be a deputy, but no one wants to do it after the other two got ate. Tom's mad he's got to go to school and I get to come here. Daisy just likes to make a bunch of rules."

"You tell Tom to come see me," Shorty said.

"Yes, sir."

Shorty walked over to some circuit boards and some other strange equipment. Mary followed.

"Teacher, what are we doing today?"

"Today, today, I find myself totally healed from my past injuries, so we'll start a new project. It will take a long time, but you will learn a lot."

"How long? What project?"

"We're going to make a robot," said Shorty. "If that pleases you."

Mary nodded with enthusiasm. "Yes sir, I would like that."

A NOTE FROM THE AUTHOR, STEVEN ROY

Well, you've done it. You've read an entire novel that is entitled Black Redneck vs. Space Zombies. It's probably not something you expected to read in your lifetime, but it happened. Life is unexpected like that.

If you would have told me two years ago that I would have written a novel called Black Redneck vs. Space Zombies, I would have offered to help you seek some medical assistance as you were clearly having some sort of stroke or had been given a powerful hallucinogen.

But, as we established, life is unexpected. A little less than two years ago, I got the idea in my head that someone should take a B-movie premise and write a serious novel, populating the book with compelling characters and creatures with an interesting biology. I kept thinking about it and soon the general idea began to have characters. I started doodling monsters at my boring day job. Not long after that I was working seriously on a novel called Black Redneck vs. Space Zombies.

I finished the book and thought I would finally get into this self publishing stuff. Besides, it wasn't like a big publishing company was going to touch a book with such a title. Big publishing, not known for taking chances.

So, I paid a very talented artist to draw a cover. The cover came out better than I could have ever imagined, and I posted to the book to Amazon with the thought that I might get more hate mail than sales.

Not much happened at first but slowly reviews came in, good ones. Stranger still people admitted to getting a little misty-eyed while reading the book. They said the book had heart and depth, but mostly readers said the book wasn't what they expected.

I hope you were also pleasantly surprised by the book. If you were, please let people know.

You could approach a group of friends and/or coworkers and say something like, "In a strange turn of events, I read a book called Black Redneck vs. Space Zombies…" I'll leave it to you to fill in the rest. I'm not bossy and trust you to handle this.

If you're one of those people who like to talk to people on the internet, feel free to leave a review on Amazon or Goodreads.

Or, if you'd just like to say hello, you can find me on Goodreads at https://www.goodreads.com/author/show/7113732.Steven_Roy
Or, you can check out my website at www.professional-liar.com

Thanks again for buying the book and supporting unexpected stories

www.ingramcontent.com/pod-product-compliance
Lightning Source LLC
Chambersburg PA
CBHW031253170626
46807CB00001B/131